Fake it 'til you Sleigh it

MÉLISA RYUN

Published in the United States by Create Mode Media, LLC. All rights reserved. Printed
in USA. First edition 2024. Cover design by Lisa Kubja.

CREATE MODE MEDIA LLC
7925 W. RUSSELL ROAD #401103
LAS VEGAS, NV 89140
eBook Edition ISBN-13: 9781947775091
Paperback Edition ISBN-13: 9781947775107

For permission requests contact:
info@melisaryun.com
www.melisaryun.com

TRIGGER WARNING: *This book contains explicit sexual content, reckless driving, extreme
profanity, references to the death of a parent, and alcoholism.*

For the guarded hearts…
may this holiday season melt your
defenses and let love shine in.

CHAPTER ONE

CHASE

"Listen up!" I shout through my megaphone. "This shot happens before lunch, or say goodbye to your holiday plans. And since Hollywood's class clown can't stay focused for more than thirty seconds—" I lock eyes with Ethan, who has the audacity to wink at me, "—you know exactly who to blame."

The crew scatters like cockroaches, actors reset, and in seconds, the soundstage is a picture-perfect cozy Irish pub again. Green explodes everywhere, like the Hulk sneezed on Saint Patrick's Day. Streamers, shamrocks, and pots of gold—it's precisely what I envisioned when I wrote the script.

My assistant Taylor materializes at my side, blondie on a mission. Eyes like lasers. Clipboard of doom in hand and looking like she could organize chaos itself.

"Chase, it's only twenty minutes until the mandatory lunch break. We can't afford another penalty and—"

"I know. See this pulsating vein in my forehead? It's doing a fabulous job reminding me just how late we're running."

Taylor's eyes soften. "If you keep scowling like that, you'll have wrinkles before you're thirty-three."

I feel my shoulders relax slightly. "Shit. Point taken. I'll try to relax. You're my lifesaver, Taylor. Have I told you today what a total badass you are?"

She grins. "Someone's gotta keep the directing queen sane in this circus."

"Not even I can control our resident pretty-boy star," I grumble, feeling my stress levels skyrocket at the mere thought of him.

My gaze darts across the set, searching for my leading man. And there he is—not at his mark, not running lines, instead he's turning the craft services table into his personal fan club. Ethan Barrett, six feet of pure frustration, surrounded by a swarm of adoring female PAs. They're hanging on his every word, laughing at his jokes, and practically melting every time he flashes that annoyingly cocky grin.

"Ethan! For the love of fucking leprechauns, GET READY for this take!"

"I've *been* ready, Chase. If you want to blame me, be my guest. But we both know you love riding my ass."

"If you could stay focused, maybe I wouldn't have to ride you so hard."

Shit. That came out wrong.

His grin widens. "You want to take me for a ride? Just say the word. I promise you won't regret it."

I walked right into that one.

"Gah! GET ON SET!"

Ethan Barrett, leading man? Hardly. More like leading *man-child*, wrapped up in an infuriatingly irresistible package. His wavy, light-brown hair is expertly styled. He has mesmerizing blue eyes and endless muscles that are perfectly sculpted to drive the opposite sex crazy. Every woman he meets falls under his spell, each wondering if she could be the one to tame his wild, exasperating heart. I cast him for precisely that reason, and yeah... he knows it.

His smile is smug—and his ego? Well, that's a package deal. His so-called charm might fool his legions of devoted fans, but not me. Ethan Barrett is an agent of chaos. He cares more about goofing off on set and posting selfies on social media than he does about memorizing his damn lines.

The Hollywood rumor mill has it right: We're not BFFs. In fact, every film we work on only intensifies our mutual dislike for each other.

He's the reason I'm consuming Tums like daily vitamins.

When I'm writing a script, I visualize it. I picture exactly where people stand, what they should say, and how everything will flow to make the audience laugh, cry, and swoon. But Ethan and his antics challenge that vision every freaking day.

He's like a Ken doll come to life that I wish would turn back into plastic.

Why, oh why am I stuck with him? Oh yeah, because unfortunately, our first Christmas movie together was a massive hit—so much so that the studio suits demanded he star in *every* film I've written since. Talk about your holiday curse.

I scrutinize the monitor, evaluating the scene. Ethan stands behind the bar, all broad shoulders, powerful jaw, and cocky grin. He looks undeniably hot in his red plaid flannel as he holds that bottle of tequila, but something's not quite right.

"Ethan, roll back your sleeves," I call out.

He lazily pushes the fabric up his forearms, revealing tanned skin and a hint of a tattoo. "How's that, Miss Perfectionist? Like what you see?"

I stride over, frustration bubbling up. "Pretty half-ass, even for you. Just... let me do it."

I clutch his muscular arm, fantasizing about strangling him with his shirt. Methodically I fold back the sleeve in a neat, even roll. *He could never.*

Ethan watches me with an insufferable smirk, his breath tickling my ear as he angles toward me. "You know, Chase, if you wanna grope me, you can just ask."

I yank on the fabric, harder than necessary. *Oopsie.* He can spare a few arm hairs.

"Ow! Are you trying to manscape me against my will?"

I step back, pause, and lean forward to undo the top two buttons of his shirt. Might as well go all in on this "sexy bartender" thing.

"Better slow down," Ethan purrs. "If you keep undressing me, the crew might get the wrong idea."

"Your look is 'approachable bartender,' not *Magic Mike* wannabe. Try to remember that."

Ethan's eyes meet mine, and for a split second, his smirk falters. "Chase, hold up. I've been running lines, and I think there's a way we can enhance this scene—"

Wait, what? Is Ethan "Eye Candy" Barrett actually trying to contribute?

But then his signature grin snaps back into place. "Let's make it more me-centric. Really showcase my natural charisma. We gotta give the people what they want."

"Just. Stick. To. The. Script."

"Aw, come on." He winks. "Admit it. You're scared the audience will be too busy drooling over me to notice your overwritten dialogue and artsy-fartsy camera angles."

"Wake up, pretty boy," I say, jabbing a finger at his chest. "My writing is what makes you seem interesting. Say the lines as written, or I swear I'll write your character as a dickless, mute monk."

Grr. How can I possibly have time for a boyfriend when this aggravating man demands all my attention? He's why my love life is on permanent hiatus.

No time to waste. I pivot on my heel and hurry to the video monitor. "Back to one, everybody!"

Staring at the screen, I catch a glimpse of my reflection. *Yikes. Did I even brush my hair this morning?* Hmm, honestly, I don't remember. I run my fingers through my long brown locks, pulling them up into an artfully messy ponytail for the umpteenth time—I call it *Bedhead Chic.*

Being a director is like herding cats, except these cats have egos the size of Texas. I'm running on three hours of sleep, six mugs of herbal tea, and half a granola bar. The bags under my big brown eyes are demanding an intervention from some miracle-cure concealer.

Whatever. I'm not here to win a beauty pageant. I'm here to make a goddamn movie!

And you know what? I fucking love it. Is it a total shitshow? You bet. Calling it stressful is an understatement—it's more like living in a perpetual state of "Oh fuck, now what?"

People call me the Ice Queen of holiday movies, but they have no clue. This job is brutal. Most days, I feel like I'm barely keeping my head above water. But being tough as nails is what it takes to create something special in this ruthless industry.

Making stories that bring people joy—that's what drags my ass out of bed at insane hours and keeps me grinding day after day. So if dealing with difficult actors and navigating studio politics is what it takes to deliver more hope and laughter, I'm all in. I'll put up with the headaches, the stress, and yes, even actors with the attention span of a goldfish *(ahem, Ethan)*. Ice Queen? Fine by me. Let them try to do my job for a day.

"Action!" I bellow.

The bar door swings open, and in sashays our leading lady, a blonde too gorgeous for words. Her face falls as she slowly slides onto a barstool—a perfect portrait of melancholy—just as we rehearsed.

Great entrance, Megan. Now don't fuck this up, Ethan.

He leans on the bar, flashing his movie-star smile that makes ovaries explode across America. "Looks like you're having a rough day. I bet I can lift your spirits—"

This is the one. The magic, the chemistry, it's all working. I mouth the words as Ethan continues.

"How about one lucky leprechaun, a lemon-laced libation that'll have you licking your lips and longing for more?"

Wait, what? That's not in the script. Before I can yell cut, Ethan starts flinging bottles like he's a goddamn stunt clown juggling flaming chainsaws. One bottle slips and—

CRASH!

"Cut! What the hell was that dumbassery?"

Ethan stares at me like I'm crazy, his puppy dog eyes wide with faux innocence. "Come on, Chase. It's a Saint Patrick's Day movie. A little bottle juggling adds some festive flair."

I pinch the bridge of my nose so hard I'm sure I'm leaving permanent marks. "The script doesn't call for 'festive flair,' you walking Calvin Klein ad," I growl. "This scene is about a heartfelt connection between the bartender and his old high school girlfriend. Maybe between your protein smoothie and your latest Instagram thirst trap, you forgot. It's this thing called acting."

"A charismatic mixologist like me would impress his girl with tricks," Ethan argues.

"You know what I find impressive about you? How quickly you derail a scene."

"My job is to embrace the character, not put the audience to sleep with another clichéd 'bartender acting as a therapist' scenario."

I feel an aneurysm forming. I start counting to ten in my head, but I only make it to six and a half before I imagine all the ways I could "accidentally" injure Ethan without getting sued.

"Look here, *Biceps for Brains*. That 'cliché' scene establishes their relationship. Now do your job. Stand there and look pretty."

"If you say so." Ethan shrugs, a little nonchalance lightly sprinkled in with disrespect. "But I still say some improv would spice it up." He turns to the crew. "Am I right?"

I can't believe what I'm seeing. Crew members nod enthusiastically. Traitors. Sorry if I'm not all cartwheels and fun, but someone has to wear the fucking mom jeans and make sure shit happens.

"More acting, less thinking, Ethan," I say, my jaw clenched so tight I could spit out tooth dust. "You're hired to tell the story as written."

"All right, all right." He holds up his hands. "One boring, by-the-book barkeep coming right up."

"From the top," I shout, my voice a blend of *I'm so done* and *I might commit murder today*. "And... action!"

Our leading lady enters the bar again, nailing her melancholy demeanor. Ethan opens his mouth... and out comes the worst Irish accent I've ever had the misfortune of hearing.

"Welcome, lassie, to thee Emerald Pub!" he bellows, sounding like a drunk leprechaun with a head cold. "Ever tried a green ale? It's so good, it'll make ye think you've found a pot of gold!"

He sticks out his tongue, and it's a shocking shade of green. The crew bursts out laughing.

"If ye think the beer's good, wait till ye see my leprechaun dance!" He launches into a complete mockery of an Irish jig. It's like he's trying to put out a fire in his pants while being electrocuted.

"Cut!" I say for the millionth time.

My assistant Taylor quickly approaches. "The executives want to see you in their office... now."

I groan, rubbing my temples. Great. More stress on top of my already stressful day. I yell into my megaphone. "That's lunch, everyone! Be back on set in forty-five minutes sharp."

As I storm off, Ethan's laughter echoes behind me—a personal soundtrack to my slow descent into madness.

***

I STRUT DOWN THE festive hallway of the studio offices, which are engulfed in garlands and fairy lights—Santa's little helpers have been hard at work. Since I've been filming a Saint Patrick's Day movie on the daily, it's easy to forget Christmas is lurking around the corner like a creepy elf on a shelf.

For the last three and a half years, I've been directing movies for the Cherish Channel—a dream job that still excites me when I'm not drowning in drama. As a kid, these love stories were my obsession. Heartwarming tales of romance and finding yourself?

Gimme, gimme, gimme! Especially the Christmas ones. They were my comfort food, my escape from reality.

I've never told a soul, but those movies were my lifeline during the holidays. Not all of us had an idyllic Christmas with matching pajamas and Pinterest-worthy gingerbread houses.

Some of us had a dad who drank too much and disappointment became the theme of our family life. But the Cherish Channel was always there, an around-the-clock escape from my unhappy childhood.

Now I'm the one in charge. The only person who can let me down is me. I have no interest in fairy-tale love myself, but I'm happy to create that dream for others. I've learned that make-believe is less painful than reality. You can't get your heart broken when it's all pretend.

I pass by the poster for my first film, *Jingle Jokes & Mistletoe*, and can't help but smile. That little gem became the most viewed movie ever on the network—so popular that Ethan was dubbed the "King of Christmas." *Gag me with a candy cane.*

The movie was so successful that the studio hired me to direct four more movies.

A dream come true... right?

Except they slapped on this one teensy, annoying-as-hell condition. One that has snowballed into a full-blown, life-ruining nightmare: Ethan must be my leading man.

In. Every. Single. Movie.

Ugh.

Four nonstop holiday headaches later, here we are at movie number five, *Shamrock Shenanigans*.

In two weeks, our latest Christmas movie, *Fa La La Love,* will premiere. When the studio credits me for their fourth blockbuster success, they'll be begging me to direct five more. And when they do, I have a plan.

Lay down the law.

Regain my holiday cheer.

Unfuck my directing career—with three simple words.

NO. MORE. ETHAN.

I'll find a better star, one who actually listens, so my life won't be a living hell. Imagine... a male lead who takes direction and doesn't use his "method acting" as an excuse for disruptive flirty shenanigans.

I take a deep breath, channeling my inner badass, and march into the executives' office. This won't be fun because my bosses—who combined are at least 483 years old—have all the holiday cheer of two constipated elves. Why they are making lighthearted romance movies is beyond me... They never smile, and I doubt either has experienced an orgasm since moving pictures were invented.

"Hello, Ms. Riley, Mr. Wiley," I chirp through a smile so fake you'd think I'd had Botox.

Their shared office is a morgue. Both in looks and temperature. I hide my shiver, not knowing if it's the frigid air or their icy stares. No decorations, no warmth. I wouldn't be surprised if the coffee machine dispenses embalming fluid.

Remember that scene in *A Muppet Christmas Carol* where Scrooge is hunched over his desk, counting his coins? That's who I answer to. They conduct two types of meetings. The first is about saving time and money. The second is... who am I kidding? It's the same meeting every time.

Miserly Wiley doesn't crack a smile. "Ms. Pemberton, you requested a budget increase for the parade scene. It's been denied."

See, told ya.

"Hear me out," I plead. "That parade pulls the whole story together. It's the big romantic scene that fans will rave about."

Wiley's face remains as frozen as a snowman's balls. "The budget calls for one pickup truck and four extras."

"I acknowledge, and I appreciate, budget constraints," I say, straining a smile. I'm not, *not* visualizing Wiley being run over by a parade float right now.

"But it's supposed to resemble the Chicago Saint Patrick's Day Parade. If you allocate just a few more resources, I can stack the extra people and a second truck and shoot it from different low angles to make it work."

"Denied," Wiley repeats, crushing my dreams like a Grinch stomping on a Who's Christmas present.

Scrooge Riley sets her steely gaze on me. "That's not all. We called you in here because—until further notice—the movie you're filming is suspended. We need you to shift your one hundred percent focus on promoting your Christmas movie, *Fa La La Love*, which releases in thirteen days."

"Promotion? But that's not my job. What do you want me to do? Film some TikTok challenges?"

"No. The shareholders are breathing down our necks. They have no interest in the existing audience; they're worried about our stalled-out subscriber accounts. Your last two movies did not bring in new fans. *We* committed, which means *you* committed, to deliver a million new paid subscribers by Christmas Eve."

ONE MILLION?!

I hide my *whatever-the-opposite-of-an-O* face is.

"I understand attracting new viewers, but let's be real. My movies have made you guys so much money."

"And the shareholders appreciate it," Wiley says, with Riley adding, "Which is why you're still employed."

How is this my problem? Where's the marketing goon squad and their social media interns? So now I'm supposed to write, direct, and go door-to-door selling my movies? What's next—dress up as Mrs. Claus and hand out flyers at the mall?

I swallow the negativity, absorbing it deep in my gut, and ask, "What kind of promotional activities?"

"You get to *direct* a marketing campaign," Wiley retorts.

I wince at his ignorant use of the word *direct*.

"You'll need to keep it festive," Riley chimes in. "Your stars should participate in interviews, social media campaigns, the works."

Despite what their decades-old business attire suggests, times have changed. There are so many entertainment options in the world now. Gaming. Social Media. Groups of Red Hat ladies choosing cards over TV.

The point is—no one gets huge numbers anymore. Those two would have a better chance of bringing color back to their faded 90s blazers. People prefer swiping on Tinder and watching cat videos to gathering in masses and supporting the nuanced art of holiday romance.

I sigh. "How am I supposed to do that? The lead actress for that movie is pregnant. We were already playing 'Hide the Baby Bump' during filming, and now I hear she's on bed rest until January."

"That's not a problem. You'll do the interviews, Ms. Pemberton. We booked one tomorrow with *Rise and Glow LA*. You and Ethan need to be there at four a.m."

Forget coal. Santa just took a massive dump in my stocking.

Then Riley drops an ultimatum of epic proportions. "You either make *Fa La La Love* the biggest hit we've ever had, or you're out. Nothing personal. Just business."

Wiley stops frowning for a second; the closest he gets to holiday cheer. "If you manage to pull in a million paid subscribers before Christmas, we will sign you on to direct ten more films."

Ten?! Holy shit. My brain glitches, then reboots at supersonic speed.

This is it.

The fucking jackpot.

The career-defining moment I've been busting my ass for, all wrapped up with a big, shiny bow.

Ten films means job security in an industry where 'stable employment' is about as rare as a unicorn in the North Pole. I could finally tell my creepy landlord to shove it and buy that dream house on Zillow. The one with space for a home office, where I can write without hearing my neighbors anger banging all night.

My mind is already buzzing with storylines. A holiday sweater designer who gets roasted online by a snarky reviewer. But plot twist—the troll is actually her secret admirer! Or the Christmas-obsessed podcaster who falls head over heels for the Scrooge-like guest who thinks the holidays are just a capitalist plot to sell more crap to children?

After all, who doesn't love a good dose of holiday cynicism with their romance?

"I promise I'll do everything in my power to ensure this promotion is a smashing success."

Then, channeling my inner negotiator *(and a touch of my inner Mafia boss)*, I add, "But I have one condition: If I hit that subscriber goal, I want final casting approval on all future projects, lead actors included."

Wiley and Riley exchange a look. "Agreed."

Holy shit! No more being forced to work with egotistical pretty boys who can't remember their fucking lines. I can handpick actors who actually respect the art of holiday movie-making. Imagine that!

For Christmas this year, I'm getting everything I want. Hello, big directing career, and goodbye, Ethan Barrett.

CHAPTER TWO

ETHAN

"I'M GONNA SINK MY teeth into you, sweetheart."

I take a bite out of the key lime jelly donut, savoring its tart sweetness. Am I sweet-talking a pastry? Only because she's my favorite and never disappoints, unlike a certain uptight director. Eating powdered sugar while wearing a red velvet suit is playing with fire, but hey, I've never been one to shy away from a little danger.

I sink into the makeup chair like it's my personal throne, ready to ho-ho-ho my way through another day of being everyone's favorite holiday heartthrob. I close my eyes, surrendering to the flurry of hands that groom and polish me to perfection. Brushes tickle my face, weaving their magic. The air is heavy with hairspray and coffee—the official scent of mornings in showbiz.

Phone in hand, I press record, unleashing the smile that's earned me my King of Christmas crown.

"Morning, beauties! Don't miss me on Rise & Glow LA today. I've got a special treat in store for you. Keep it sexy."

I wink and hit *Post*, feeling the familiar twinge of... something. Emptiness? Nah, probably just hunger. Nothing another donut can't fix.

But it's not all pussy and presents being the King of Christmas.

Every day, it's 'Ethan, say something charming,' or 'Ethan, give us that smolder.' I love spreading holiday cheer like it's my job *(which, technically, it is)*, but sometimes, beneath all the tinsel and twinkling lights, I wonder if anyone sees the real me. The artist. The guy with actual thoughts in his surprisingly handsome head. The actor who wants to be more than a holiday hottie.

Don't get me wrong, the role has its perks. There's no shortage of gorgeous women vying for a spot on my "nice" list. It's a jolly way to pass the time between movies. But lately, this gig has left me feeling like a regifted sweater—slightly worn and wondering if I'll ever find someone who wants to keep me for more than a season.

Every romantic scene I perform lately has me questioning if that kind of love truly exists, especially for a guy like me. Still, I keep playing the part.

Charming smile? Check.

Witty one-liners? You bet your ass.

Gratuitous shirtless scenes? If you've got it, flaunt it.

But deep down, I'm terrified that's all I have to offer—a pretty face with a knack for selling bullshit. However, I've made a commitment. The Yuletide show must go on... for now.

BANG!

The door flies open. There she is: Chase "Killjoy" Pemberton. Game face on and ready to conquer the world—or at least make this morning talk show her bitch.

"Prep time, Ethan," she snaps. "Don't forget to plug the snowman scene. Make sure you tell them how hilarious it is."

"Smokin' hot snowman. Got it, boss." I wink.

She rolls her eyes.

Score one for Ethan.

Getting under her skin is my favorite game to play. Her very warm, smooth skin.

That citrus shampoo scent of hers is like a time machine. One whiff brings me back to when we first met. It's subtle but intoxicating, and it messes with my head every damn time. Her voice, with its rich, velvety husk, doesn't help either. It still does things to me, firing up parts that should know better by now.

This woman drives me nuts, but I can admit it: Her signature ponytail and high cheekbones are a deadly combo. Sure, she wears that brunette topknot so tight, you can almost hear her scalp begging for mercy. But there's no denying she's gorgeous, with those captivating brown eyes and lashes that cast their own spell. And that athletic build? Let's just say her full, pursed lips are making it really hard to stay focused.

But then she speaks, and it's like a cold shower on my warm thoughts. Not to mention she's decked out in an all-black suit... for a morning talk show. Her outfit is basically screaming "Fuck off" in a room full of holiday cheer. It's a harsh reminder of the ice queen underneath. Suddenly, my dick wants to crawl into a hole and hibernate for the winter.

"Dingleberry, focus up! The second agenda item is the Christmas karaoke scene," she says, pacing. "Since this is the first movie you sing in, we gotta hype that up. Audiences will go wild for it!"

I nod along, trying not to laugh at her intensity. Sometimes Chase takes herself way too seriously. Okay, all the time. I wonder if there's some alternate universe where a more laid-back version of Chase exists—one who'd actually laugh at my jokes and be fun on set.

But here's the catch: she's the best damn director I've ever worked with. Her eye for detail, her vision, the way she can coax a solid performance out of even the worst actors—it's fucking impressive. Not that I'd ever admit that to her. I've got an image to maintain, and it doesn't involve kissing the director's ass. Even if she looks incredible in those tight pants she wears.

No matter how hard I try with each movie, she remains unimpressed. Thank God the network forced her to hire me. It was a hit to my ego, I'll admit. I'm used to women throwing their panties at me. But Chase? She sees me as an annoyance she can't shake off, like gum stuck to her shoe. Which, frankly, makes me want to irritate her more.

After five films together, I'm still trying to break through her ice queen exterior. I've got ambitions, damn it. I'm not here only to play the heartthrob. I want to make a real impact and help these films shine. Who knows, maybe even direct someday? Working with Chase is a challenge, but it's also a masterclass in filmmaking—if you can endure it.

Like how I'm enduring this talk show etiquette lecture as if I haven't already nailed the morning show game. Hell, I could teach a course on winning over hosts while being half-awake and nursing a hangover.

"Finally, and this is critical," she continues, her nostrils flaring like an angry bull. "We *need* more Cherish Channel subscribers. Tell them it's the perfect gift for Christmas. First month is free—emphasize that."

"Whoa there, Holiday Huckster," I say, ignoring the fire igniting in her eyes. "Why are you all worked up? It's a morning show... light banter. Ya know, fun and festive."

Chase huffs out a breath, putting a slight pause in her manic pacing. "Easy for you to say. I have never done a live interview before."

Holy shit! Is Chase actually nervous? She may be Darth Director behind the camera, but that look in her eyes is unmistakable... pure panic.

Usually, I'd be on this like powdered sugar on a donut, but surprisingly I'm feeling... protective? *Huh, that's weird.*

"Relax. We'll just go out and do some friendly chit-chat. Try to enjoy yourself."

But she looks like she's about to pee her pants, throw up, and faint all at once. I can't have her melting down on camera, or we'll both look bad.

"Hey, chill! What's the worst that could happen? You mess up and become an internet punchline? Like that 'Side-Eyeing Chloe' girl or the 'Double Rainbow' dude? I mean, yeah, your dignity would be toast, but think of all the sweet meme money!"

Nailed it. Yeah, I'm basically a life coach.

Chase looks worse now. I pretend like that was helpful and spin towards Tiffany, the blonde makeup goddess who dives right back in, doing her thing on my face.

She smooths foundation over my defined features and dabs a little concealer under my eyes. *Let's be real—it's not like I need it. I wake up this handsome.*

"So, Tiff, any wild holiday plans?"

"You know I do. Get this. Flights out of LA are so cheap..."

As Tiffany launches into the story of her upcoming Vegas girls' trip, I sneak a glance at Chase from the corner of my eye. Her shoulders drop a fraction, which I take as a good sign. She settles into the makeup chair next to mine and starts breathing again.

"Hot damn, Ethan," Tiffany purrs, giving my jawline one last stroke. "This red suit is sinful. You look like a snack."

"Thanks!" I say, letting my famous panty-dropping smile linger—the same one that launched a thousand housewife fantasies.

"What's your deal? I'm guessing a sexy holiday vacay." Tiffany pries.

"Nah, I'm counting down the hours until I head home for Christmas. My family goes all out—the tree literally sags with ornaments, the gingerbread house showdowns are intense, and get this—my dad dresses up as a retired Santa, complete with flip-flops, a red bathrobe, and a hat that says *off duty*."

"Aww, that's adorable," Tiffany coos. "Your parents gotta be so proud. Their son being the King of Christmas and all."

"Oh, without a doubt. My mama's more obsessed about Christmas than Santa himself."

Tiffany's assistant, Kate, a bubbly girl with pink hair, starts to apply makeup on Chase. With a bright smile, she asks, "What about you? Any fun holiday plans?"

"Christmas vacation? Hard pass," Chase says, her voice flatter than my abs *(which, for the record, are spectacular)*.

Both makeup artists gasp.

"I do the same thing every year," she continues, dripping with the disdain of a teenager forced to hang out with their parents. "I rent a cabin in Lake Tahoe where I can focus on writing my next script. No family, no drama. Just me. Alone. Preferably buried under ten feet of snow."

Okay, pooh-poohing Christmas I can not condone. Time to poke the Chase-bear again. "Really? No family to order around like minions on Christmas Day? I'm sure you have some secret holiday tradition... Maybe watching *It's a Wonderful Life* and rooting for Mr. Potter?"

Chase's death glare could make Satan himself piss his pants. *Worth it. So fucking worth it.*

Tiffany puts the finishing touches on my hair. She grins at me in the mirror. "You're perfect," she says, then adds with a giggle, "Not that you weren't perfect before. You're even more perfect-er."

Kate examines her blush palette before selecting a soft-pink shade. I can't help but enjoy the sight of Chase looking utterly miserable in the hot seat.

"I love your cheekbones," Kate gushes. "I'd throw away my favorite vibrator for bone structure like that."

"I'm flattered," says Chase coldly, distancing the compliment. "Keep it natural," she instructs. "No red lips. I'm a director, not an actor."

"No warm colors, please," I stage whisper to Kate. "She likes to keep her face in *Ebenezer Scrooge mode*. And God help us if she ever smiles. You best run for your life—it's a sign of the apocalypse."

"I have no desire to participate in this absurd interview," Chase grumbles. "If your co-star wasn't knocked up, I wouldn't be here."

I smirk. "Don't blame a baby for your stage fright."

She narrows her eyes. "Ethan, I need you to be irresistible out there. We need new subscribers as badly as we need oxygen. That's our top priority. Do something big, I mean it."

I waggle my eyebrows. "Sure thing, boss. Should I give the host a lap dance?"

"Yes, if that'll bring in more viewers," Chase says without missing a beat.

"Relax, I've got this shit handled. Let me work my magic. After all, I'm the King of Christmas."

***

"**AND WE'RE LIVE! CHRISTMAS** is sneaking up on us—less than two weeks away! We're celebrating the best of the holidays every morning. I'm your host, Madison Morgan, and you're watching Rise and Glow LA."

Madison sparkles under the lights. With her flawless smile and her sleek blonde bob, she's everyone's bestie. Her excitement is contagious, and the audience dances along as she struts around, high-fiving fans.

The holiday set is a straight-up winter wonderland, like the North Pole got a Hollywood facelift. Pine garlands decked out with sparkling ornaments line the walls, and snowflakes dangle from the ceiling, glinting like tiny diamonds. Every available surface has been yassified.

Chase and I are perched on our chairs, waiting for our cue like obedient circus animals. I'm channeling my inner sexy Santa, cooler than a cucumber in a friggin' ice bath, while Chase is... *Holy hell!*

I catch a whiff of what I can only describe as "Eau de Panic" wafting off her. It's a delightful bouquet of flop sweat, the mint gum she's been furiously chomping, and the unmistakable scent of fear. Her knees are bouncing like she's got a goddamn earthquake happening in her pants. At this rate, she's gonna rocket off that chair like a jittery jack-in-the-box.

Is that genuine fear in Chase's eyes? Shit, it is. The woman is trembling, much like I was when she made me reshoot a kiss scene forty-seven times in sub-zero temperatures... during a snowstorm! Where the hell is my iron-willed director—the one known for making grown men cry on set? Since when did I start caring about Chase's feelings? *Damn. I must be coming down with something.*

I place a hand on her thigh. "Easy there, Sonic," I whisper. "You need to spit your gum out. And settle down before you drill a hole through the floor."

"Touch me again, Barrett, and you'll be singing 'Jingle Bells' in a voice so high, Mariah Carey will be jealous."

"Copy that," I whisper, removing my hand but not my gaze. I'm about to tell her to take a breath when—

"Today I'm here with the hunky star of the new Christmas movie, *Fa La La Love,* on the Cherish Channel. He's the *King of Christmas.* Let's hear it for Ethan Barrett!"

The audience erupts in applause. I live for this—the attention, the showboating. I love an audience that just wants to have a good time. I give an appreciative grin and wave. "Thanks for having me, Madison. Always a pleasure to spread some holiday cheer."

"And with you is your co-star, Chase Pemberton," Madison continues.

"Actually, I'm the writer and director," Chase corrects, her tone so icy it could freeze my balls off. "His co-star, Erin Calloway, is on mandatory bed rest, so... here I am."

Oof. The audience's enthusiasm deflates faster than a dollar-store air mattress.

"We're all really thrilled for Erin," I cut in with practiced ease. "She's about to have a happy, healthy baby boy."

The crowd collectively 'awws,' and just like that, we're back on track.

Madison launches into our backstory, explaining how many movies Chase and I have done together. Then, as if our 'let me do the talking' convo never happened, Chase jumps in.

"I actually discovered Ethan," she says, a hint of pride in her voice. "It's a really funny story."

Oh boy. Here we go.

"He was a nobody. Ethan was doing foot fungus commercials before I cast him."

"What can I say? You saw what a fun-GUY I was, so you had to scoop me up, didn't ya," I joke, steering us back to safer waters. "But seriously, we have such a strong connection. I mean, how else do you explain us collaborating on film after film? We can practically read each other's thoughts."

I shoot Chase a "shut the hell up" look, and her eyes narrow. *Message received.*

Madison presents to the camera with a glimmer in her eyes. "Chase, tell us why you love making romantic movies about the holidays. You must have had amazing Christmases as a kid. Your movies are so magical."

Chase freezes, like Santa getting caught by Mrs. Claus on Grindr. "Well, umm..."

Oh my God, Chase. That was an easy one.

"We both love to sprinkle in that childhood charm," I jump in smoothly. "My family absolutely loves Christmas, so it's a piece of cake for me to bring that joy to each character I play. It's the best holiday there is."

The women in the audience swoon and clap. One of them yells, "We love you, Ethan!"

I pretend to blush and blow a kiss. "Right back at you, gorgeous!"

Chase regains her voice. "So, um, the Cherish Channel has this super cool... promotion thingy. For Christmas. New subscribers get their first month free! Isn't that... neat?"

"Let's take questions from the audience," Madison says, ignoring Chase's lead.

A woman stands up, wearing a shirt that reads *All I Want for Christmas is Ethan Barrett* with my face plastered on it *(gotta get me one of those)*. "I want to know about your real-life romance, Ethan," the fan gushes. "Who will you be kissing under the mistletoe this year?"

"Hold up... Is that really what you're curious about?" I say, playing coy. "Who I'm dating?"

I saw this one coming a mile away. It's always the same question. My dating life is a never-ending parade of starlets, and the gossip sites can't get enough.

The audience bursts into applause and loud catcalls.

Madison shouts over the rowdy crowd. "Stand up ladies, and cheer! Let's convince Ethan to stop dishing on his movie and instead dish on his love life!"

I can feel Chase's rage burrowing into the side of my head. *Sorry, princess, but they love me, not your precious writing.* Chase has her Resting Grinch Face on, but then, strangely, her face changes, as if she's solved an impossible equation.

Madison motions for them to sit back down, then leans in. "Okay, Ethan. Spill the tea. Who's the lucky lady warming your bed this holiday season?"

I open my mouth, ready to serve up my usual charm-and-dodge routine, but—

"It's me," Chase blurts out. "Ethan and I are a couple!"

Wait, what?

My stomach drops.

Freefall.

"We've kept it hush-hush so far," Chase says, her voice filled with fake sweetness, "but eager Ethan here has been bursting to announce our love to the world. Right, honeybunch?"

I nod. Mechanical. Smile frozen. Inside? Screaming.

Madison's eyes go wide. "Hold the phone! You two? But I thought... I mean, aren't you guys notoriously at each other's throats?"

"You know how romance goes... Opposites attract!" Chase chirps. "But seriously, our movie, *Fa La La Love,* mirrored our love story in the most insane way." She turns to me, her smile sharp. "Ethan, tell them about the karaoke scene."

"I, uh..." *Words. Where are my words?*

"Don't be shy!" Chase pinches my cheek.

Is this what they call an out-of-body experience? Because I'm pretty sure I'm watching my career implode in real time.

"Let me tell it," Chase says, her eyes twinkling. "So, during filming, Ethan was trying to drop hints about his feelings, but I was totally oblivious. I mean, Ethan's always so charming, it's hard to read the signs!" She winks at the audience. "There's this adorable karaoke scene in *Fa La La Love*—and let me tell you, Ethan's voice is to die for—and when I called 'cut,' he started serenading me with 'All I Want for Christmas Is You.'"

The audience lets out a collective "Aww," and I wonder if it's too late to make a run for it.

"Don't even get me started on the snowman scene," Chase continues, clearly on a roll. "Let's just say Ethan needed some serious help with his snowman-building skills."

I try to regain some control. "I didn't need her help, but she's always there, offering it regardless."

Chase turns to the audience. "Ladies, he's as romantic as you think. Ethan planned this whole moment on set during the snowman scene. He waited until I called 'cut,' then wrapped his arms around me and whispered, 'You know best. That's why I always listen to you... and also I love you.'"

"That's not exactly how I said it," I interject.

"Oh, you totally did! You even set up this whole romantic scene with the props department, making fake snow fall on us. And then, with tears in your eyes, you kissed me right there and asked me to be your girlfriend."

"Well, it wasn't exactly tears," I say. "A fake snowflake got in my eye. Those things are made of soap, so my eyes were stinging like hell."

"That is so beautiful," Madison gushes.

"Isn't it?" Chase says, her expression turning serious. "We were two people caught off guard by love. It wasn't in the script, but life writes its own story. Love swoops in and turns your world upside down."

I nod, utterly defeated. *What else can I do?*

"Oh, this is a juicy exclusive!" Madison says, looking stunned.

The audience jumps to their feet, whistling and hollering.

Chase beams, proudly taking in the immediate, ecstatic reaction.

"So, will you two be spending Christmas together?"

"Of course! We're spending it with Ethan's family," Chase says. "I'm excited, Ethan's excited. His whole family is excited!"

I'm a pretty good actor, but I can't sell "excited" at the moment.

"Ethan's family goes all out for Christmas. There are gingerbread house contests, and we'll be decorating the tree together." Chase starts to fake giggle.

I listen in shock as she repeats my words from earlier like they're hers.

"And Ethan's dad dresses up as a retired Santa in flip-flops and a red bathrobe. It's so cute."

"Sounds incredible. And where are they located?" Madison asks.

"Well, you know... they're Ethan's family. I don't want to speak for him."

Chase fixes her manic eyes on me.

"Florida," I manage to croak out.

"Florida?" Chase echoes, her voice rising an octave. "Yup, that's right. So many fun things planned for Christmas in... Florida."

Chase wraps her arm around mine in a move that's about as smooth as a middle schooler at their first dance. "You should follow Ethan on social media for special sneak peeks of the movie... and us, being in love... right, sweetie pie?"

I pat her hand awkwardly. "Soooooo much love."

Note to self: Next time, do these interviews alone or hire a body double for Chase, or better yet, don't let there be a next time.

"Well, you heard it here first! Holiday love is in the air. Don't miss out on their new movie premiering in twelve days on Christmas Eve. Only on the Cherish Channel! And when we come back, we'll show you how to wrap the perfect Christmas gift... with your feet!"

Chase, subtle as a sledgehammer, blurts out one more agenda item, "And buy your loved ones a subscription to the Cherish Channel for Christmas. First month's free!"

What in the sweet mother of fuck just happened?

CHAPTER THREE

CHASE

"HUMAN! I WANT TO talk to a freaking human!" I screech into my phone, teetering under a mountain of Ethan's fan gifts. Plushies and glittery packages threaten to bury me alive. There's a stuffed reindeer making out with my left ear, approximately 372 helium balloons plotting my airborne escape, and is... that gift box ticking?

A robotic voice chirps back, "You are number seven. Please stay on the line to talk with the next representative."

Cue the hold music from hell. The first two lines of "We Wish You a Merry Christmas" start playing. And then they repeat. And repeat. *Great.* Now I'm being aurally assaulted by the world's laziest Christmas carol.

I groan, staggering toward my car. Not only was that interview a complete dumpster fire, but now I'm stuck playing Santa's little helper to all things Ethan. Fan-fucking-tastic.

The music loops again, mocking me. "We wish you a merry Christmas, we wish you a merry Christmas—"

"I wish you'd answer my damn call!" I snarl at the phone.

"We are currently experiencing a high call volume for the holiday season," the robotic voice informs me cheerfully, "but you are next in line."

Yeah, next in line for a straitjacket, maybe.

What the actual reindeer poop was I thinking? Declaring myself Ethan's girlfriend to the entire universe? I had a game plan, damn it! Promote the movie and gain subscribers. Logical. Simple. Obvious.

But no, it turned into The Ethan Show.

Ethan's smile.

Ethan's hair.

Ethan's ability to impregnate a virgin with only a wink.

He lapped it up like a dog with a bowl of eggnog, while my beloved movie got shoved aside quicker than a bad Tinder date. That's when it hit me: Give the people what they want.

I figured I could redirect their Ethan obsession straight to the movie. In theory, it was genius. More movie hype equals more new subscribers. In reality, I signed myself up for the Hollywood gossip circus. I'm going to get more intrusive questions than a contestant on *Jeopardy*.

Unlike Mr. 'I'd Stream In My Shower If You'd Let Me' Barrett, I prefer my life on the down-low. I don't want the world to learn about me, my love life *(or lack thereof)*, or my childhood. I'm a behind-the-camera gal. I don't post personal moments because—newsflash—they're PERSONAL!

I want this ten-movie deal so freaking bad. If I had more time, I could've cast someone else as Ethan's girlfriend. *Grr.* Stupid Wiley and Riley, ambushing me like that.

No, I can spin this. I can make this work. I'll write the story the fans want—a real-life romance *(that is secretly an elaborate PR stunt)*.

Sure, Ethan has a revolving door of supermodels, Hollywood star-lets, and occasionally, influencers who can't spell their own names. But they'll believe we're a couple. *Right?*

Fuck, who am I kidding?

Okay, Chase. Breathe. You can pull off being Ethan's girlfriend. It's just acting. And you're... well, you're adjacent to actors all the time. How hard can it be?

THWAP!

What the—? Something just hit me in the face. Oh, sweet baby Jesus. Are those...? Gross! Nothing says "I love Christmas" like crotchless panties.

I spot Ethan in the parking lot, holding court with his adoring public. His dazzling grin has them hanging on his every word, re-minding me of our polar opposite roles, both on and now off set. He gets the praise, and I get the fucking headaches.

As I watch the women fawning over him, a small voice in the back of my mind whispers: What if someone looked at me that way? Not for what I can do, but for who I am... Goddammit. I shut that thought down hard. I've got a job to do, and it doesn't involve dreaming about being noticed or... whatever.

As "We Wish You a Merry Christmas" continues to blast in my ear, I create my own version.

"I wish you a hairy ass fart. I wish you weren't on my shit list," I sarcastically sing. "I'm gonna throw a shit fit if you don't pick up my call."

The robotic voice chimes in again, "We are currently experiencing a high call volume for the holiday season, but you are very important to us." Aaannd... the hold music drones on.

Another pair of lacy red underwear slips out from the pile and onto the parking lot. *Oh, hell no.* For a moment, I'm tempted to leave it there, but I need these fans' support now more than ever if I want to keep my job. I give the panties a swift kick towards the car. God only knows what Ethan does with stuff like this. Let's keep it that way.

I finally reach my trusty white Toyota Camry hybrid—my mobile office and now current storage unit for Ethan's fandom treasures. I open the back door and load in the gifts.

The balloons have other ideas. They're refusing to cooperate, bobbing and weaving as I try to shove them into the back seat. The tinny Christmas music is stuck on repeat, and every "we wish you" is making my blood pressure skyrocket.

I glance down at the lacy underwear on the ground. It mocks me with its presence. Using the corner of a Christmas card envelope—because there's no way in hell I'm touching that STD specimen directly—I gingerly pick it up. A photo slips out, and on reflex, I catch it.

My brain short-circuits like a cheap toaster. It's a nude picture of a fan with flaming red hair, who has strategically placed Christmas cookies barely covering her... holiday assets. The message scrawled across the bottom makes me gag: *Ethan, all I want for Christmas is your candy cane inside my fuzzy wreath.*

"Holy shit," I blurt out, right as a chirpy male voice answers on the phone.

"And a very merry holiday to you too! How can I help you to-day?"

I toss the photo into the car, wishing the image out of my mind. "Hi, yes," I say, attempting not to sound like someone who just saw

Santa's naughty list come to life. "I'm calling about my cabin reservation in Lake Tahoe. My plans have changed, and I'll be arriving later than expected. I'd like a refund for those days."

"I'm sorry, ma'am," Mr. Holiday Cheer responds, "but we can only offer a refund if you cancel the whole reservation."

This day keeps on getting better. I look at the sea of balloons still refusing to fit in my car, and I've had enough. I grab a long-stemmed rose from the gift pile, and with vindictive pleasure, I pop a few balloons with its thorny stem.

POP! POP! POP!

Take that, false holiday cheer.

"Nope, keep it," I tell the cabin guy. "I'll be there on Christmas Day."

I end the call and turn to face the fan frenzy swarming around Ethan. "We gotta go!" I yell, but he ignores me, posing like he's auditioning for *America's Next Top Douchebag*.

"Un-fucking-believable," I groan. *That attention whore is incapable of listening—probably because he can't hear anything over the constant cheering in his head.*

I watch the spectacle and notice the fans' attire. They're decked out in more Ethan merchandise than a clearance sale at a teen heartthrob convention. T-shirts, water tumbler stickers, socks with his face plastered on them. Who is pumping out all this unlicensed crap?

I can't take this shit for another second. I storm over to the fan huddle. As I push through the crowd, trying to reach Mr. Popularity, a woman materializes, blocking my path like she's beamed down from the fangirl mothership.

Her vibrant red hair and striking green eyes are the first things I notice, but it's her attire that really steals the show. She's not wearing normal clothes. Her outfit is a full-body prayer to the Church of Ethan.

Exhibit A: Crop top. *Ethan's Future Wife* plastered across her chest. Because nothing screams "stable" like wearing your delusions.

Exhibit B: Jeans. Ethan's face. On. Each. Ass. Pocket. Left cheek, right cheek, a butt cheek sandwich with a side of crazy sauce.

Exhibit C: Water bottle. A pic of Ethan's shirtless abs with text that reads, "Sip it in, ladies." What are we sipping? The Kool-Aid of wishful thinking? The tears of Ethan's one-night stands?

The pièce de résistance...

Exhibit D: Necklace. An actual mold of Ethan's puckered lips. *For emergency smoochies*. Feeling horny? Make out with this necklace!

I stand there, stupefied. Is this what it feels like to be Ethan? Surrounded by people who see you not as a person, but as some weird item to be worn and displayed? I kinda feel sorry for him.

"Hey there, pushy pants," she hisses. "There's a line. You need to wait your turn."

I freeze, a chill running down my spine.

Shit. I know her.

She's the Christmas cookie flasher. The woman from that X-rated photo I just crammed into my car, with baked goods barely covering her—

"I've seen your tits," I blurt out before quickly correcting myself. "Er, um, I mean I'm Chase, and I'm actually Ethan's girl—"

"Yeah, I saw your little performance on TV," she interrupts, her eyes slanting with suspicion. "You're the 'surprise girlfriend.'" She gives me a cold once-over. "I thought you might be competition, but now I'm not worried."

Ouch.

"You don't even know me, so—"

She flips her hair. "Chase Pemberton, 32, Capricorn, from Evanston, Illinois, with a fashion sense as tragic as her social media presence."

Shit! I forgot about social media. The only thing I post regularly is my... who am I kidding? I don't *post*.

"I'm just... private."

"Don't worry, we totally respect that," the red-haired siren says, patting my arm as if I'm a lost puppy. "I mean, it's not like Ethan's fans are interested in every tiny detail of his life. Oh wait, we totally are!" She laughs maniacally, and her minions join in like it's a cult initiation.

The redhead turns her back on me and pushes her way to Ethan. *Sure, the crowd parts for her.* I try to follow and am immediately blocked by a wall of Ethan-worshippers. The woman giggles and squeezes next to him, putting her hand on his waist with the familiarity of a long-time friend... or something more.

"Ethan?" she coos, her voice dripping with sugar-coated venom. "Aren't you going to introduce me to your... girlfriend?"

Ethan, finally remembering I exist, comes over. "Chase, this is Gail. She's the president of the Ethan Addicts fan club."

"We just met," I manage.

Gail eyes me skeptically. "We were all shocked to hear about your relationship, weren't we, ladies?"

A chorus of agreement rises from the fan collective.

"Ethan's never had a serious girlfriend before, at least not one he's told us about." She winks at Ethan, and I swear I see him blush.

Put on the spot, I fumble for a response. "Yeah, we wanted to keep things secret until we knew it was serious."

"And how long have you and Ethan been dating?"

"Four months," I say confidently, just as Ethan says, "A couple weeks."

For the love of...

Gail's smirk widens. "Fascinating," she muses, "because you're nothing like the dream girl he described in his last interview. What was it again, Ethan? A hot yoga instructor who loves rescuing kittens and white water rafting."

My heart is doing backflips in my chest. *How am I supposed to make this human lie detector believe I'm smitten with this jackass? Five seconds ago, I was ready to chuck my shoe at him.*

Come on, get a grip. You've written approximately eleventy billion of these scenes. I frantically run through my mental archive of every rom-com I've created.

Gaze lovingly into his eyes?

Ha! I'd rather make prolonged eye contact with the camera during an awkward sex scene.

Snuggle up to him?

Hell no! I'd rather freeze my tits off cuddling a life-size Ethan ice sculpture.

Maybe a cutesy nickname?

Snookums? Honeybear? I'd sooner call him *"Fuckboy Mc-Dreamy."*

I've got nothing.

What would his typical airhead dream girl do? Probably laugh at his jokes and compliment him relentlessly. "Oh, Ethan, your muscles look particularly bulgy today, especially the bulge in your pants."

Gross. Fuck no.

In my movies, couples bond over something quirky and cute. But Ethan and I? The only thing we share is our mutual disdain for each other. Why is this so hard? I've written a dozen screenplays about fake relationships!

Screw it. If I can't be the dream girl, I'll be… whatever the hell I am.

I force a laugh. "You know how it is. Sometimes love jumps up and bites you like a venomous spider. Next thing you know, you're mating and the female bites the man's head off."

Ethan breaks the awkward silence with a pity chuckle and says, "She's a writer, this one, always making jokes."

"Aren't jokes supposed to be funny?" Gail quips.

Time to change the subject before I bite Gail's head off. I address the crowd. "You're all going to love Ethan in *Fa La La Love*. He sings in it."

"The viewing party is already on the calendar," Gail says. "We see everything Ethan stars in because he's a true leading man." Her eyes narrow even further *(if that's possible)*. "I just hope you're ready for the attention that comes with dating Ethan. His fans can be quite… passionate."

What the hell is with this lady? I've faced down studio execs with god complexes and actors who think their hair is the center of the universe. *Sorry, Gail. You don't intimidate me.*

"I can handle it," I say, wrapping my arms around Ethan's and ignoring how unexpectedly nice his bicep feels. "In fact, why don't you keep an eye on Ethan's social media? You'll get all the spicy details about our romantic getaway to Florida."

Ethan nods, a beat too late. "Yeah, it's gonna be… great."

Her smile is all teeth, no warmth. "We'll be watching alright. Very, very closely."

Gail and I lock eyes in a battle of wills. It's all arched eyebrows and razor-sharp smiles, a silent showdown of "bring it" and "game on." May the best badass woman win.

Ethan, sensing the impending catfight, steps in. "Sorry, ladies, we really need to go. Thanks again for coming out to support my—I mean *our* new movie."

"Bye Ethan, we love you!" Gail calls out sweetly as we turn to leave. Then, loud enough to ensure I hear every syllable, she says, "We'll be monitoring those relationship updates!"

As we make our escape, I can feel Gail's stare burning holes in my back. It's quickly replaced by Ethan's growl.

"You," he whispers, "have some serious explaining to do, Director Pemberton. Why the fuck did you just broadcast to the whole damn planet that we are an item?!"

CHAPTER FOUR

ETHAN

I FOLLOW CHASE INTO her apartment, and it's like... I walked into a sensory deprivation chamber. Everything is either white, beige, or that soul-sucking shade of gray they use in prisons. Does she have a vendetta against color? And what's with all the minimalist furniture and decor blending in with the walls?

I venture into the kitchen, my eyes searching for any sign of life—a boyfriend, a half-dead cactus, hell, even a dirty dish would suffice. But there's jack shit. This place takes the cake for the strangest apartment I've ever seen, and trust me, I've been in plenty of women's places *(don't judge)*.

Chase thought it best to go somewhere private to discuss what had just happened. With pictures of us already blowing up on social media, I wasn't the only one wanting answers. Although now part of me wonders if she lured me here like a sadistic serial killer because her place gives me the fucking chills.

"Jesus, Chase," I say, running a finger along a spotless countertop. "Do you actually live here, or is this some kind of movie set?"

Chase taps away on her phone, not even looking up. "Don't touch anything. I'm getting my laptop. We are going to handle this mess before it gets out of hand."

She leaves the room, and that's when I spot it—a sign of life. A stack of movie scripts are scattered across a sleek glass coffee table. Of course, the only personal touch is work-related.

Don't get me wrong, I didn't expect a dog, but my money was on a hamster or at least one of those... what do you call 'em? Those depressing fish that live in a sad little jar... A beta. You know, the type of thing that can live without mutual love or human connection.

"Ethan!" Chase shouts from her bedroom. "Shoes off, Barrett. I don't want you tracking your ego all over my floors."

"Sure thing, boss," I yell back, kicking off my sneakers. "Seriously Chase, where's all your shit?"

Chase struts out, laptop in hand. "Some of us prefer a tidy space to a hot mess. Unlike your place, which I imagine looks like the 'lost and found' bin at a strip club."

For a moment, I imagine rolling in the sheets with a control freak like her. Clipboards, timers, the works. Performance reviews in bed? Pass. I swipe left on that idea faster than my last one-night stand.

I smirk playfully. "Well, the bedroom is the only room that matters—because that's where the magic happens."

Chase scoffs, rolling her eyes. "Yeah, maybe if you prefer your living space filled with regret and hepatitis."

"I wouldn't call this living. You don't have a single photo in this place," I say. "Surely someone must have tolerated you long enough to get a picture with you?"

A flicker in her eyes. *Was that... sadness?* It's gone in a blink.

"My personal life is not your business," she says, her voice clipped. "Or anyone else's. I don't feel the need to plaster my life over social media for likes."

"Hey, my fans appreciate my openness."

"Your fans go crazy for your shirtless selfies," Chase fires back. "They don't know the real you. And if they did, they wouldn't like it."

Damn. That's harsh.

I'm well aware that my fangirls love the persona of Ethan Barrett—the holiday romance movie hunk who looks good in nothing but his abs and a Santa hat. And yeah, that's part of me. I've spent years crafting that heartthrob image.

But the real Ethan?

Heck, these days I don't even know if *I* know him.

Chase sits in her sleek, gray armchair, its sharp angles unyielding to her body. The narrow armrests are rigid and uninviting, so much so that I'm uncomfortable for her. But she seems accustomed to it as she opens her computer and types. Her fast clicks fill the stark, sterile room.

Across from her, I flop onto the rock hard sofa. *Oof.* It's so stiff it makes a *FWUMPF* sound like it's never been sat on. The fabric is scratchy. Definitely not comfortable enough to fuck on *(just saying)*.

"Did you bring me here to bang me? All you had to do was ask," I wink. "No need for elaborate schemes."

Chase's stare could cut the balls off a brass monkey. "In your dreams, Barrett."

"Nah, in my dreams, you actually smile," I quip. Then my tone turns deadly serious. "Cut the bullshit, Chase. What the hell is all this? You announced to the whole fucking world you're my girlfriend, and my phone's exploding with people wanting answers. Which includes me, damnit."

She takes a deep breath. "The network is demanding we bring in one million new Cherish Channel subscribers before Christmas. But don't worry, I've got a plan."

"Hang on. What?" I sputter. "A million subscribers in less than two weeks? I'm popular, but I'm not freaking Santa Claus."

"Which is why my brilliant fake relationship scheme is the answer. Just listen to my pitch. We'll leverage your social media presence and your rabid fanbase to promote the network. Those subscriptions will be pouring in."

"You saw how my fans reacted. It was like watching kids open socks on Christmas," I say, leaning back with a smirk. "And re-member Gail? Can you honestly picture Gail rooting for us to be together? Didn't think so."

"Oh, I don't think anyone could forget Gail. Seriously, Ethan, I know you'd sleep with a toaster if it had boobs, but—"

"Whoa, timeout!" I interrupt, making a T with my hands. "I have not slept with Gail. There's 'crazy in bed,' and then there's 'might actually murder me in my sleep.'"

"Sure. Whatever," she says, unconvinced.

"I'm not lying. No way I'd hook up with that one."

"Well then, that's where your charm comes in. Work your fan magic. Make them love me."

"That's asking the impossible. No one likes you."

"The crew likes me," she insists

I put a hand on her tense shoulder. It's like trying to comfort a marble statue. "Uh no, they don't. They all call you 'Ice Queen' behind your back. Though, if we're being honest, the B-word is the top pick."

I wince, realizing I might have gone too far. I'm about to apologize when—

"Like it or not, we're stuck together," she says, her voice tight. "We need to convince a million new fans to subscribe to the Cherish Channel, and I've come up with an elaborate PR stunt."

Chase spins her laptop around. *BAM!* My face. Everywhere.

There I am, grinning from dozens of photos, each with a different stunning woman on my arm. Actresses, models, even a couple of pop stars. It's a veritable who's who of Hollywood's most eligible bachelorettes.

Click. Click. Click.

Website after website. All about me... well, my love life.

"This," Chase says, pointing at the screen. "This is a story I can write. It's got everything the fans will be rooting for."

I stare at the images, feeling a strange mix of pride and discomfort. It's the Ethan Barrett brand in all its glory—the Hollywood "It Boy," the playboy with the heart of gold.

Chase continues, "You're the guy every woman wants to tame. The eternal bachelor. It's classic. Cary Grant. George Clooney. Now, Ethan Barrett.

Chase opens up my Ethan Addict's fan page. Photos of me hitting the gym, grabbing coffee, posing with nothing but a Santa hat. Then, a stream of women—one gorgeous lady after the next. *Okay, maybe my dating life has gotten a little out of hand.*

Click. Click. Click.

"If everyone thinks we fell head over heels during filming, they'll be like, 'Oh my God, I gotta see this movie!' It's like we're offering a two-for-one special on romance—buy the on-screen love story, get the behind-the-scenes one free. They'll subscribe faster than you can blink, all to peek at our supposed off-camera chemistry. And voilà! A million subscribers for the Cherish Channel."

I shake my head. Hard. "Won't work because A) my fans all want to bang me and B) they know me... Well, they know my type." I look her up and down, taking in the power suit and severe ponytail. "And you're—

"I get it. I'm not a bombshell."

"I didn't say that. You're plenty..." I trail off, suddenly aware I'm navigating a minefield in flip-flops.

Beautiful? True, but I'd eat my Santa hat before giving her that kind of ammunition.

Smart? She'd probably take it as an insult to her other qualities.

My brain scrambles for a safe adjective, coming up empty.

"You're fine," I end up saying. I instantly regret it.

"You're an asshole," she says, slamming her laptop shut.

"Yes, people love me. That doesn't mean I can make people like *you*. I'm not a magician."

"Get ready to pull a rabbit out of your ass, because this is happening. We have two weeks to convince everyone we're madly in love."

Something's off. Chase is wound tighter than usual, which is saying something. She's holding back, but what?

"You have no idea what you've done. The media circus, the rabid fans... it's not all autographs and selfies, you know."

Chase scoffs, waving a dismissive hand. "Please. You do it. How hard can it be?"

I laugh. "It's a full-time job. The constant updates, the carefully curated posts, dealing with the die-hard fans. Tell me, have you ever been followed into the bathroom? You think directing is stressful? Try having millions of people watching your every move, hanging on your every word."

"I can handle it," Chase insists, her jaw set in that stubborn way I've come to know all too well.

I stand up. "No. I'm not doing it. I'm not participating in some subscriber scam."

Her eyes narrow dangerously. "If you don't..."

She hesitates. Since when is she so careful with her words? I can feel it, like when a performance isn't genuine. Chase is many things—bossy, frustratingly attractive, probably plotting my demise this very second. But indirect? Not her style. *So why does this feel like she's hiding something?*

For a moment, her voice goes soft, like she's temporarily possessed by an actual human being. "Ethan, I.. I need this or..." Then, faster than I can say "what the fuck," she's back to her usual bossy self. "Or you can kiss your 'King of Christmas' crown goodbye. The network's drawn the line: a million subs, otherwise we're both fired."

What she says hits me like a gut punch. I need this job. The money, the fame—it's not just for me. I have people who rely on me, but there's no way in hell I'm telling Chase that.

Then again... maybe this PR nightmare is my golden ticket out of rom-com purgatory. I've been dying to do more than just flash my abs and dazzle old ladies with my smile. This could be my chance to go from handsome face to Hollywood heavyweight.

I shrug. "Maybe I'm done being typecast. My agent's been pushing me to move into action flicks. Says this body's being wasted on feel-good movies." I flex for emphasis, enjoying the way Chase rolls her eyes. "There's this surfing biopic that's got me pegged for the lead."

"Oh, please," Chase snorts. "Christmas owns you. And you love it."

I lean in, my voice low and cocky as fuck. "Face it, ice queen... You need me more than I need you. I'll play along with your little scheme, but only if we do it my way."

Chase leans back, arms crossed, holding in her rage. "I'm listening. But this better blow my mind, or I'm swapping you out for a blow-up doll. It'll give a more convincing performance."

"Starting with shit like that. You might be a hotshot director, but social media is my kingdom. You need me, my fans, and my brilliant fucking ideas. It takes a lot more than just pretending we're a couple. If this is a social media campaign, we're equal partners, sweetheart."

"Absolutely not," Chase fires back.

I shrug, turning towards the door. "I guess I'll be hitting the waves. Cowabunga, dude!" I mime riding a surfboard and then wave goodbye with a hang loose sign.

Chase pinches the bridge of her nose. "Wait, okay," she grits out. "Partners."

I grin, dropping back onto the sofa. "Next, I want you to go to bat for me with the executives. I want to direct a movie."

The laugh that bursts out of Chase is so sudden and loud, it echoes off the bare walls. "You? Direct? Oh... you're serious?"

"Yeah. Why is that funny?"

"Pretty boy, you have no idea how difficult my job is. You can't just smile your way through it. Directing is hard work."

"Look, I'm not an idiot," I say somberly. "But I need to level up and explore new aspects of my career. I can't ride off my good looks forever."

Chase studies me for a long moment, her expression unreadable. Finally, she sighs. "Okay. I'll put in a good word. But don't get your hopes up."

"Thank you," I say, genuinely grateful. "One last thing."

"There's more?" she groans. "Seriously, do I need my lawyer present?"

"You gotta sell it as my girlfriend around my folks. I'm not kidding, Chase. You might enjoy being alone in a cabin like some kind of psycho, but I love going home for Christmas."

"Not everyone loves the holidays," she snaps. "That doesn't make me a fucking psycho."

I backpedal faster than when a fan asks me to sign her chest. "Look, what I'm saying is, my family goes all out. We have a ton of traditions. I haven't been home in a year because of work and I don't want you to—"

"Fuck it up?" Chase finishes.

"No! I mean, yes. I mean..." I rake a hand through my hair. "I just need you to act like you're into me and actually enjoy the damn festivities. Think you can manage that?"

Chase's eyes widen in horror. "You mean like physical contact? Hell no."

I chuckle. "Whoa there, Handsy McGrabby. That's where your mind went first? I mean, I know I'm irresistible, but get a grip, woman."

A flush creeps up Chase's neck, and I'd be lying if I said it wasn't kind of adorable. "That's not—I didn't—Oh, go fuck yourself, Barrett."

"Is that your way of saying we have a deal?"

"I'm going to regret this, aren't I?" She looks up at me, resignation written all over her face. "Fine. Deal."

"Shall we seal it with a handshake? Or would that be too much physical contact for you?"

Before she can protest, I pull out my phone and start filming for social media. "Hey there, Ethan Addicts! I'm here with my girlfriend. We are packing for Florida!"

I put my arm around Chase, who looks about as comfortable as Scrooge searching for a character witness. "Are you excited, darlin'?"

Chase grimaces, her attempt at a smile. "I-I-I'm speechless!"

Just to really get under her skin, I give her ponytail a little ruffle.

"We wanted to come on and ask for your help to make our new holiday movie, *Fa La La Love*, the biggest movie of the season! Let's show the doubters that we believe in love. We need one million new subscribers to watch the movie when it premieres on Christmas Eve. What do you say, Ethan Addicts!"

Chase adds awkwardly, "Give the gift of the Cherish Channel this Christmas."

"We love you!" I say, ending the recording.

Chase gruffly pushes me away. "Next time, warn me when you're going to touch me!"

"Ooh, so feisty. Exactly why I fell in fake love with you."

Chase shoots me an intense stare. "You know that feeling when you look into someone's eyes and just know, deep down, you're definitely not *ever* meant to be together? That's us."

"Right back at ya." I wink. "Now, get packed. We're taking the red-eye to Miami tonight."

"Tonight?" Chase sputters.

"Pleasure doing business with you," I say, heading for the door. As I reach for the handle, I turn back with a grin. "Oh, and pack for the beach. Christmas in Florida is still pretty warm this time of year."

As I close the door behind me, there's a look of sheer panic on her face. It's priceless, maybe even worth all the chaos about to come our way.

Chase Pemberton, the ice queen herself, pretending to be my loving girlfriend for two weeks? This is going to be one hell of a Christmas.

CHAPTER FIVE

ETHAN

"Oh my God, this humidity is a fucking disaster," Chase complains.

We step out of the airport in Miami, and her hair goes full poodle. Picture if Medusa, Einstein, and a startled porcupine got together and said, "Let's make a hair monster." And they did.

"You look like you fucked a light socket," I joke. "Most people need a whole glam squad to get their hair so teased out. You're like a one-woman homage to Twisted Sister."

"I hate this place already," she groans, trying to tame her frizzy mane.

We're standing in the rental lot, surrounded by a sea of shiny vehicles roasting on the asphalt. I wipe the sweat from my brow. The humidity is so intense you practically have to swim through it. Planes roar over us, and I can feel Chase melting down from the combination of heat, moisture, and noise. Seeing her so miserable, I realize... this is gonna be fun!

"Florida's a whole different ball game. You either fall in love with it, or you're booking the next flight out."

The woman has been a nonstop complaint factory since we boarded the plane. First, she criticized my 'excessive manspreading.' Then she found fault with my 'obnoxious' chewing of the complimentary pretzels. She also went on a tirade about my 'incessant knee bouncing' and how my 'unnecessarily large biceps' were invading her personal space.

But then, miracle of miracles, she fell asleep... on my shoulder. I didn't dare move a muscle. I sat there, stiff as a board, terrified that the slightest twitch would wake the sleeping beast and unleash fresh hell. There was one little bonus from the flight—that fact that I can still smell her alluring citrus scent on me.

And now she's wearing all-black again for our fun Florida getaway. She views it as professional while I see it as a sad, misguided storm cloud crashing a beach party.

I pull out my phone, stand next to her, and snap a quick selfie. "Smile!"

I dictate the caption, enjoying how it makes Chase squirm. "Meet *The Frizzinator*: my girlfriend's new look, courtesy of Florida's sultry embrace. #HairGoneWild."

"If you post that —"

"Whoops," I say, tapping *Post* with a smirk. Before she can smack me, I tuck a wild strand of hair behind her ear. "This is what you signed on for. Unless you wanna call it off, darlin'?"

Chase fixes me with a piercing gaze. "Don't. Call. Me. That."

"What's the problem, pookie?" I lean in. "Not a fan of pet names, sweetheart?"

"Not from you. And especially not 'darlin' or 'sweetheart.' I'm your director, not your actual girlfriend."

She yanks her suitcase handle with enough force to take down a small child and starts marching through the row of cars. I follow behind, watching the sway of her hips. Even pissed off, she's got a walk that could stop traffic.

"Come on now, honeybun. How else will my family be convinced of our steamy romance? Buttercup? Snookums? Ooh, I know, how about sugar tits?"

She whirls around so fast I nearly plow into her. Her chest heaves *(hey there)*, and I force my eyes up to her face. Her very angry face. "How about you call me by my name? Or better yet, don't talk to me at all."

"Now where's the fun in that, pumpkin?" I smirk.

"I've got a few choice names for you," she growls, jabbing a finger into my chest. "Jackass. Egomaniac. Walking HR violation. Take your pick."

I catch her fingers, pressing them firmly against my pecs. Her palm is warm, and I can feel my heartbeat pick up. "Careful there, lovebug. A guy might think you're coming onto him with all this touching."

Her eyes darken, and for a moment, I think she might actually kiss me. Or kill me.

She yanks her hand away. "Touch me again, and I'll make sure you can't sit comfortably for a week."

"Kinky..." I wink. "I always knew you had a wild side, baby."

"You're impossible," she mutters, pulling away.

"Impossibly charming? Devilishly handsome? Irresistibly—"

"Annoying."

"You love it," I tease, falling into step beside her.

My grouchy travel buddy rolls her eyes and takes a breath. I can almost see her counting to ten in her head. "Let's find the car so we can get some AC."

I slam the button on the key fob. A cherry red Mustang convertible chirps back like it's happy to see us. Chase's face goes through a dozen different expressions in one fleeting moment, landing somewhere between *I'm gonna hurl* and *Do they have the death penalty in Florida?*

"A convertible? In this sauna? Are you out of your goddamn mind?"

"My turf, my rules. Equal partners, remember?"

"I didn't think it was possible to hate you more than I already do. Congrats, you've outdone yourself."

"Oh, you wait. We've got two whole weeks ahead of us."

We climb into the car. I rev the engine and peel out of the parking deck. The Florida sun hits me with its warm caress, and I feel something inside me uncoil. I'm home.

Miami is its own world—a cocktail of cultures served in a glass rimmed with beach sand and tourist traps—and I love it, but what I love more is the moment I hang a left onto Highway 41, head toward the Everglades, and leave the concrete jungle in my rearview.

I'm alive!

The landscape opens up around us, wild and untamed, just like yours truly.

"Where are you taking me?" Chase asks, her voice laced with suspicion. "I thought you lived in Miami?"

"I said I live *close* to Miami. Marco Island is my home," I reply, puffing out my chest like a proud peacock.

"Is that a real place, or did you just make that up to mess with me?"

I chuckle. "Oh, it's real. Sit back and enjoy the drive. We're taking the scenic route."

As we cruise along, I drink in the sight of the endless wetlands covered in green sawgrass—cypress trees scattered across the shimmering waterways. It's a scene from a movie, but better. The beautiful blue sky—no L.A. smog—and pure, puffy white clouds.

This. Is. Livin'.

Don't get me wrong, Hollywood's a crazy ride, but there's something about the untamed terrain of Florida that blows L.A. out of the water.

I take a deep breath, savoring the mix of earthy wetland aromas and rich swampy smells. I glance over at Chase, expecting to see her equally enraptured by the view. Instead, she's gagging dramatically. Her face is scrunched up like she's caught a whiff of a particularly ripe dumpster.

"What in the ever-loving fuck is that smell?" she chokes out. "Did something die?"

"That's nature's perfume," I say, patting the steering wheel affectionately. "Nothing rivals the smell of the wetlands."

"Please, put the top up. I will pay you $500. I'm seriously going to throw up."

I grab the pine-scented air freshener off the rearview mirror and toss it to her. "Here, I'll enjoy the swamp, and you can protect your nose with the manufactured scent of Christmas."

"You had to grow up in Florida, didn't you?" she complains. "This is not Miami. This is a wasteland. How are we supposed to promote the movie in Dump Water, Nowhere?"

I give an empty chuckle, trying to shake off Chase's judgment of my childhood, my values, my home. *You invited yourself here, you selfish little*—I stop myself, smiling with satisfaction at how miserable she is.

She can wallow all she wants. I'm in my happy place.

"Trust me, Christmas in Florida is magical. It's not like any other place on Earth," I say, my hometown pride taking over. "My family has lots of fun holiday traditions that don't involve freezing our butts off."

"Let me guess... Instead of an ugly sweater contest, it's an ugly bikini contest?" she snarks.

"When you report back to your leader, Satan, can you ask him if you're allowed to wear a bikini while you're here and maybe smile a little? I know he has a strict 'no fun in the sun' policy."

"You're such a dick."

"That's why you love me, sweetheart," I say, blowing her a kiss.

We roll down the sun-kissed stretch of road, the Sunshine State showing off her best. I'm grinning ear to ear, but her face suggests she's considering jumping out of the moving car. There's lush greenery everywhere and critters that most people only meet on their TV screens.

A group of herons wade through the shallow water, and I gesture out the window. "Check that out. Pretty amazing, right?"

Chase barely glances up from her phone, her brow furrowed in concentration. "Mmhmm," she mumbles, unimpressed.

"Picture this: *Christmas in the Keys*—a Cherish Channel original. Sun, sand, and sizzling vacation romance. It'd be unforgettable, don't you think?"

She shakes her head. "No snow, no Christmas movie. That's not my rule—that comes straight from the Network. Now shut up. I'm trying to work."

And she's back to her phone, frowning at the screen. "God, the reception out here is awful."

I reach over and gently lower her phone. "Hey, Workaholic. You do realize you're missing out on a live-action National Geographic special? Actual living creatures surround us on all sides. Do you really want to ignore this natural wonder to check emails?"

Her eyebrows raise, and she glares as if I've suggested we strip naked and wrestle gators, but then her face softens. "Fine," she says, slumping back in her seat. "So, tell me about this redneck Christmas of yours. Does Santa bring moonshine instead of milk and cookies?"

"Fair warning, you're about to witness the Barrett Family Christmas Extravaganza. It's like a Vegas show meets the North Pole. And you? Well, let's just say you might want to tap into some of my holiday spirit. You're gonna need it."

Because her dark, brooding cloud of holiday loathing won't cut it when we get there. My family? They make the Griswolds look like amateurs in the holiday cheer department.

"My mom's gonna want to know all about you. So, tell me some stuff."

"Like what?"

"I dunno. Your childhood, your parents?"

"Nope, I don't discuss that." Her tone leaves no room for argument.

"My mom is going to ask."

"Then you'll need to tell her that it's personal."

"So, what am I allowed to tell her? Give me something here, Ice Queen."

Chase sighs, acting as if I've asked her to donate both kidneys and maybe a lung. "Tell her I'm from Evanston, Illinois. I've always wanted to direct. I went to USC to get my filmmaking degree. My job is my whole fucking life."

"Well, that's depressing," I say before I can stop myself. "Isn't Northwestern a film school around there? Why didn't you go to that university? Too many corn fields?"

"Because I needed to get as far away from that hellhole as possible."

There's definitely more to that story. I'm about to ask my next question when her phone chirps.

"Network update," she mutters, scowling at the screen. "They've created a real-time subscriber counter app. We've pulled in 10,000 new paid subs for the Cherish Channel so far."

"That's awesome!" I say, feeling a surge of excitement.

"That's it?! You've got over a million social media followers. Where the hell are they, and why aren't they coming over? Ten thousand is not gonna cut it. This plan is doomed."

"You're looking at this all wrong. Most of my followers are already subscribed. You're welcome, by the way! That means we gotta reach new people—lots of them, since you've set the bar sky-high. It's doable, but you have to believe. That's how Christmas magic works."

Now I'm being looked at like I've sprouted antlers. "Magic? What are you, five?"

"What made our first movie blow up?" I ask. "You didn't see it coming. Neither did I."

"It was my writing and my directing."

"Nah, it wasn't even my rock-hard abs or my irresistible charm." I shake my head, grinning. "It was Christmas magic. And for those who believe, it comes every year."

"We need a strategy, a social media campaign. Not a general feeling of goodwill."

"I know," I say nonchalantly, pointing to my head. "I'm working on a plan as we speak."

"I don't know if you should be thinking and driving. That's asking a lot from that pretty boy brain of yours."

"You can knock off all the bull—"

"*AARGH!*"

Chase screams, "Oh my God, oh my God, I swallowed something! I freaking hate this disgusting, sticky, bug-infested hellhole!"

"Lighten up. It's a bug. Probably a mosquito." I wink at her. "They're the state bird of Florida, you know."

She coughs and hacks, as if trying to expel a demon. Then she grabs her water bottle and starts chugging, trying to drown the bug. In her frenzy, she spits out the side of the car.

Straight. Into. The wind.

The spray comes right back, splattering her face.

I lose it, howling with laughter. Chase looks like a cat that fell into a bathtub—frizzy hair, streaky makeup, and soaking wet.

"Hey, look on the bright side," I say, gasping between chuckles, "at least the water's blending in with all that sweat. Florida's natural moisturizer, baby!"

She is not amused—that oh-so-familiar look of murder on her face once again. "I hate you, and I hate Florida."

CHAPTER SIX

CHASE

"Oh, thank God. I can smell the ocean."

The salty breeze washes over me, a refreshing change after the miles of muggy misery. I take in a deep, cleansing breath, purging the swamp and bug guts from my nostrils.

"Sorry to break it to you, but that's not the ocean. It's the Gulf of Mexico."

"Oh, thanks for the mansplanation. How about I womansplain where you can stick your condescending attitude? Here's a hint: It starts with 'up' and ends with 'your ass.'"

Maybe Floridians get all hot and bothered about different bodies of water, but the rest of the world? Couldn't care less. Especially me. Then we round a bend, and holy crap, Marco Island pops up like a freaking vacation commercial. I soak in the view, and suddenly, I hate him a little less.

The island is too much—a beautiful blend of sand and civilization. Palm trees hula dance in the breeze on long, clean beaches. Quaint sailboats. Shimmering water. Orgasmically blue skies. I want to live here... or at least write my next script here.

"What a relief," I admit. "I was starting to think Florida was one big smelly swamp that farted you out. That stench was un-freaking-bearable."

"You're unpleasant. To work with. To travel with. You know that song 'Shut Up and Drive'? Let's try that."

"I'm trying to be nice. I thought you were dragging me to some swampy hellhole, but instead… well, let's just say you've redeemed yourself. A little." I smile, taking in the sand, city, and sky.

Ethan smirks. "I'd hold off on thanking me just yet." He turns the wheel sharply, steering us into a dense patch of trees on a two-lane gravel road. Seconds later, it looks *(and smells)* awfully similar to the Everglades.

"Where are you going?" I ask frantically. "You said you lived on the island!"

"Oh, yeah, about that. I meant to say I live *near* the island."

"You're such an asshole. I can't fucking stand you."

"You're gonna need that rage for where we're going. Destination: Mosquitoville. Population: ALL OF THEM."

As we plunge deeper into Jurassic Swamp, my mind reels with questions. How does someone go from a redneck in Shrek's backyard to a leading man in Tinseltown, USA? This is Ethan Barrett, for crying out loud. A man who's made swooning an Olympic sport. He should be another Hollywood blowhard lounging in Malibu mansions—not playing Tarzan in the backwaters of Florida.

"So, you actually grew up here?" I say, feeling some serious swamp PTSD.

"Born and raised. Learned to swim with the gators before I could walk."

"You're full of shit," I say, narrowing my eyes. I try to picture a mini-Ethan paddling alongside scaly death machines. "You're messing with me."

"Maybe. But I did learn to airboat before I got my driver's license."

The sun's rays pierce through the canopy of trees, casting dappled light across my face. The trees overhead are doing a piss-poor job of blocking the sun, and I've become a sweaty, irritable mess. As much as I can't stand the sweltering heat, I hate the smug bastard behind the wheel even more.

If he doesn't wipe off that condescending grin, I'm going to push him out of this fucking car.

"How much longer? I desperately need a shower. I'm starting to smell like your homeland."

Ethan chuckles. "It won't do you any good. My dad refuses to turn on the AC."

"Please, for the love of shit, tell me you're kidding."

"Adapt or die."

"Or go home."

"That's always an option, sweetheart. No one will miss you."

That one stings. Time to tell this jerkoff where he can stuff his—

"We're here! Put on that smile. It's showtime!"

"I'm gonna have to act my ass off to pretend I don't want to kill you," I mutter.

"Oh, that pep talk was all for me, sweet cheeks. Pretending to love your always delightful ball-busting personality? That's the performance of a lifetime."

Silence. We both stew in our mutual hatred. *Oh my God. How did I think we could pull this off?*

As the car crunches up the gravel driveway, I get my first look at Casa de Barrett. The quirky light-gray house is perched on hurricane stilts like it's ready to run *(girl, same)*. The home itself is a large, middle-class structure that is worlds apart from the cramped apartment I grew up in. It's idyllic, really, if not for the swampy surroundings. Then I see the lawn—I'm gaping.

Imagine Santa's workshop and a Florida souvenir shop hitting rock bottom and deciding to liquidate their assets in a tacky "going out of business" sale. It's an extravaganza of bad taste.

Plastic pink flamingos wearing tiny Santa hats.

Inflatable alligators in reindeer costumes.

Garish green wreaths made from palm fronds and pine cones hang on the house.

Spanish moss adorned with Christmas lights.

And then there's the twelve-foot blow-up Santa on a surfboard wearing a Hawaiian shirt.

My mind immediately starts cataloging the challenges of making this tasteless wonderland "Christmas cute" for our social media posts.

This is a total nightmare. And not the fun *Nightmare Before Christmas* kind.

A petite woman with long blonde hair stands out front, stringing up even more tacky, colorful lights. She's decked out in a blindingly bright flamingo romper, accessorized with enough jingle bells to wake the dead. The moment she spots our car, her face lights up brighter than her decorations.

"Ethan!" she squeals, abandoning her light-hanging mission and racing towards us.

Before Ethan can even get out of the car, she's pulled him into a bear hug that defies her small stature. I awkwardly exit the vehicle and approach the love fest, trying to plaster on my best 'meet the parents' look.

When Ethan finally extricates himself from his mother's embrace, she turns to me with a smile that rivals the Florida sun. Her lipstick is the exact hot pink shade of the lawn flamingos, and it's so quirky it's almost endearing. I can't help but wonder—which came first?

"And I'm so excited to meet your girlfriend!" she gushes.

"Chase, this is my mama, Darla," Ethan says, gesturing between us.

I extend my hand, summoning every ounce of politeness I can muster. "It's a pleasure to meet you, Mrs. Barrett. Thank you for having me."

Darla looks at my outstretched hand like it's a foreign object from another planet. "Oh honey," she coos, "we don't do formal here!"

She pulls me into a hug with the grip of a python. The scent of sugar cookies and peppermint Schnapps invades my senses, and I fight the urge to sneeze directly into her tinsel-adorned hair.

After what feels like forever, Darla releases her grip and gives me a once-over. "Well, you're just as stiff as Doug on our wedding night." She follows with an exaggerated wink. "If you know what I mean."

I'm still reeling from that mental image *(stop it, brain)* when Ethan's father makes his grand entrance. He emerges from the front screen door looking like Ethan's stunt double from the future. His light-brown hair is peppered with silver, and his kind blue eyes crinkle at the corners as he smiles.

His outfit, though? Pure Florida dad on a bender. Khaki shorts, boat shoes, and a T-shirt that proclaims *Merry Gator-mas!* with a cartoon alligator rocking a Santa hat. It's like he's trying to win the "Most Florida" award.

Ethan and his dad launch into what appears to be a secret hand-shake-hug hybrid, clearly perfected over years of practice. I stand uncomfortably to the side, feeling like an intruder on this family moment.

Finally, he notices me. "Where are my manners?" he says, turning in my direction. His eyes widen as he surveys me. "I'm Doug. Aren't you a beauty? Ethan, she's a real knockout. I can see why you fell for her." He pauses, glancing at his wife. "Not as beautiful as your mother, though."

I force my mouth to smile. "It's nice to meet you, Mr. Barrett."

Doug's face scrunches up like I've just insulted his alligator shirt. "Oh my. We like to keep it casual around here."

"You can just call us Doug and Darla. Now let's go inside before the mosquitoes smell fresh blood!" she says, wrapping her arm around mine.

"State bird of Florida," I blurt out.

Doug's face lights up, and he gives me a hearty slap on the back. "That's right! Come on in, you two. I just made my special Christmas Gator punch!"

As we follow the Barretts towards the house, I shoot Ethan a panicked look.

He whispers through his arrogant expression, "Welcome to the family, sweetheart."

***

I'M STANDING IN WHAT I assume is the Barrett family's entryway, though "chaos containment unit" might be more accurate.

In the cramped corner of the room, there's a makeshift holiday punch station. The punch bowl? A life-sized alligator head, jaws wide open, filled with some suspicious liquid. Its plastic teeth gleam under the lights as Doug reaches for a glass.

"You're gonna love it, I guarantee!" he says.

I take a sip of the murky green concoction, half expecting the goo to wink at me. "How did you get it to be so... slimy?"

Doug's face lights up. "My Gator Punch is a concoction of coconut rum and pineapple juice mixed with melon liqueur," he begins, chest puffing out with pride. "But to get that swamp-like texture... I use gravy mix."

I swallow the liquid, miraculously not gagging. The drink slithers down my throat, a bizarre mix of tropical sweetness and savory thickness. It's as if he blended fiber powder into what would have been a tasty piña colada.

Meanwhile, Doug downs his entire glass in one go, smacking his lips with satisfaction. "You can't even taste the gravy!"

I consider dumping the rest of my drink in the nearest potted plant, but think twice. In this backwoodsy place, it'd probably come to life and eat me. I've seen enough horror movies not to risk it.

My eyes dart around, searching for any hint of organization. *Ha! As if.* There's a bench by the door, buried under a mountain of shoes, jackets, and what looks like every umbrella ever manufactured. The "Florida survival corner" is stocked with enough sunscreen and bug spray to last through the apocalypse, and is that... gator repellent?

"Where should I put my things?" I ask.

Doug just laughs. "Anywhere you can find a spot, darlin'! We're not picky."

Clearly.

I set my suitcase down, and I swear I hear it whimper.

They're wearing shoes. Inside. On the carpet—it's permanently painted in footprints.

My inner neat freak screams.

Darla starts excitedly talking to Ethan and me, but mostly Ethan, "You look so good, honey! And bringing home your girlfriend, we're thrilled to bits. Nolan is down at the shop, but he'll be back for dinner. He can't wait to meet Chase!"

"Yes, Chase is also excited to meet my twin brother Nolan," Ethan says matter-of-factly.

Twin brother? Shit. How did I not know about this? "Yes, of course," I say, trying to sound nonchalant. "Those two goofballs and their twin misadventures."

First thing tomorrow—Google "Ethan Barrett twin."

Darla is full-on chattering about family members I've never heard of when she leads us into the living room. I hesitate at the threshold.

My first instinct is to wince. The room is a riot of color and kitsch. There's so much holiday and tropical-themed decor, it's like someone walked into a Margaritaville restaurant and weaponized Christmas cheer.

Plastic flamingos peer from every corner.

Over-the-top floral patterns clash against equally chaotic floral wallpaper.

Hawaii called, and they don't want their patterns back.

Above the countless alligator knick-knacks stands their ruler; a six-foot inflatable alligator wearing a Santa hat and dominating a corner of the room. Its toothy grin is somehow both ridiculous and heartwarming.

The lawn was just the appetizer for this feast of tackiness. But just when I think I'm ready for anything this house can throw at me, my gaze travels deeper into the room—and something shifts. Something I did not expect.

There, beneath the layer of "holiday cheer gone wild," lies the true heart of the home. Scuff marks on hardwood floors tell stories of Barrett boy shenanigans—teaching the twins to wrestle, impromptu Nerf gun battles, and victory dances. The old sofa and its well-worn cushions bear the imprint of years of family togetherness.

My eyes catch on a wall near the kitchen, where pencil marks climb like a wonky ladder. Each line is carefully labeled with a name and date—a display of growing children and passing years.

A lump forms in my throat. This house has been lived in... loved in... invested in. A lifetime of family memories has made this place what it is. No set designer could replicate the intangible warmth that permeates every inch of the space. This is not just a house... It's a home.

The realization hits me like a sledgehammer to the heart. Ethan had something I didn't have growing up: a loving family. No wonder he's so damn happy all the time, prancing around like he's got sunshine shooting out of his ass.

For a moment, I imagine growing up in a home like this... I see myself as a little girl, having family dinners and playing in the backyard, curious and carefree. My eyes start glistening. *Oh hell no.* I need to get off this emotional roller coaster before it gains any more speed.

Quick, find a distraction. Any distraction.

Is that... their tree?

It's a plastic palm tree playing dress-up as a Christmas tree. A tropical imposter. The ornaments are a gaudy mix of seashells, mini surfboards, and tiny plastic crabs wearing Santa hats. The star on top? A light-up margarita glass.

This is the tree version of a shameless dad wearing socks with sandals.

I can already picture the network execs having synchronized aneurysms at the thought of something so nontraditional in one of our movies. The Cherish Channel has a very specific idea of what Christmas should look like, and *(spoiler alert)* it doesn't involve palm trees or alligators in Santa hats.

My eyes land on a wall covered in framed photos. At first glance, I think, *Oh, cute, they're really into Halloween.* Seriously, why else would an entire family be dressed as pirates, wizards, or in cheerleader uniforms? But then I take a closer look, and with a growing sense of *WTF,* I see that every pic features them on a beach next to a Christmas tree. Then it clicks...

"Are these Christmas cards?"

"Why yes, sweetie, they sure are. It's a family tradition. We choose a theme each year and all dress up. Isn't that fun?"

I smile through my bewilderment. "Oh, absolutely. Very... creative."

Darla, pleased by my response, continues, "So, Chase, we wanna be hospitable. You got any special family traditions you'd like us to include this year?"

Oh joy, my favorite game: *Dodging Personal Questions About My Less-Than-Perfect Childhood.* I'd rather walk barefoot over Legos than discuss my family's nonexistent holidays.

Hell, I'd rather do my taxes.

On Christmas Eve.

While sober.

"I, uh…"

"Yeah, we're so curious and excited. We wanna know all about you," Doug chimes in as he gulps down another full glass of swamp juice. "The stories Ethan has told us, well, they don't paint the best picture."

Darla pats her husband's arm affectionately. "Now, Douggie, you and I weren't all rainbows and catfish from the get-go. Chase, we were like two feral cats, always hissing and clawing at each other. I never would've thought we'd end up purring in marital bliss."

I turn to Ethan, my eyes narrowing. "Well, I hope Ethan had *some* good things to say."

An awkward silence descends on the room. Darla, bless her relentlessly cheery heart, rushes to fill the void. "Let's start fresh. Give us your story, Chase."

I shift uncomfortably in my seat. "Well, um, I'm not really one to share. And there's not much to tell."

Ethan jumps in. "As you know, Chase is a director. She went to USC, the same college as Steven Spielberg."

"Oh, he did that *Jaws* movie, didn't he?" Doug nods sagely.

"I still get chills every time we take the boat out on the water," Darla adds with a shudder.

Doug lunges at his wife, pretending to chomp on her neck like an overgrown, slightly inebriated shark. Darla dissolves into a fit of giggles, playfully swatting at him.

"Excuse us," Darla says between giggles. "Doug is a big ol' cuddle bug, and he can't stop showing off how much he loves me."

"Can't stop, won't stop. Why would I want to?" Doug agrees, peppering Darla's face with kisses.

Awesome. Nothing like a little public make-out session to make things super comfortable.

"You two don't need to hide your love from us," Darla says, turning her attention back to Ethan and me. "We show affection in this house."

Before I can protest, Ethan's arm sneaks around my shoulders. I tense up, gritting my teeth to stay composed. "We're used to hiding our love at work," I say, gently shoving his arm off me.

The room falls silent again. The skepticism radiating from Doug and Darla is palpable.

"I think I need some more of that delicious Christmas Gator punch," I blurt out, reaching for my glass on the coffee table.

That's when I notice it. Amidst the clutter, an overly lifelike, four-foot-long alligator decoration sits on the ground. *Unnerving.* I study its scaly tail, then scan its rough, prehistoric body all the way to its blunt snout under half-lidded eyes. *So much detail.* I'd swear it was breathing... if it wasn't wearing a Santa hat and holding a cheesy stuffed flamingo in its mouth.

Weird.

Then.

It.

MOVES!

I scream, clinging to Ethan.

"Oh, that's just Bubbles," Doug says casually, as if having a live, forty-pound alligator in one's living room is normal. He scoops up the gator with two hands, hugging it affectionately like a super-long wiener dog. "He's friendly. See?"

Before I can protest, Doug sets Bubbles onto my lap, wrapping my arms around the scaly creature. Terror courses through my veins. I'm literally paralyzed.

This creature is hefty. Its powerful tail, nearly as long as its body, shifts side to side like a sunbathing cat in a window. Then the animal settles, breathing in a slow, steady rhythm as its body rises and falls gently against me.

In its mouth is a mutilated pink flamingo plushie with gator teeth holes on all sides and stuffing leaking out. Darla, oblivious to my distress, plucks the toy from Bubbles' mouth. "Looks like Feathers is gonna need us to restuff her again."

Fuck! Now the alligator's mouth is wide open—its piercing, jagged teeth facing me. I look at Ethan, silently pleading for help, horror etched across my face.

"Don't move," Ethan says seriously... before smirking. "Great idea, babe. Let's show the fans!"

Ethan grins at his camera phone and starts filming. "We made it home. Chase is meeting the family! This is Bubbles, a dwarf alligator and my dad's latest pet project. Ha! See what I did there, called it a pet project. You like that one, Dad?"

Doug and Darla wave enthusiastically, and Ethan *(the fucker)*, waves Bubbles' webbed foot at the camera. I sit, frozen, like I'm a hostage to the world's strangest terrorist group.

Ethan stops recording and senses that I'm about one alligator tail swish away from a full-blown meltdown. He mercifully lifts the reptile off my lap and hands the "pet" back to Doug. "Well, Dad, I think we can safely say they're not going to be BFFs anytime soon."

"You'll fall in love with him soon enough," Doug says, smothering the gator with kisses. "I'm training Bubbles to be an emotional support alligator. He's the third one I've raised. You'd be surprised how smart they are."

Hmm. A super-intelligent animal with razor-sharp teeth. What could go wrong?

I guess when your *fake* boyfriend says his family is "a bit unconventional," he really means "batshit crazy with a side of deadly reptiles."

Wake up, Chase! Because this is one seriously fucked-up dream.

CHAPTER SEVEN

ETHAN

"You washed my Christmas SpongeBob sheets? Aww thanks, Mama!"

I stride into my childhood bedroom, and it's like I never left.

There are wall-to-wall memories, from my Pikachu posters to my Harry Potter magic memorabilia. My heart sings! And that desk in the corner? It's like my high school yearbook in 3D. The playbills and trophies are a warm reminder of where my acting journey began.

I flop onto my bed, grinning. "The gang's all here! Santa Sponge-Bob, Polar Patrick, Snowman Squidward!"

Mom beams, then turns to Chase. "Ethan got those sheets when he was twelve. He loved them so much, I caught him trying to stuff them in his suitcase when he moved to L.A."

"Boys and their silly toys," Chase manages. "And where will I be sleeping?"

"With me, of course." I waggle my eyebrows and pat the bed.

"Oh... good. That's what I was hoping for."

"She tries to hide it, but she's a big ole snugglepuss." I leap up and squeeze her into a smooshy, overly sappy hug.

Huh. This feels... different.

For once, Chase isn't her usual rigid self. She's clinging to me, all soft curves and warm skin, setting my nerves ablaze as if someone struck a match. The scent is back—an intoxicating citrus aroma—wrapping around me like a sensual fog, and clouding my judgment.

For a heartbeat, I'm off script, lost in the moment. I forget we're putting on a show.

Holding her is kinda... nice.

"Bless your heart, Chase. I don't know how you do it," my mom says, waking me from my haze. "Ethan sleeps like he's tanglin' with a gator, but hey, maybe that's your cup of sweet tea. I ain't one to judge."

Chase's arm slides behind my back. Her fingertips brush against the thin fabric of my shirt, sending pleasant shivers and raising goosebumps in their wake. The sensation is electric.

Well, damn. She's got the touch of an angel. Or, more accurately, a she-devil wearing one hell of a tempting disguise.

Why am I suddenly imagining her touch *everywhere*?

Her body goes rigid against mine. Before I can process the loss, pain explodes in my side.

What the actual fuck?!

The pinch is so vicious, I'm pretty sure she just removed a chunk of my flesh with her fingernails. I half expect to see blood.

Our eyes meet. For a second, something flashes on Chase's face.

Confusion?

Lust?

The beginning stages of food poisoning?

We let go of each other faster than you can say "flustered." I'm slightly wobbly, feeling like I just got off a roller coaster. My side hurts, my heart's racing, and I have the strangest urge to hug her again.

"Now, this is the Jack and Jill–style bathroom," Mom chirps, gesturing dramatically as though she's showcasing a luxury spa. "Nolan's room is on the other side of that door."

Dad clears his throat. "Sorry, the door's a bit jiggly."

"You mean the lock that's been broken for twenty years?" I jest.

"And I'm gonna fix it," Dad justifies. "One of these days."

Mom's face suddenly lights up. "Douggie, go grab our special gifts for them!"

"Oh, you didn't have to get me anything," Chase says, her expression showing she'd rather take a bullet than accept a gift from my parents.

"Well, shucks, I know I don't have to. I love to," Mom replies, glowing.

"Gift-giving is my mama's love language," I say and then whisper to my mock girlfriend, "Mine's physical touch, in case you were wondering."

My lips brush against her ear, and once again, a little tingle catches me off guard. My eyes linger on the curve of her neck, the gentle fall of her hair, and the way her chest rises and falls with every breath.

Mom interrupts my gaze, bouncing with excitement. "And I've got an even bigger surprise for you guys tomorrow!"

Dad returns, arms laden with two gift boxes. Before he can hand them to us, Mom can't stop herself from squealing, "They're Christmas jammies!"

"Let's all put on our holiday PJs and wear them to dinner!" Dad suggests, his enthusiasm rivaling a kid on Christmas morning. "Your mom made Bubbles his own sweater this year!"

"Ethan, we're having breakfast for dinner," Mom adds. "Your favorite!"

I glance at Chase, who's teetering on the edge of an implosion.

"That all sounds fun. But can you give us a minute to settle in? We'll be right out after we catch a quick rest."

Mom pulls me into another hug. "We are so tickled pink that you're home!"

The moment the door closes, Chase, a tiny, furious tornado, whirls on me. "Ground rules, now!" she snaps. "I need to be told before you're going to film. Before you touch me—"

"Nah, that ain't gonna fly. My family is always around. Am I supposed to say, 'Hey, Mama, this may sound weird, but my girlfriend likes me getting permission before I put my hands on her body.'"

"Ugh, fine. I get your point. But when we are filming, you need to warn me. You can't just sneak attack me with the camera."

"Sorry, no can do, buttercup. I'm an artist. Inspiration strikes when it strikes."

"You're enjoying this, aren't you?" she accuses, her eyes blazing.

"More than Buddy the Elf loves syrup."

Chase's eyes narrow to slits. "The bed is mine. You can sleep in the bathtub for all I care."

"Nice try, sweetheart. Despite this being my time off, you're expecting me to be camera ready twenty-four-seven. And this mug"—I point to my face—"needs its beauty sleep to keep lookin' this good. You can have the floor. I'll even throw in my SpongeBob pillow."

Her eyes scan the discolored, worn-out rug from my teenage years. She seems resigned, and for a moment, I've won. Then the door handle rattles.

Uh-oh. This is gonna freak her out.

The door flies open, and Bubbles waltzes in like he owns the place. Which, to be fair, he kind of does.

"Oh yeah," I drawl, enjoying the way Chase's eyes bulge out of her head. "Did I forget to mention he can open doors with his tail?"

"Jesus Christ!" she screams, maneuvering me to be her human shield. "Fine, we'll share the fucking bed!"

Chuckling, I usher Bubbles back out of my room and shut the door, jamming a chair under the handle for good measure. When I turn back, she's having a full meltdown.

"I'm in hell. I must have died and been sent to Florida for crimes in a past life. How did I get stuck in this... this... swamp, doomed to spend eternity with tacky holiday decorations and a bunch of weirdos who are one gator short of a full zoo? And you—"

"Watch it, Your Highness. That's my family you're trash-talking."

"I can put up with a lot of shit, but who the hell raises pet alligators? Any other insane surprises I should know about? A shark in the shower? A python guarding the fridge? Seriously, what's wrong with your family?"

"Screw you. My parents have been nothing but welcoming," I snap. "You don't like it here? Go do the holidays your way. Visit your own damn family."

She goes quiet, her face pale.

"Don't dish it out if you can't take it, darlin'."

Even more awkward silence. *Well, fuck me.*

I run a hand through my hair, trying to dial it back. "Listen, roomie. This whole 'crashing my family vacation' idea was yours, not mine. So suck it up. We do Christmas the same way every year. Keep your opinions to yourself or go home."

I wrinkle my nose, catching a whiff of something funky. "How about you take a shower? You smell like Bubbles marked you as his territory, and I don't want your stink ruining my dinner."

"Gladly," she mutters, grabbing her suitcase. "I'll try to keep my opinions to myself, but your family is... a lot."

"Hey, Stinky," I call out, tossing her a gift box. "Don't forget your festive jammies. Just cause you pissed me off doesn't mean you should offend the whole family."

Chase catches the box. "Do not come into this bathroom under any circumstance," she warns.

"Don't flatter yourself."

The bathroom door slams with enough force to rattle the windows.

I drop back onto my bed with a groan. I give her three days tops before she has a complete breakdown.

I whip out my phone and check the Cherish app: 12,000 paid subscribers. Only a handful more since earlier, but it's a start—I'll take it. I swipe it away and open Instagram, checking on my recent posts.

Yeesh. The fans are really going after my new girlfriend. Some of these comments are savage.

What's with those funeral clothes...? Her photos give me frostbite... She's as interesting as a bowl of oatmeal.

Guess I've got my work cut out for me. *But hey, fake it 'til you sleigh it! Right?*

As I read through the comments, a realization hits me like a shockwave. They might not be digging our love story, but they sure as hell enjoy Chase being humiliated. Dang... The more she squirms, the more *the likes* skyrocket.

Interesting. I can work with that.

My eyes land on a comment from Gail: "I'd rather see Ethan date a burnt sea slug than her." It already has 1500 likes. I chuckle. Gail's always been my number-one fan.

And critic.

And possibly future stalker.

The shower kicks on with a hiss, and suddenly my brain is hosting a one-woman show featuring Chase—buck naked and bold as brass. She's a goddess in that steam, water dancing down her body, tracing paths my fingers ache to follow. Her breasts are unrestrained and magnificent, and I hear delicate moans slip from her mouth while the water showers her with adoration. It's music to my ears.

I give my head a sharp shake, trying to evict the mental image. No indulging in enemy-related fantasies! Even if that enemy has legs that stretch forever and a backside that deserves its own Pinterest board.

Damn it, Ethan, she hates your guts, she'd love to see you crash and burn, she's completely off-limits—and she's your fucking boss. You still have to work with her when this is over.

Logic kicks in, and I opt for a quick snooze. If Chase's naked body makes an appearance, that's on my subconscious.

A little shut-eye later... *CRASH!*

A noise from the bathroom awakens me.

"Chase?" I yell out. "You good?"

Silence.

"If you're trying to make a break for it, no need. I'll buy the plane ticket and drive you there myself!"

Still nothing. Not even a sarcastic *fuck off*. Now I'm concerned.

I hear a muffled sound that might be *help*. But then, she screams.

"HELP!!!"

In a split second, I scramble to the door. "Hey, what's going on?"

I put my ear to the door... Nothing.

"I'm coming in."

I swing open the door, steeling myself for whatever chaos awaits. I imagine the worst, but instead...

It's equal parts hilarious and arousing. Chase is standing there in her underwear, battling a red sweater that's trying to swallow her whole—arms stuck up in the air, head completely engulfed, and shirt barely covering her bra. She's a modern-day mummy, but with way more underboob and a lot less dignity.

"Help!" she yells again. "I'm trapped!"

I rush over, stifling a laugh. "I am going to put my hands on you. Try not to get turned on."

"*Now* you ask for consent?"

"Do you want my help or not?"

"Your mom's PJs are the size of a toddler's onesie!"

"Be still," I command, grabbing on to the bottom of the sweater and yanking downward. "Man, this thing is on tight!"

"What the hell are you doing?" Chase shrieks. "Get it off, not on!"

I switch tactics, pulling on the shirt's sleeves. "Why are you wearing this?"

"Huh? These are your mom's stupid Christmas jammies."

"This is so small, it's obviously Bubbles' sweater. There are flamingos on it."

"Everything in this house has fucking flamingos on it!"

Chase flails wildly, banging into the door and knocking toiletries off the sink. "I can't breathe!" she says. "Seriously... about to... blackout."

"Bend over," I instruct. "I'm going to pull it off from the bottom."

I grunt with effort as I tug, but the damn thing won't budge. It feels as though it's been superglued on.

"For love of... Santa's saggy ball sack," she gasps out, her breathing growing more and more ragged. "G-G-Get m-m-me out of this s-s-straightjacket!"

Oh crap. She's having a panic attack. Her breaths are quick and shallow, which sends my heart racing. *I gotta do something drastic. Fast!*

I grab a pair of scissors from the drawer. "Don't move," I order.

"Ethan, what are you doing? S-S-Stop," she says, wheezing, "and t-t-tell me wh-what you're—"

"Stay calm, I'm cutting through the fabric," I say softly but firmly. "Trust me."

I quickly cut through the back of the shirt, ripping it off and tossing it to the floor.

Chase breathes in large gulps of air—finally freed.

Only then do I realize she's not wearing a bra.

Her breasts are fully exposed *(oh holy night)*, and they are spectacular.

The universe just gave me VIP access to the most incredible show on the planet. These aren't ordinary breasts—they surpass the ones in my dreams: firmer, fuller, and begging to be worshiped.

"You cut my bra?!"

Before I can respond *(or stop gawking)*, the other bathroom door swings open. On instinct, I clasp my hands over Chase's breasts. Did I want to cop a feel? Yes, but I'll claim chivalry to my death.

Nolan, my brother, stands in the doorway to his bedroom. He looks at me and a half-naked Chase with my "hands bra" still in place. His expression is so neutral, he could be a sculpture dedicated to the art of indifference.

"Hey, bro," I say, trying to sound casual. "Chase, this is my twin brother, Nolan. Nolan, this is Chase. She's, uh, trying on her Christmas outfit."

Nolan's eyes flick between us, his expression unchanging. "Mom says it's time for dinner," he announces flatly. "I'll tell her you're having dessert first."

Without so much as a backward glance, he shuts the door.

Awkward silence.

The warmth in my hands begs me to squeeze, to lose myself in the softness of her skin. Her breasts rise and fall with each breath, and I can feel her heart pounding under my palms—a frantic rhythm that echoes my own racing pulse. Every breath she takes makes it harder and harder to resist.

Chase's voice snaps me out of it. "Take your hands off my chest."

I can't resist one last jab. "Warning. I'm going to be removing my strong, capable hands from your fabulous breasts now. Just giving you advance notice, like you wanted. Wouldn't want to deprive you of my touch too suddenly—"

She shoves me hard enough to make me stumble. "Get out!"

"Next time I save your life, I don't need a boob grab as payment," I retort. "A simple thank-you will do."

CHAPTER EIGHT

CHASE

I WAKE UP AND I'm totally confused. I feel like I just got tased. As my eyes adjust to the dim light filtering through the curtains, I become aware of two things:

1. I'm sprawled across Ethan's chest like it's my own personal Tempur-Pedic mattress.

2. The Great Wall of Pillows I constructed between us last night? Demolished. Obliterated. Bye-bye.

Fantastic. Just fucking dandy.

I lift my head, ready to ninja-roll myself out of this awkward situation, when my gaze lands on something that makes me freeze. Squidward's giant schnoz is staring at me in... 3D. *Oh shit!* It's not his nose. There, proudly tenting the SpongeBob sheets, is Ethan's morning wood.

Holy barnacles! That's not a tent—it's the whole damn circus.

My brain malfunctions. I'm caught between erupting into un-controllable giggles or bolting towards the door. I try to move, but his arm is wrapped around me like a muscular python. When the hell did that happen? And why am I not bothered by it?

"Stop overthinking," I mutter to myself. "Just get up. This never happened."

Easier said than done. We're basically fused together.

Then Ethan stirs.

His hand moves. Down. Under the sheets. *Oh God.*

He reaches between his legs—rearranging his impressive morning salute—when he mumbles something that sounds suspiciously like my name.

No. Way.

Is he dreaming about... me?

His hand moves faster. Squidward's nose bounces.

Up.

Down.

Up.

Down.

It's hypnotic and scandalous. SpongeBob looks absolutely horrified.

Is this a scratch he plans to finish? I'm not sticking around to find out. I scramble off the bed, my cheeks flaming. Grabbing my clothes, I bolt for the bathroom.

I ease the door shut and slink to the floor, trying to calm my racing heart. It's no use. Heat courses through me like an inferno as I think about Ethan's embrace and his very impressive erection. Why am I tempted to climb back into bed with him and see what happens? I can almost sense his strong hands commanding me, his lips trailing kisses down my—

No. Hell no. The biological reaction to sharing a bed is messing with my head. Nothing good can come from thoughts like this.

Except maybe multiple orgasms. I could march back into that room, straddle Ethan's hips, and...

I need a cold shower! Or maybe a hot one, where I can take care of this ache between my thighs myself. Because right now, the only thing I want to subscribe to is whatever Ethan's offering under those sheets. And that is a recipe for trouble.

***

THE CAR RUMBLES ACROSS the bridge, and Marco Island looms ahead like a beacon. Sparkling water peeks between buildings along the shoreline. Sunlight dances on the waves. My eyes drink it all in. A blessed distraction from...

Nope. Not thinking about Squidward's... nose.

Brain, I swear to God, if you go there one more time.

I shake my head so hard I nearly give myself whiplash.

"You alright there, Chase? You're looking a little... twitchy." Ethan's voice oozes amusement.

Busted. "So, what's the plan?" I squeak, clearing my throat. "How are we convincing everyone we're more lovey-dovey than a Cherish Channel romcom?"

He flashes me that grin—the one that makes even grandmothers swoon and nuns question their life choices. "Don't sweat it, sweetheart. I've got this under control."

I bite back a snort. The day Ethan Barrett has anything under control is the day I'll chow down on one of Darla's flamingo-shaped oven mitts.

"I want details. We need a subscribers' plan."

"Relax, Chase. Social media's my playground. It's my turn to take the lead." He pauses for dramatic effect. "But first, my mom has a surprise for us."

We pull up to a cluster of shops, each painted in soft pastels like a row of charming dollhouses. Charming brick walkways link them together, giving off such an adorable small-town vibe. You half expect a baker to pop out with free cupcakes.

My eyes land on a sign that reads "Darla's Craft & Joy." *Oh no.*

"Your mom owns a craft store?" I ask, already dreading the answer.

"Yup. Act like you already knew that, okay, fake girlfriend?"

We step inside. My retinas scream.

I'm bombarded by a kaleidoscope of colors and knick-knacks. Flamingo can openers wink at me from one shelf. Alligator toilet paper holders grin toothily from another. And there's an entire holiday section entitled *Santa Got Wasted in the Everglades.*

I'm speechless, trying to process the sensory overload.

How am I supposed to fit in here? I'm a woman who color-codes her sock drawer and arranges her tea cups by size, color, AND frequency of use. This place looks like it was organized by a blindfolded monkey throwing glitter bombs.

My palm itches to grab my phone and take a quick glance at my schedule—just a small reminder that order still exists in the universe. But I resist, barely.

Suddenly, a lanky figure materializes next to me, and I nearly jump out of my skin. It's Nolan, Ethan's twin, looking about as comfortable as I feel.

Ethan greets him with a bear hug and a double back pat that screams "bro love."

Nolan swivels towards me, his eyes curious. "What do you think of the shop?"

"Wow," I manage, plastering on my best fake smile. "It's... even more... better than Ethan described."

Nolan nods thoughtfully. "I keep thinking we should expand into other animal crafts. Like, what about... pelicans? They're the *flamingos* of the sea, don't you think?"

How the hell do you even answer that?

I offer weakly, "I guess you'll never know until you try."

While Nolan rambles on about aquatic bird merchandise potential, I can't help but study him. How in the name of all that's genetically possible are these two twins?

Ethan is literally a walking, talking romance novel cover. Chiseled jaw, bedroom eyes, and a body that makes women *(including me)* want to "accidentally" fall into his arms. On purpose. Repeatedly. *What is the deal with my brain today?*

Nolan, on the other hand, is like if you ordered Ethan off Temu. Same basic model, completely different outcome.

He's tall and slender, with a softness to his features. His light-brown hair looks like he started styling it and then got sidetracked. And his expressive brown eyes have a shy, almost nervous energy that makes me want to give him hugs and bake him cookies.

But yikes, that shirt.

It's a gray polo covered in grinning cartoon alligators wearing reindeer antlers. *Is it just me, or is he trying to blend in with the merchandise?* As if becoming one with the tackiness would make his social anxiety fade away.

"Mom wants to see you guys in Ethan's Corner," Nolan says softly before disappearing.

"What's Ethan's Corner?"

He grins at me. "You're gonna hate it."

"For once, I believe you."

He leads me to the back. There, in all its glory, is a special section fully dedicated to Ethan Barrett merchandise. It's official. I've entered some bizarre alternate dimension. It's less *display* and more *altar* to Ethan's oversized ego.

"Oh. My. Fuck," I blurt out. "Is this a cult? Are you a cult leader?"

He beams, completely missing *(or ignoring)* my disdain. "Isn't it great? Check out this life-size body pillow of me. Perfect for late-night selfies and impromptu cuddle sessions."

"Oh yes, because nothing says 'sweet dreams' like waking up to those dead eyes staring at me."

I'm gearing up to unleash when Darla's voice rings out sharply. "There's my favorite couple!"

I turn to see Darla, her smile brightened by her signature pink flamingo lipstick. Today she's sporting a shirt covered in flamingos that proclaims, *Let's jingle and flamingle.*

She grabs my hands. "I've got the biggest surprise for you!"

What's it gonna be? A coconut bra bedazzled with googly eyes? Sparkly beer can fanny pack? Seashell-studded toilet seat that scratches your ass? *Oh God, please don't let it be an alligator-themed sex toy.*

But no. It's so, so much worse.

She proudly whips out a T-shirt that says *Chathan* in large, garish letters. Painted on the shirt is a bizarre rendition of Ethan's and my faces, with Bubbles the Alligator crudely drawn in.

"It's your couple name!" Darla squeals. "Get it? Chase plus Ethan!"

I force a smile so fake it makes my cheeks hurt. "Wow. I didn't know we had a couple name."

"You do now! Try it on," Darla urges, shoving it towards me. "Nolan did an amazing job with the design."

Ethan's immediately stripping off his shirt like it's no big deal. *And, damn.* His abs should come with a warning label: *Caution: May induce spontaneous licking.* There's a light dusting of hair trailing down his stomach, disappearing into the waistband of his jeans, and I find myself wondering where that trail leads.

I close my eyes, trying to dislodge the X-rated thoughts. Nope, boner Squidward is still chilling in there. *Fuck.*

Ethan pulls on the ridiculous shirt, and I watch, mesmerized, as the fabric stretches across his muscles. Even the monstrosity of Chathan can't hide how sinfully attractive he is.

I force myself to actually look at the "art." Our faces look like they were sketched by a drunk toddler:

Using crayons.

With their nondominant hand.

A grotesque mashup of us. My head is uneven, the eyes are definitely cross-eyed, and Ethan's chiseled jawline looks like a lumpy potato. It's horrifying. Total nightmare fuel.

But to give credit where it's due—Nolan nailed my frizzy, humidity-induced hair with startling accuracy.

"So, what do you think?" Darla asks, her eyes sparkling with hope.

I open my mouth, close it, then open it again. I'm doing a fantastic impression of a fish out of water.

Oh boy. How do I answer this? Darla's radiating more maternal warmth than a Cherish Channel movie marathon, and it's... nice. Touching, even. But her style is—

"She's speechless with joy. Aren't you, sugar plum?" Ethan says so smugly that I want to smack him in his stupidly handsome face.

Before I can object, his hands are at my waist, fingers skimming my skin as he lifts my shirt. "C'mon, babe," he purrs, "try it on. Show some Chathan pride!"

I swat his hand away. "Back off. I can do it myself."

I pull the shirt over my existing one just as Nolan reappears, holding a jar filled with little slips of red and green paper.

Ethan gushes, "Bro, you outdid yourself this time!"

Darla beams. "How lucky am I having such talented boys?" She turns to me. "I don't know if Ethan told you, but Nolan has transformed our business, getting us on the interwebs."

Great. Now the Chathan pandemic will spread beyond Florida's borders.

"Make sure to tell your friends and family, sweetie. They can get their shirts only on our Etsy store," Darla says.

"Yes, I definitely will," I lie through my teeth.

"These shirts have been selling like hotcakes since you two announced your relationship," Darla gushes.

Nolan, in his soft-spoken way, adds, "We've sold six so far."

Only six?! Oh fuck. We're screwed. I edge close to Ethan, whispering urgently, "This fake relationship is not going to save our jobs."

But Ethan, the optimist *(or as I prefer to call him, the delusionist),* is supremely confident. "I'm not worried. I had a revelation last night."

"Care to share? What's with the jar?"

Instead of answering, he whips out his phone and starts filming a live video. *Oh no. No, no, no.*

"Good morning, Ethan Addicts! Check out this awesome shirt my brother made. You can get it on my mom's Etsy store, Darla's Craft and Joy."

Darla pops into the frame, brash as ever. "Hey ladies, free shipping and guaranteed delivery before Christmas! And if you order in the next hour, we'll throw in a lock of Ethan's hair!"

She snips a piece of his hair from the back and holds it up to the camera. *I'm pretty sure this is how cults are born.*

Ethan swings the camera towards me. "Sweetie, tell everyone what you love most about the Chathan design."

I freeze like... like that animal... the one that freezes in headlights. Only I'm not cold. I'm very sweaty and uncomfortable. "Oh, the drawing is very... colorful." *Nailed it.*

But he's not done torturing me. He faces the camera to himself. "The term Chathan. You came up with that name, right?

"S-S-Sure did," I stutter... Is it possible to die from embarrassment? "But your brother Nolan gets all the credit. He drew this... not me!"

Ethan, apparently hellbent on my complete humiliation, starts another subject. "So last night, this girl—my girl—got stuck trying to squeeze into a Christmas sweater three sizes too small. She had it halfway on, and she looked like a human corndog, half-dipped in batter—her arms were sticking out like the wooden stick. It was hilarious, right, babe?"

He laughs and turns the camera onto a non-laughing me. I quickly fake smile, fake laugh, and "real" push the camera back to him.

"And that gave me a great idea," he continues. "After I got her out of her sweater and enjoyed some boob-squeezing thank-yous, I came up with this."

I barely stop myself from crawling under a nearby display of alligator-shaped wind chimes.

He holds up the jar Nolan brought over. "This is what I'm calling the *10 Days of Holiday Dares*. Some are nice, most are naughty. And if you wanna see Chase and me do all ten, you gotta help us out."

Oh shit. What fresh torture is this?

"We're aiming for a million new subscribers to the Cherish Channel by Christmas in support of our new movie, *Fa La La Love*," Ethan explains. "What's our number up to today, sweet cheeks?"

I check my phone. "Fifty thousand."

"If we all work together, we can double it by the end of the day. If we do, Chase and I will—"

He motions for me to pull out a slip of paper from the jar. Darla, ever the encouraging mother, provides a drumroll sound effect.

I reach into the jar, feeling like I'm fishing for my own doom. Plucking out a green slip of paper, I read it cautiously, "Do a polar plunge."

Ethan grins wickedly. "Sweetie, you did say it ain't Christmas without the cold."

"I regret saying that now," I quip.

"You've got six hours, Ethan Addicts!" he announces to the camera. "Tell your friends to subscribe! C'mon, who doesn't love the Cherish Channel? And if we reach our goal of fifty thousand new subs, I'll do the plunge in my Santa Speedo."

He winks at the camera in a way that probably just impregnated half his viewership.

That's his plan?! A Speedo?! And now this attention-obsessed monster wants to freeze my lady bits off. What the fuck have I done?

***

IF THIS IS THE life of an actor, you can shove that candy cane right up Santa's chimney.

Ethan's been parading me around town all day, showing me off like his personal Instagram accessory. Every store we've hit has turned into an impromptu meet-and-greet, with adoring fans lining up for selfies. Mr. Charm happily obliged each request, always reminding the starstruck fans to subscribe. He also invited every single one to our polar plunge this evening.

I hate to admit it, but I'm lowkey impressed. Watching Ethan in action has given me a new appreciation for what he does and how well he does it. Unfortunately, it also stirs up something I thought I'd buried long ago.

See, I've been in this industry for years, fighting for every bit of respect. At first, I tried being nice, but that only led to actors ad-libbing my carefully crafted scripts and crew members 'forgetting' my instructions. So I raised my shields and became the Ice Queen of directing. Because it's not a popularity contest. People don't have to like me; they just need to know I'm the damn boss and I get the job done.

So why does seeing Ethan interact with people make me feel so conflicted?

"More ice!" Ethan yells, getting the excited crowd to chant with him. "More ice! More ice!"

We're standing on a tiny stage in a park, in front of the massive Marco Island Christmas tree. It's almost as tall as the palm trees around it, all decked out with twinkling lights and tropical ornaments like seashells and starfish.

And what's right in front of us? A not-so-hot tub that Ethan has converted into a giant polar plunge jacuzzi, decorated like Santa's sleigh. Because nothing says Christmas like frozen nips.

I've heard jumping into ice baths is a trend or something. It's good for your circulation, celebrities do it, blah blah blah. Ethan loves it, claiming it "makes you feel alive." *I'm alive enough, thanks.* Besides, I'm pretty sure that hypothermia makes you feel dead.

"Can't we just pretend it's cold?" I ask.

"No way. It's gotta be authentic, sweetheart. The fans will know."

"Sorry, but you think people wearing shirts with Chathan on them are smart enough to know the difference?"

"This is why you need me," he responds. "You don't respect the fans."

"I know what the subscribers pay for," I argue, bristling at his accusation. "My movies. They love the stories that I write."

"Getting them to watch the movie is one thing," Ethan says. "But getting them to keep coming back for more? That's a whole other level. It's like the difference between a one-night stand and a committed relationship."

"You've never had a real relationship, so how would you know?" I snark.

For a hot second, I catch a glimpse of something in his eyes. It's quick, but it's there. A flash of... hurt? Before I can dive deeper, Nolan materializes next to Ethan, holding a cooler filled with ice.

"Okay. It's cold," he deadpans, dipping his hand in the water.

"Keep pouring ice till it'll freeze off a snowman's dick," Ethan instructs his brother.

I lift my gaze, and the number of admirers has tripled since we got here. Ethan raises his phone and shoots a quick video. "Only thirty subscribers to go. Time to call your mom's Bunco pals or your long-lost cousin. We need them. We're so close."

He posts the video and then keeps waving at all the loyal supporters waiting for a pic.

His tactics make me cringe, but I can't argue with their effectiveness. Sure, we're not even close to a million, but damn if the man doesn't know how to rally people to a cause. It's annoyingly impressive.

Darla runs up to us wearing a Chathan shirt with boundless enthusiasm. "Wow, hun. Great crowd," she gushes. "Oh look, there's Mayor Seabrook!" She waves frantically. "Hiya, Teddy!"

"Darla, you don't sell scuba suits at your store, do you?" I ask.

She gives me a playful arm slap. "You're funny, Chase. That must be why my boy loves you."

If she only knew.

"Sweetie, we gotta get your dad a picture. He's running late at work."

I want to protest, but Darla's already staging Ethan and me close together. She takes a few steps back. "Smile!" she says, holding up her phone.

After a moment, she frowns. "Shucks, that's not it. Ethan honey, how about you dip Chase? That'll be cute."

I whisper rage, "Ugh. Will you just dip me and get this over with?"

The second Ethan pulls me in and leans me back, the crowd swoons with applause.

"Oops, I missed it," Darla says cheerfully. "No worries. I want to get the whole tree in the shot. Hold on."

As Darla repositions herself, I notice Nolan, emotionless, pouring yet another cooler of ice into the hot tub. My nipples pop out at the sight. This is gonna suck.

Ethan tosses his phone to Nolan. "Be ready, bro. Go live right at 6:00."

Nolan responds with the enthusiasm of a mannequin, his face a masterpiece of neutrality. Ethan seems to take it as, *You got it, bro.*

"Sweetie, give Chase a kiss for the picture!" Darla calls out.

I whisper under my breath, "What the fuck is happening? Tell her I'm not comfortable with PDA."

Ethan gives me a light kiss on the cheek. Everyone *(except me)* groans in disappointment.

"A real kiss. Hurry up," Darla insists. "Ain't no time to be shy, lovebirds. The audience is waitin'."

"She's not gonna stop," he warns.

"Fine, just make it quick."

"Trust me, I will."

He leans in and gives me a quick peck on the lips. I breathe a sigh of relief.

"I need you to hold the kiss so I can get the picture!" Darla pipes up again.

Stage Mom is relentless.

Then hell rains down on me as the enthusiastic crowd joins in, chanting, "Kiss her! Kiss her! Kiss her!"

Ethan shrugs apologetically. "Sorry, fans want it. And you want fans. We're doing this."

God, this is humiliating.

I regret everything—I don't want to be here. I close my eyes...

Ethan leans in, crashing his mouth onto mine. His lips are soft at first, and then his kiss deepens, becoming more passionate, more demanding. He pulls me closer, and the obnoxious chanting and excited squeals fade to a whisper. My heart pounds wildly as he cups my face in his hands. The intensity of his touch surprises me.

I regret nothing—I *sooo* want to be here. *It's fucking electric.*

My brain goes haywire as he devours my mouth. My inhibitions vanish, swept away by a flood of desire. I feel him shudder as I trace his bottom lip with my tongue. He presses his rock-hard erection against me, and goddamn—the jolt of pleasure nearly knocks me off my feet. I moan, and he swallows the sound. My spine tingles, every nerve ending a live wire, crackling with electricity.

I've filmed Ethan kissing lots of leading ladies. It took countless hours to manufacture a kiss that looked magical. Still, I always dreamed about what it would feel like. No wonder women throw their panties at him—if I'd known his kisses could set me on fire like this, I might have jumped him years ago.

Darla's voice cuts through the noise. "Okay, you can stop. I probably got a good one. I took at least fifty, just in case."

I yank myself away, but my head's still spinning like I just downed a bottle of vodka and jumped off a merry-go-round.

Ethan and I lock eyes.

All dilated pupils and swollen lips.

What. The. Hell. Was. That?

His alarm goes off. Ethan's expression changes instantly, and he switches to his announcer voice. He points to Nolan, who holds up his phone to start the livestream.

"We did it. Fifty thousand new subscribers for the Cherish Channel. Holy smokes! That means now we have to..." he pauses, inviting the audience to echo his shout. "Take. The. Plunge!"

Ethan rips off his shirt—the crowd goes wild.

He rips off his pants—they lose their shit!

He's wearing a Santa-themed Speedo. I can't look away. His package is wrapped better than any gift under the tree, and I'm suddenly feeling very... festive.

But then I remember why we're standing here, at the edge of this ice-filled abyss. He grabs my hand, his fingers tightening around mine.

"Ethan, I changed my mind. I don't want to—"

We're airborne.

The fans are screaming. I'm screaming. My hoo-ha is screaming in anticipation of the ice-cold doom.

We hit the water with a force that knocks the air from my lungs. The cold is a thousand knives slicing through me, stealing my breath and freezing my screams.

Fuck me. I haven't felt this alive in years.

CHAPTER NINE

ETHAN

I'M FLOATING ON A cloud of pure ecstasy.

The world around me is hazy, but my mouth is working overtime, savoring the sweetest taste I've ever known. God, her lips feel amazing. So moist and warm. With every swipe of her tongue, I can sense myself getting harder.

My hands wander to her breasts, and I squeeze, feeling their weight in my palms. The more I ask, the more this girl's body gives me. Her touch wanders down to my cock. Damn, her fingers are soft and friendly, just how I like it. I want this woman.

The throbbing between my legs intensifies as she squeezes. I long to be inside her... now!

The woman is a mystery, a blurred form with a voice that reverberates in my head as speaks. She sounds familiar but far away, like a memory. "Ethan, you're doing it all wrong. There's no chemistry. It's like you're kissing your grandma. Where's the sex appeal? I need less 'background extra' and more masculine star power."

I pause, confused. That ball-breaking voice...

My eyes fly open. *What the actual fuck?*

My heart's pounding faster than a reindeer on Red Bull. I blink rapidly, trying to shake off the lingering fog of sleep. That was the most bizarro dream ever. I was kissing... Chase? But as I become more aware, I realize it isn't all in my head.

Chase is in my bed, her head on my chest, and her hand... *Hmm. How to say this delicately?*

Her hand is wrapped around my dick.

We're tangled together under my Santa SpongeBob sheets. I glance down at my crotch. Squidward's giant nose keeps moving up and down. What the fuck is happening? She is completely zonked out, but her fingertips are doing some serious exploration. Her thumb is gently stroking my tip...

Stroke.

Stroke.

Squeeze.

God, that feels good. Really fucking good.

Shit. I gotta get out of this bed before I come on her hand. Chase would never let me live that down. I try to shift away, but her grip tightens like she means to finish the job.

She makes a deep, throaty sound. I'm so turned on. The expression on her face shows she's immersed in a steamy fantasy.

Is she dreaming about me?

No way. Absolutely not. The girl doesn't even want to be here, much less in my bed. She's made it clear she thinks I'm a fucking idiot. As if this trip hasn't been awkward enough, I know this would push my fake-girlfriend-with-accidental-benefits to her limit. I have to slip out without waking her.

She exhales a very sexy moan and wraps her leg over me, grinding her pelvis into my thigh. I groan under my breath, "Mother... of...

fuck." I feel precum dripping on her thumb as she glides it over my tip.

This isn't working. I mean, yes, it's technically working. I sense my North Pole becoming slicker by the second as she continues her unconscious adventure. But Chase isn't aware of what she's doing, and if I don't make a move soon, I'm going to light up like a Christmas tree.

I whisper to the smiling faces of SpongeBob and Patrick on my sheets. "Alright gang, F is for friends, remember? So let's do this together."

One. Two. Three!

I give the sheet a mighty yank and tumble to the floor with a thud. I lie there, completely still, holding my breath. Another sultry sound drifts down from her, and I risk a quick glance.

Chase is sprawled out, facedown on the bed like a starfish. Her black pajama shorts are riding up to reveal a peek of purple lace panties.

I lick my lips at the sight. *Shower. Stat.*

I stumble into the bathroom, flipping on the water. The warm stream flows down my back as I grip my cock in one hand and prop the other against the tile. Visions of Chase fill my head. Her gorgeous face... those soft, kissable lips... the way her tits spilled into my palms... the undeniable heat between us when we kissed.

God, she's hot. Sure, she's awful, mean, evil, and... most importantly, she hates me. But so fucking hot.

And why is her bossy attitude such a turn-on?

I feel myself getting close, and I need my mind off you-know-who. *Think of another woman, any woman!*

I can't.

Chase was stroking me moments ago. That's all I can imagine as I seize myself harder. Within seconds, my balls stiffen, and my cock jolts as I come all over the shower tile. The pleasure ripples through me in one long, sweet release.

Oh fuck, I just jerked off to the enemy."

***

"YOU TWO ORDER WHATEVER you want. It's on us," Dad announces, opening his menu.

"Dad, I'm 33, fully employed, and—" I protest, but Dad's already waving me off like I'm a pesky mosquito.

"Can't. It goes against Dad Code. Especially since you have your lady here."

Chase seizes on the moment. "You'll have to forgive Ethan. He's not great at taking direction."

"This guy has to listen to me. He knows if he doesn't, I'll dad-joke him into oblivion."

"Fine," I surrender. "But no dad-dancing."

"No promises!"

We're at the Wise Owl Grill, a quirky little joint in Naples, about twenty minutes from home. It's our annual family pilgrimage to sample their special Christmas entrées, which are as authentically Latin as I am a convincing actor *(if you ask Chase, that is)*.

The vibe? Imagine if a food truck worker got drunk in Cancun, on Christmas, and decided to settle down and open a restaurant. You've got traditional Mexican murals that look like they were painted by someone who once saw a postcard of Mexico, mixed with enough bamboo to build a tiki bar. Because nothing says "authentic Latin cuisine" quite like... bamboo?

There's a small stage for live entertainment, which tonight promises to be... interesting.

Chase is eyeing the menu like it might bite her. Maybe it will. You never know in Florida.

"What do you recommend that won't turn my stomach into a war zone?" she asks, her nose scrunching adorably. "The Enchiladas de Navidad or the Merry Mole Burrito?"

I lean in close, my lips barely grazing her ear. "Alcohol. Focus on alcohol. You're gonna need it."

Her eyes narrow dangerously. "Ethan Barrett, if you don't tell me what's going on, I swear I'll—"

"Can we get a pitcher of some Ho Ho Ho Rita's over here?" Dad's voice booms.

Mom squeals, "Yes! Let's kick off this holiday shindig!"

Chase moves close, her voice low. "Spill it, pretty boy. What is happening?"

"Remember all those times I asked for the scripts the night before shooting? So I could practice the new scene changes? But you were always 'fine-tuning it,' leaving me to memorize everything at the last minute. This is payback for that, darlin'."

She groans and rolls her eyes. *Shit.* She's adorable when she's pissed.

This morning, we posted our video challenge and smashed our 50,000-subscriber goal in just three hours; making our grand total 150K subs. Today's assignment from the naughty or nice jar? *Ethan chooses a secret dare for Chase.*

It's been driving her nuts all day, and I've been savoring every second of her squirming.

Except secretly, I'm the one squirming every time I recall her *(almost)* sleeping hand job this morning. The sensation of her smooth, soft fingers grabbing my—*hold up. Not going there. Think unsexy thoughts.*

Grandmas twerking. Airport diaper changes. The spectacle we're about to see. Chase in those delicious purple lace undies—*Dammit!*

I casually shift to adjust my growing hardness under the table, praying no one notices how she's getting to me.

"So, Ethan," Mom chirps, yanking me from my increasingly reckless thoughts. "Are you gonna give us a hint about Chase's dare?"

"Sorry, Mama. This woman luu-ves surprises," I drawl. "Don't want to ruin it for her."

Mom turns to her. "Ooh, I bet it's a doozy! Our Ethan's always been a creative one. When he was five, he decided to 'improve' the neighbor's nativity scene with dinosaurs. You should've seen baby Jesus being cradled in those triceratops horns. It was a hoot!"

Dad adds, "He's an idea guy, just like me. I bet he's giving you good ones for filming all the time."

My 'girlfriend' forces a smile. "Oh, he's a nonstop bundle of ideas. Can't shut him up most days."

From day one, Chase has had me on her shit list. I remember that second week of filming like it was yesterday. I'd just wrapped a take and was pretty damn proud of myself. But Chase? She responded with a silence that was deafening. Her disapproval filled the air, choking me with every breath. I was bracing myself to be fired, or maybe replaced by a cardboard cutout she'd consider "more believable."

But then there's this other side to her. This tiny nod she'd give after a scene, so subtle you'd miss it if you blinked. And fuck if it didn't make my chest swell like I'd just won an Oscar. It's been an emotional rollercoaster ever since, complete with loop-de-loops and unexpected drops.

She's got this gift for making me feel like I've personally offended her by existing. It's a special talent, really. And here's the kicker—I actually *care*. Me, Mr. "Hit It and Quit It" Barrett, is as desperate for her approval as a puppy begging for treats.

Don't get me wrong, I'm used to people loving me. It's my superpower. I flash a smile, crack a joke, and ta-da! Instant adoration. But Chase is immune. Like trying to charm a brick wall—a very talented, incredibly intimidating brick wall.

And it's driving me insane. Why? Because I respect the hell out of her. When I told her I wanted to direct, I wasn't just blowing smoke up her perfectly sculpted ass. She's the real deal, a genius behind the lens.

Next to her, I'm a kindergartener with a disposable camera.

I doubt she knows how closely I watch her on set. The way she frames each shot, how she draws performances out of even the most difficult actors (yours truly included). She's got an intuition for the heart of a scene.

I want to tell her I genuinely admire her work. Explain how I've rewatched her films to the point of obsession, dissecting her techniques like a film school geek. I've got stacks of notebooks filled with observations from our shoots. But every time I open my mouth around her, something idiotic comes out.

Her opinion matters to me.

I wish it didn't.

But it does. Fuck, it does.

I glance at her, but she avoids my eyes. She's scanning the room, clearly plotting her escape.

Mom giggles as a pitcher of pale yellow liquid, tangled in a web of twinkling Christmas lights, lands on the table. "Sip, sip, hooray!" she chirps, raising her glass.

We clink glasses and drink. Chase's expression twists like she's just sucked on a lime dipped in chili sauce. "That's an odd flavor."

"Spiced eggnog margarita," Dad explains. "It's a real taste explosion!"

Chase spits the drink back into her glass. "So, where's Nolan?" she asks.

"Oh, don't you worry, hun," Mom says with a wink. "He should be here any minute."

The manager appears at my side. "They're ready for your introduction," he says discreetly.

"It's go time, sunshine!" I say.

The way her face panics? It's priceless. If I could capture that look of sheer terror—memeify and sell it—I'd be richer than Jeff Bezos on Prime Day.

I bound up to the little stage, grabbing the mic. "Good evening, beautiful people of Naples! I'm Ethan Barrett, your friendly neighborhood Christmas hunk."

The small crowd erupts in cheers and applause. One woman shouts, "I love you, Ethan!"

"I love you too!" I reply automatically. It's become a reflex at this point. "But tonight, it's not about me. Ladies and gentlemen, get ready to jingle and mingle for the most festive, fun-filled event of the season. Our Holiday Drag Show features the glitter-tastic, tinsel-terrific, absolutely fa-la-la-bulous... KRINGLE KWEENS!"

Mom and Dad cheer from our table, "Woo! Kringle Kweens!"

The lights dim. The room transforms. It's like a disco ball having intercourse with a Christmas tree. Three stunning drag queens sashay onto the stage, dressed as candy canes so sexy they'd make a dentist weep.

The queen in the red dress takes the mic, her voice sultry and playful. "I'm Candy Cane Couture, and honey, I'm about to make your holidays very merry indeed."

The crowd roars.

"But first, we need a volunteer. Can the lovely Chase Pemberton please come to the stage?"

I dash over to her, whipping out a pair of light-up antlers and planting them firmly on her head.

"No, absolutely not. Hell fucking no."

I pull out my phone and hit *Go Live*. "Hey Ethan Addicts! Here's your special treat. My sugar plum is performing, tonight only, with The Kringle Kweens!"

The crowd cheers. Chase downs her eggnog margarita in one gulp—accepting defeat. She reluctantly allows me to guide her to the stage.

I tilt my head in her direction. "Don't worry. I promise you'll be safe. Nolan will take good care of you."

Her eyes snap to the drag queen in front. "That's *NOLAN*?!"

Candy Cane Couture winks at Chase. "Don't be shy, sweetie. I promise I won't bite... unless you ask nicely."

The thumping bass kicks in, vibrating the tacky decorations on the walls. Chase stands on stage, stiff as a board, while

Nolan-as-Candy leads her through a series of increasingly ridiculous dance moves. She's like a mannequin trying to do the *Macarena*—always one step behind.

"Come on, sugar!" Candy coos. "Shake your snow globes like they're full of glitter!"

I'm laughing so hard I can't hold the phone steady. Chase's dancing is a crime against rhythm. I give her credit, though. She's flailing those long legs like she's a soulless Rockette robot, with grim determination on her face that's usually reserved for yelling "CUT!" on set.

And then, as if by some sort of Christmas miracle, it happens. She starts to smile. Not her usual "I'm imagining your slow, painful death" smile, but a real, honest-to-God grin. Her whole face lights up.

For a moment, I forget I'm filming. I'm lost in this version of her—letting loose and having a blast. She can't dance for shit, but God, it's endearing watching her try.

As the song reaches its climax, Chase attempts a spin that sends her careening toward the Christmas tree. Nolan catches her just in time, dipping her low as the crowd goes wild.

She catches my eye. I smile at her, and—

Time stops.

Suspended in this infinite heartbeat, I take in every detail. Her cheeks are flushed—her eyes sparkle with laughter—her hair is a glorious mess.

It's a part of her I've never witnessed.

I'm struck with the urge to make her smile like that again.

She's never been more gorgeous.

CHAPTER TEN

ETHAN

MORNING HITS, AND I'M stiff as a board... and I am not talking about my abs.

Chase is draped over me like a sultry blanket... again. I could get used to this. Her breasts press against my chest—her pelvis just a subtle back arch from my cock. She's dripping with sensuality. I need to have a quick sidebar with my dick.

Knock it off, goddammit. This woman drives you nuts!

I tell myself it's morning wood—purely physical, nothing personal.

Sharing a bed has been more of a challenge than I expected. *Shit.* I need another shower.

Seconds later, I step under the warm spray, groaning as it cascades down my back. I grip my cock, desperate to take the edge off, but all I can see is her.

Naked.

Dripping.

Yearning.

Stop it, penis!

Maybe I actually want to anger-bang her? We can't stand each other, after all.

Is this some subconscious dirty bucket list thing?

Fuck! My orgasm shreds through me once more, all because of the she-devil who's hijacked my horny second brain.

After my shower incident, I spent the morning dodging Chase like she was radioactive. Fortunately, Dad filled the silence with endless swamp trivia during our drive through the Everglades. Chase hardly spoke, just gazing out the window as if she was contemplating her life choices... Except when she thought I wasn't looking and I caught her sneaking glances at me. *Interesting.*

Now it's the ass-crack of dawn and I'm standing outside an alligator theme park sweating my balls off. The Cherish Channel cooked up a brilliant plan to put us on TV at a time when sane people are still drooling on their pillows. We're about to appear on the local news, showcasing our totally-not-fake romance for all to see.

But here's the thing—I'm not exactly bringing my A-game today. Why? Because I find myself continually fixated on Chase. My mind is a chaotic swirl of conflicting thoughts. It's like I'm viewing two movies at once with completely different plots. I'm not sure if the heroine is likable or a vicious, back-stabbing serial killer. Either way, I can't stop watching.

I see the uptight Chase *(aka the sexy serial killer),* and she's bossing me around, micromanaging my every move. Then I see the charismatic Chase—the one who got on that stage last night. She's...

Smiling. Laughing. Fun?

I remember her genuine laughter at the show, and I grin. Never would I have dreamed infectious joy could come from that woman.

I mean, holy hell! She was a totally new person. What pushed her to let go? And what other Chase-shaped mysteries are hiding in there? Why do I keep thinking about her? Is she thinking about me?

Enough, Ethan. You're assigning magical properties to her. It's not real; this is Chase we're talking about. The boss who's made your career a daily obstacle course of criticism and unreachable standards. The director who scrutinizes your performances like she's hunting for flaws with a magnifying glass.

But damn. Her smile cancels out all my frustrations in an instant.

Her hair blows slightly. It's swept up in that signature tight ponytail, and... why do I want to grab her locks and pull on them like reins? She's not in her usual all-black attire today. She's poured into a pair of snug green cargo shorts that hug her curves and make her ass look incredible. That fitted white button-down is doing wonders for her breasts, and the rolled-up sleeves really showcase her tanned, toned arms.

She's a knockout, and I want her to direct me in a porno called *Raiders of the Lost G-Spot.*

Fuck! Get it together, man!

She's brutal, heartless. How many times have you lost sleep over her insults? Hell, remember that one time? She brought you to tears. She gets off on making you feel like you aren't good enough. She's a sadistic drill sergeant, breaking you down to nothing. She wants you feeling worthless and talentless. Don't fall for it.

I start tallying the reasons she's the absolute fucking worst:

1. She's an agenda-setting dictator who can't be spontaneous.

2. Her heart is colder than a penguin's nutsack.

3. She micromanages everyone on set, especially me, like it's her God-given mission—

"Do I have something in my teeth?" Chase whispers, snapping me out of my thoughts. Dammit, she's even cuter when she's nervous. My stomach does a backflip.

Penis 1. Brain 0. Quit calling the shots, Little Ethan!

"Your teeth are fine. Your personality, however… that needs work."

"Okay, thanks, I'll get right on that. Right after you stop being a cocky dickhole. Deal?"

"Ah, so you're finally doing nicknames now? Okay, snuggle tits."

Penis 1. Brain 1. Ha!

We're not-so-patiently waiting as a busy news crew works frantically to make last-second adjustments. I try not to fidget. Try not to think about how easy it would be to reach out and take her hand.

And hold her.

And kiss her.

Dammit, Little Ethan!

"Ready when you are," the cameraman says, giving the reporter a thumbs-up.

The reporter—all bouncy black curls and luminescent smile—does a final fluff of her hair. She's pretty in that "I eat kale for breakfast" kinda way, but my eyes are glued to Chase—despite her forced scowl and even if she is pulling away from me like I'm wetland ooze.

"I'm Ashley Barnes, standing in front of the Swamp Life Haven here in the Everglades. With me is hunky holiday movie star, Ethan Barrett, and his co-star girlfriend, Chase Pemberton."

"I am not an actor," she says. "I'm the director and also the screenwriter."

"That's my girlfriend. She's got a mile-long list of quirks, but she's all mine." I say, glossing over Chase's rudeness. "Ashley, appreciate you coming out."

The reporter's eyes light up. "You two are adorable! Everyone's buzzing about Chathan! Tell me, what's it like working together and filming those romantic scenes? Do you ever get jealous?"

Chase's laugh sounds like a rusty hinge. "Jealous? Of what? Ethan's ability to forget his lines five seconds after I call action?"

"Oh, sweetheart, maybe I forget my lines because you're rewriting them every five seconds. For someone who loves her precious words so much, you sure love changing them—"

Ashley's smile falters. "Next question! You're currently filming your fifth movie together, right? You two really know how to create movie magic."

"We're a great team," I agree with sarcasm. "I act. Chase yells 'cut' every thirty seconds. Then somehow, thirty miserable days later, we end up with a movie."

Chase fires back, "What Ethan is trying to say is that we have a very... collaborative process. I collaborate, he processes. Eventually."

Ashley, a true professional, barrels into her next talking point. "Ethan, your family must be thrilled to have you home for the holidays with your girlfriend."

"Oh yeah, they're over the moon to see me—I mean, us. Both of us."

"It's been great," Chase says, her tone suggesting it's been anything but. "Ethan is great. His family is great. They're just so... present. Like, they're always around, everywhere we go. All the time."

I throw an arm around her shoulders, feeling her stiffen. "Chase is a shy one. She's not used to so much Barrett family love. Are you, snookums?"

"Definitely not, sugar bear. But every day is a gift, and I'm counting them down until I get to open the big one. Then... Christmas will finally be over."

Chase flashes a smile so strained, it takes me a second to remember the cameras are rolling. I let out a forced laugh and she casually shrugs off my arm.

"Honestly, she's got this relentless, exhaustive energy that keeps me on my game, no matter where we are. I can't get enough of it."

Ashley picks up her pace, eager to move the interview along. "Your hilarious dares have had me giggling every day. Say, would it be possible to pick today's challenge live on our show?"

"Absolutely," I say, whipping out the dare jar as if I were a gambler laying down the winning hand.

The reporter turns to Chase. "So you both have no idea what's on those slips of paper?"

"Trust me, I wish I did." Her voice is tight and controlled. I know that tone. She hates not being in charge—hates the unpredictability. She looks so uneasy that part of me wants to comfort her. The other part...

"This one's a control freak, Ashley. But we're both loving all this good ole clean fun as we promote our new movie. Right, Chasey poo?"

Ashley nods enthusiastically. "Your movie premieres in a mere eight days. And your goal is to have a million new subscribers watching *Fa La La Love* on Christmas Eve. Is that right?"

"First month free!" Chase chirps, sounding like a deranged parrot.

"Exactly," I say, "and we've raised 150,000 subs so far. Everyone's having a really good time with us. Let's see what dare we're doing today." I hold the jar up to Chase. She reaches in like she's grabbing a live grenade.

Her eyes go wide as she reads the slip. "Kiss an alligator? WHAT?!"

My face radiates with excitement. "This one's such a big dare that we gotta hit one hundred thousand new subs today. That's a lot, but we're on the edge of history here, folks. I'm shaking in my boots, and Chase just pissed herself. Okay, not really. So get all your friends to sign up. You don't want to miss this!"

Ashley's face lights up like she hit the jackpot. "That is genuinely terrifying. And we are here for it. Stay tuned for more Chathan! Next up, Swamp Santa will be cruising the Everglades on his airboat, delivering special gifts to kids in need."

The camera stops rolling and she dismisses us. "Great show, guys." She joins her crew as they head off to capture B-roll of the alligators.

I brace myself, ready for the fallout. I'm not surprised to see Chase looking paler than freshly fallen snow.

"Don't worry. My dad is an alligator trainer here. It'll be fine. He's kissed plenty of them."

"Okay, A: That's super weird. Do you hear yourself when you talk? And B: That in no way makes me feel better."

I know it seems crazy to an outsider, but my dad's never had an accident. I grew up learning to respect the danger while enjoying the excitement. The stunts, the showboating—it's all for the tourists.

It's *(almost)* as safe as a magic act. I wish she could relax and enjoy it.

This sudden desire to pull her close is... unexpected.

"Come on. We've got some time to kill while we wait. I'll show you around."

"Time to kill? Is that a threat or a promise?"

"With all these alligators around? Could be both," I quip.

A huge sign reading *Merry Gatormas* greets you at the entrance of Swamp Life Haven. It's part zoo, part theme park. Playful alligator statues wearing festive scarves and Santa hats lurk among the palms, their jaws in perpetual, toothy grins. Garlands of red and green tinsel drape the fences, intertwined with strands of twinkling lights reflecting off the murky waters. Every few feet, signs warn of gator crossings.

Don't be fooled by the signs—they're just for show. All reptiles are securely contained behind electrified chain link fencing.

"Welcome to gator haven," I announce, spreading my arms wide. "Where the stockings are hung by the swamp with care, and Santa's sleigh is pulled by reptiles with a hunger for reindeer."

"Charming. Do the elves wear Crocs?"

"Was that a joke? From the woman sentenced to death by gator kiss?"

"When in Florida, do as the Floridians do."

"Go ahead, act like you're not wooed by their charm. Wait'll you see Santa surfing on a wave of eggnog."

There's a glimmer of a grin on her lips. That near-smile does something strange to my heart.

"As a child, this place was basically our backyard." I steer her past a group of excited children digging in a giant sandbox filled with "snow" *(aka white sand)*. "Nolan and I caused so much trouble, I can't believe they didn't feed us to the gators."

"That's because it's illegal to feed the alligators here. I saw a sign," Chase deadpans. "And you were just a kid. But now, you're an actor, and actors are considered nuisance animals by Florida state law."

"I'm a *nuisance animal*?"

"How else do you explain all my on-the-job stress headaches?"

"Whatever. It's okay to confess you love directing me."

"Directing you is like trying to wrangle Godzilla."

"So you're saying I'm bigger than Godzilla?"

"You have the same ego. But talent? That's debatable."

I lean in close, unable to help myself. "You know what they say about guys with big egos..."

Chase pushes me away. "That they're compensating for something?"

"I was going to say 'great screen presence,' but I like where your mind went," I say with a wink.

I guide her to the boardwalk that gives us a prime view of Alligator Lagoon. The sunlight dances on the water, catching the scales of dozens of gators as they chill in the murky waters.

"Check out that big fella over there. That's Brutus. He's the head honcho of this place. And if you–"

SPLASH! An alligator lunges playfully.

Chase jumps like she's just touched a live wire, grabbing onto me and clinging firmly. My arms instinctively wrap around her—every nerve in my body tingles.

Time seems to slow, and suddenly we're caught in our own little bubble of sexual tension. Our eyes meet, and I'm drawn into her gaze. Then my attention shifts to her lips, slightly parted and tempting as hell. Chase sucks in a breath, and I can practically taste her mint toothpaste on my lips. Her pulse is racing at the base of her throat, and my heart feels like it's about to beat out of my chest. My body's screaming at me to kiss her again, to see if it's as fucking incredible as the first time. I start to lean in—

But then Chase pulls back. "Are the gators always this restless?" she asks, trying to act normal, but I can see desire in her eyes. It's the same urge that's clawing at my insides.

"Only when they're hungry, which is typically once a week. Don't worry. Gators prefer sunbathing over anything else. Chase, serious question. Do you trust me?"

She eyes me warily. "Do I have a choice?"

I ignore her negativity *(years of training)* and steer her toward the Reptile House. She stops dead in her tracks at the doorway. "I get the idea—gross, slimy, scaly things. I don't need to see them up close."

"Let me show you something cool," I say, offering my hand to her, palm up. I hold my breath, waiting for her response.

She pauses, rolls her eyes with award-winning flair, and then grudgingly takes my hand. Her fingers are warm and delicate, and I can't resist giving them a comforting squeeze.

The darkness inside covers us like a heavy blanket. Chase inches closer, her body pressed against mine, and I'm vividly aware of every point of contact. That sweet citrus scent of hers—it's all around me again. I long to bury my face in her hair and breathe her in.

It's strange seeing her so uncertain. The Chase I know from work is relentlessly confident. This Chase is vulnerable, and it does something to me. Makes me want to be... better somehow.

We step into a room filled with illuminated glass terrariums. She eyes the reptiles suspiciously, her hold on my hand tightening. "Yup, just as I thought: gross, slimy snakes."

I guide her to a large glass case. Inside, the humid air fogs slightly at the edges, where rocks and greenery mimic a miniature jungle.

"This one is my favorite. The coral snake."

Coiled on a large rock, the striped serpent is a showstopper. Its bands of vibrant red, black, and yellow deliver a warning and an invitation all at once—kind of like Chase. It's nature's way of saying, "I'm hot as fuck, but I'll kill you if you get too close."

"Wow," she breathes, her face softening. "Okay, it's actually pretty cool."

I take a deep breath, deciding to share a piece of myself. "Want to know a secret? When I'm prepping for a role, I give my character a spirit animal. Helps me get into their personality."

Chase turns to me, genuine curiosity in her eyes. "Really? That's ... fascinating. Why haven't you told me about your process before?"

Her question takes me by surprise. I swallow hard, deciding to risk the truth. "Honestly? Because whenever I try to bring things up, you shut me down."

Chase winces, and for a second, I think I've ruined the moment. I'm about to make a joke, to brush it off like I always do, when she surprises me.

"I'm sorry," she says softly. "I should've... I mean, I want to hear your process for developing characters. Your idea is intriguing." A small smile tugs at her lips. "What animal did you use for Connor, the barkeep? Let me guess, a peacock."

I chuckle. "Nah. It was a chicken, actually."

"A chicken," she repeats playfully. "The sexy bartender was a chicken?"

"Hey, chickens are badass!" I defend. "They're social, enthusiastic. Great listeners. Plus, they care for chicks that aren't their own. Kind of like bartenders, they sense when they're needed."

"You know, Ethan, you might actually have some depth under all those muscles."

"Careful, Chase. That almost sounded like a compliment."

She turns back to the snake, but not before I catch the smile she's trying to hide. My gaze drops to our still joined hands, and I'm struck by how perfectly they fit together.

***

WELCOME, FOLKS, TO THE Jingle Gator Jamboree!" Dad's voice booms across the amphitheater, a perfect blend of showmanship and genuine enthusiasm. "I'm Doug Barrett, and we've spruced up this lagoon for a festive good time!"

I grin, leaning forward in my seat. This never gets old.

There he is, my old man, standing proud in the middle of this outdoor spectacle. He's swapped out the usual Florida retiree getup for khaki shorts and a sharp shirt, looking every bit the adventurer he is—minus that worn-out Santa hat perched on his head.

Weather-beaten benches form a semicircle around a murky pool, hinting at more danger than your typical Christmas gathering. A chain-link fence surrounds it all, a flimsy barrier between the audience and potential reptilian chaos. Every seat is packed with sunburnt tourists, cameras at the ready, eyes wide with anticipation.

I turn to Chase, seated beside me. "Dad's been doing this show since before I could walk, and it still gives me goosebumps."

"I see where you get your showmanship. Your dad's a natural. Too bad you didn't get his good looks."

"Funny stuff. Really. But to be clear, people tell me daily how handsome I am."

"That's because you're famous; Gail and her scandalous Christmas cookie photoshoots don't count. Though I have to admit, that woman has a talent for strategic icing placement."

"How do you know about that?" I ask, caught off guard. "Hold on, are you jealous?"

Whoa—she blushes.

My brain blushes right back.

Then she smiles.

Wow, she's so beautiful when she smiles.

Dad's voice snaps me back to reality. "I want to introduce you to Bubbles, my dwarf alligator. While some gators live in the wild and others are kept as pets with the proper permits, Bubbles is neither. He is being trained as an emotional support alligator."

He holds the reptile in his arms like a scaly, potentially lethal toddler—stroking the gator's head as if it were a dog. The crowd awws—I can't disagree. The cute animal's friendly smile and wagging tail make it impossible to imagine this "puppy" chomping your hand off.

"He's four years old, and he loves it when you say hello. Everyone wave and say hi to Bubbles!"

The onlookers all coo in unison, "Hi, Bubbles!"

"With his tail, he's four feet long and weighs in at forty pounds. He's packing eighty razor-sharp teeth. But Bubbles is uniquely different—he loves a good snuggle, watching YouTube videos, and can never get enough hugs and kisses."

To demonstrate, Dad hugs the half-sized gator and plants several kisses on the alligator's snout.

Chase leans in, her breath tickling my ear. "Yup, still weird."

I stifle a shiver, feeling my heart rate kick up a notch. *Keep it together, Barrett.* You know the drill—list the reasons she's not your type:

Cold.

Controlling.

Silky hands.

Soft, luscious lips.

Fuck.

Dad passes Bubbles off to an assistant. "But today, I'm going to show you some tricks with the biggest gator we've got. Say hi to Brutus!"

As Dad launches into his spiel, I start giving Chase the play-by-play. "Watch, he's gonna make a Christmas joke."

"If Brutus wrote to Santa, his list would be short: 'Dear Santa, all I want for Christmas is… more snacks!'"

The crowd laughs and then cheers as Dad tosses a fish to Brutus, who catches it mid-air. His powerful jaws close around it in milliseconds, showcasing remarkable speed and accuracy.

"Alligators have exceptional sensory abilities. Their integumentary sense organs can detect the slightest changes in water pressure. They track prey in the murkiest waters, and the best part? They never lose their car keys."

Chase snorts, a sound that should be unattractive, but on her is somehow endearing.

"You know, growing up, I wanted to be my dad—an alligator wrangler. It's why I love being called the King of Christmas. I get to bring joy to people like he does." I turn to her, curiosity getting the better of me. "What was your dad like when you were little? Was he your hero?"

Chase's expression droops like a wilting flower, her eyes reflecting a hint of sadness. "Let's just focus on the show," she snaps.

I sense there's more to this story, a depth of feeling she's trying to hide. I want to pull her close, to unravel the mystery that is Chase Pemberton, but—

The crowd's collective gasp yanks my attention back to the show. Dad's got his hand in Brutus' mouth, playing a game of "Will I Keep All My Fingers?" It's nerve-wracking the first time you see it... *Okay, maybe even the one thousandth time.*

The second my father pulls his hand out, Brutus chomps down hard, his jaws closing with an audible snap. The audience lets out a mix of relieved sighs and excited squeals.

Dad, ever the showman, beams at the spectators. "Ladies and gentlemen, prepare yourselves for my next stunt. The face-off! This ain't your everyday trick. No, this one is extra dangerous. Get those cameras ready. If I mess up, I *will* lose my face!"

Chase pivots, facing me with wide-eyed horror. "Oh my God, what the hell's he gonna do?"

"He's sticking his head into the jaws of the alligator. It's awesome!"

My dad's voice booms, building up tension. "Do you know what kind of pressure Brutus' jaws can exert? A bone-crushing, mind-blowing two thousand pounds per square inch! That's like having a car dropped on your face!"

Dad takes a deep breath and dramatically opens the alligator's gnarly jaws. He steadies himself and peers inside. Then, in one swift motion, he places his head into Brutus' mouth. The group holds its collective breath. For a moment, it's so quiet you could hear a mosquito fart. Then Dad removes his head, and Brutus' jaws snap shut. The amphitheater erupts in cheers and camera flashes.

He raises his hands for silence. "Show's not over yet, folks. We have two special guests in the audience, and they'll be helping me with an extra trick today." He pauses, amplifying the suspense. "Now, I'm proud as Gator Punch of my son. You know him as the King of Christmas. Let's welcome him and his beautiful girlfriend, Chase, to the stage. Because they'll be giving Brutus here a big ole sloppy kiss!"

The crowd cheers, but all I can focus on is Chase's sharp intake of breath. Her hand finds mine, gripping tight.

"I'm gonna be sick," she whispers, her voice trembling.

A fierce, overwhelming, all-consuming need to protect her surges through me, unlike anything I've ever felt before.

"I won't let you get hurt. Trust me," I say, surprised by the intensity in my voice.

She meets my gaze, and her vulnerability tugs at my heart. *Who knew the Ice Queen could melt?* She gives a subtle nod, and we step forward together, fingers intertwined.

Dad locks Brutus's jaws with a special strap, but it does nothing to untie the knot in my gut—not for my safety, but for Chase's. I trace her knuckles with my thumb, trying to calm her nerves. The excited chatter of the crowd turns into white noise as my focus goes entirely to this woman.

Despite her fear, fire flashes in her eyes. "If my face gets chomped off, I'm going to haunt you every day, not just Christmas," she says.

A chuckle rumbles in my chest. Even terrified, she's all spark and sass. "I wouldn't have it any other way, sweetheart."

Her palm is sweaty against mine, but I'd face down a whole swamp of alligators before I'd let go. The thought should scare the hell out of me, but instead, it steadies me.

My dad's voice cuts through the haze. "Alright, Brutus. Pucker up!"

I give her hand a comforting squeeze, and together, we lean in towards Brutus' snout.

CHAPTER ELEVEN

CHASE

How is Ethan talking me into these batshit crazy stunts?

The speedboat rocks beneath my feet as I eye the stepladder like it's a trapdoor to hell. My "Santa's Naughty Helper" costume makes Cardi B's music video outfits look downright modest. This red satin bikini is barely holding in the twins, with the life vest doing its best to keep things PG-13. But my ass? It's having a full-blown "main character" moment.

I squirm, painfully aware of how much skin I'm showing. Today's stunt is even more outrageous, but hey, Ethan's tactics are working. Not to kiss and tell, but we grew an additional 50,000 subscribers overnight after our alligator make-out session. Apparently, nothing screams "like and subscribe" like a potential trip to the ER.

And then today, *BAM!* We hit our 100k goal daily challenge within a few hours. We're up to 400k subs now! I can't believe it. Seven more days to go, and I'm feeling pretty freaking good about hitting our target.

Get those wallets ready, Wiley and Riley!

But first it's time for me to give the fans what we promised. I take a deep breath, steeling myself for the descent. Ethan is already perched on the ladder, his stupidly gorgeous blue eyes shining up at me. He looks annoyingly amazing in his red swim shorts. Those broad shoulders and sculpted arms? They're impossible to ignore.

I've seen Ethan shirtless before. In Hollywood, you can't swing a clapperboard without hitting a topless Ethan.

But this?

This is him in his natural habitat—half-naked and fully aware of the effect he has on women. *Or, more specifically, this woman.*

I need to remind myself that he's an actor. Just yesterday he was explaining to me his process. Maybe he's already figured out my spirit animal and how to sweet-talk his way into my pants. Nice try, guy, not happening.

"Hey there, sweetheart. You need a hand?" His voice is nonchalant, as if he's asking if I want fries with that.

"No thanks," I insist because I'm not some damsel in distress. But as I start to climb down, his hands find my waist, and oh my God, his touch is a pure shot of espresso.

"Careful now. Things tend to get slippery when wet," he murmurs as I descend the access steps.

Each time his fingers graze my skin, sparks shoot through me, igniting a fire low in my belly that I'm desperately trying to ignore.

As I reach the base of the ladder, his palms slide down to my hips, then lower. I can't hold back the gasp as he gives my ass a squeeze that's anything but innocent.

"Ethan!" I hiss, throwing him a scowl over my shoulder.

He grins, completely shameless. "What? Just making sure the director knows she's in good hands."

His voice rumbles through me, all low and husky and irritatingly sexy. I'm supposed to be immune to his charms, but my knees are buckling. I mentally draft a strongly worded letter to my body: *Knock this shit off.*

For a moment, his eyes, usually twinkling with mischief, are dark and intense. I find myself drawn in by some magnetic force I can't resist—

"Hold on to this for me?" Ethan says, breaking the spell and handing me his life jacket. Without hesitation, he dives headfirst into the water, swimming swiftly towards a two-person raft.

I watch him slice through the current, trying my best not to notice the way his muscles ripple with each stroke. Definitely not admiring. Except... okay, fine, it's mesmerizing.

He reaches the inflatable and pulls himself up with an effortless heave. Liquid cascades down his body, and I am transfixed. Droplets cling to his abs, catching the sunlight. They're like tiny, sparkly glitter bombs, and I'm fighting the urge to start a rave of my own...

On his stomach.

With my tongue.

Hold up. What the hell?

I close my eyes, trying to banish these utterly inappropriate thoughts. No, I do not want to lick him like a delicious ice cream cone on a hot summer day.

Who am I kidding? I totally do. God help me, I do.

He sits up, steadying the raft. "Coming aboard? Or are you just gonna keep enjoying the view?"

I roll my eyes. "You wish I was staring, Barrett."

"Pssh. I know you were." He smirks, extending his hand.

I grasp it, doing my best to ignore the spark from his touch. "I've got it, thanks—"

And then with the grace of a clumsy stripper... I slip.

His strong arms catch me, and he falls onto his back. My hands are splayed on his pecs, and I can feel his heart racing beneath my palms.

"If you wanted to get on top of me, there are easier ways."

I push against his chest, attempting to get up. "In your dreams."

His embrace tightens around me. "Oh, trust me, my dreams are a hell of a lot more interesting than this."

"Guys?" Nolan calls out from the boat. "You ready to get into position?"

"Always on point with your timing, bro," Ethan remarks playfully.

We awkwardly separate, and I try not to mourn the loss of contact. *What is wrong with me today?*

Ethan helps me turn onto my stomach, his hands lingering as he guides mine to the raft handles. Every touch feels deliberate, charged. His fingers trail fire across my skin, and I have to bite my lip to keep from making a very inappropriate sound.

"Comfortable, darlin'?"

"About as comfy as you can get when you're about to risk your life for some likes," I grumble.

Am I crazy, or is Ethan being extra touchy-feely today? I mean, every little brush of his skin is saying, "Hello, fire department." Or is this his usual MO with all women? Perhaps he's just keeping his game sharp while he's stuck playing my fake boyfriend?

"Live a little, Chase. It'll be fun."

"Your idea of fun and mine are vastly different."

"Oh yeah?" he says, voice low. "What's *fun* for you?"

Images flash through my mind, all involving Ethan and significantly fewer clothes *(which says a lot, given my skimpy outfit)*. "Not something you need to know."

"You sure about that? I'm pretty confident I could change your mind about what fun we could have."

I turn my head to look at him, ready with a snappy comeback, but the words die in my throat. His eyes are dark, intense, fixed on me as if I'm the only thing in the world.

"Chase," he continues softly, "I—"

Nolan shouts, "Alright, guys! Ready for the signals? This means start." He makes a thumbs-up gesture. "And this means stop." He demonstrates, making a motion with his palm facing out. "Got it?"

Ethan and I nod, the moment broken.

We're being dragged at least a jillion miles an hour on a giant inflatable death trap. Okay, maybe not quite that fast, since a Jimmy Buffet booze cruise just floated past us. But I'm clinging to this tube like it's the last life preserver on the Titanic. Praying to every deity I can think of that the rope isn't as flimsy as my dignity.

How, in a matter of days, have I gone from respected director to jackass stuntman?

"Are you sure this is safe?" I ask, my voice embarrassingly squeaky.

"Totally. Nolan and I did this all the time growing up."

"Yeah, and I bet you also thought Tide Pods were breath mints and Sharpies were fun to smell. Your childhood shenanigans aren't boosting my confidence here."

"You want proof you'll be okay? Fine. Look at me. I'm alive. And you will be too."

He's too cocky to even realize we're in danger. We're about to be dragged through the water at *oh-shit-miles-per-hour* on a glorified pool floatie, then launched off a ramp forty feet into the air.

What could possibly go wrong? Oh, I don't know... EVERY-THING?

The reality of the impending disaster settles in. My chest tightens—I'm having a panic attack.

"Chase, nothing bad will happen."

"*If* the rope doesn't snap or decapitate us," I counter. "And if we don't get devoured by a Kraken. There's still a high probability of drowning."

"Krakens aren't native to Florida."

"Neither is common sense, apparently!"

Ethan's eyes soften, and he takes a real, long look at me. He lays a calming hand over my white-knuckled grip on the tube handle.

"I won't let anything bad happen to you."

I melt. I believe him.

Damn him and his sexy reassurance. It's one thing for his ardent fans to fall for this act, but me? Why is my body reacting this way? Every cell of mine is screaming, "Girl, forget the hate. Let's get it!"

I pause, realizing what this is, and admit it to myself. I haven't had sex in a very, very long time. My vagina has turned into a deserted playground, with rusty rides and no visitors in sight.

Staying single is common in Hollywood. Usually, the dating process lasts longer than the actual relationship. That's certainly been my experience with guys in LA. So why bother? But right now, with Ethan's thigh pressed to mine, "Why bother?" is starting to sound similar to "Why not?"

He shifts, turning onto his side to pull the phone from his pocket. He secures it into a wrist holder with a tight Velcro strap and connects the phone with a cord. No chance it's falling off in the water. He lies back, this time his entire body presses into mine—and good Lord, do I like it. A lot.

An endless GIF of this morning's scenes keeps replaying in my brain. I woke up, draped over Ethan like he was mine. My face was snuggled into his neck—my lips grazing his stubble. Damn, it felt good.

I wonder how it would feel if my mouth accidentally landed on his.

My focus catches Ethan's eyes roaming over me in a slow, sensual sweep, as if he's mentally peeling away my skimpy bikini, revealing every inch of skin. His gaze drops to my mouth, and my heart races wildly.

I swallow hard, resisting the urge to lick my suddenly dry lips. *Does he want to kiss me as badly as I'm dying to kiss him?*

Gah! All of this fake relationship crap is really messing with my head. Maybe if I get a "fake boyfriend" tattoo, my body will get the message.

This is just a job.

A job to save my real job.

To save who I really am—who I want to be.

These feelings aren't real. They're... method acting.

I'm playing the part of Ethan Barrett's girlfriend... for now. For a few more days. Soon, I will escape to my Christmas cabin and start writing my next movie.

One that doesn't star Ethan "Walking Wet Dream" Barrett.

Nolan yells at us from the helm of the idling speedboat. He waves his hands until he sees he has our attention, then gives us a thumbs-up. That's the signal.

My mock boyfriend holds up a hand, palm facing his brother, signaling to wait.

"Okay, sweetheart, it's showtime."

Ethan taps his phone, going live. "What's up, Ethan Addicts! I know you've been waiting for this. We got some high-flying aquatic action." He turns to me with a wink. "Any last words, babe?"

"I hate this. I hate this. I hate this!" I slur the words together.

He wears a devilish grin as he turns back to the livestream. "She's having the time of her life, folks. She just doesn't know it yet!"

I glance at the phone screen—within seconds, the viewer count shoots up into the tens of thousands. Viewer hearts and comments fly by faster than my rising blood pressure, with a blur of emoji vomit.

Ethan starts greeting his adoring fans. "Well, hello there, Gail!"

Gail. Even her name tastes bitter on my tongue like I've licked the bottom of a public trash can. I can picture her smug face now, probably glued to her phone—her only lifeline to this obsession.

Ethan chuckles. "Gail's comment says, 'Ten bucks you chicken out and jump ship, but if you don't, then she prays for a wardrobe malfunction,'" he teases. "And oh, there's more, lots more."

No doubt this girl has her manicured talons poised to spread more venom the second I fail. The psycho lives for this shit, feeding off drama like an emotional vampire. *Get a life, lady.*

"I'm paraphrasing here," he continues, "but basically she wants you to drown so hard, even the fish will be saying, 'Damn, that's brutal.'"

The rage bubbling inside me is so hot I'm a volcano of "Bitch, please." *Who does this discount store groupie think she is?* She could never land someone as hot as Ethan, famous or not.

Oh, Gail. You poor, delusional little gnat. I'm in Florida. Just this morning, I've eaten bigger bugs than you for breakfast.

I flash a sugary-sweet smile to the lens. "Be careful what you wish for. If I go down, Ethan goes with me."

That's it. I'm turning this tube ride into a middle finger so big it'll be visible from space. *Gail wants a show?* I'll give her a goddamn IMAX experience of her crushed dreams with surround sound and complimentary popcorn.

I wink at the camera teasingly. "First, how about a good luck kiss?"

Then, before my brain can catch up with my body and scream, *What the hell are you doing?*, I grab Ethan's face and plant a big ole kiss right on his lips. *Take that, Gail. Choke on it.*

I pull back, riding high on adrenaline and spite, only to see the shock in his eyes. He wasn't...

Expecting. Feeling. Or wanting that kiss.

Oh shit.

My stomach drops faster than we're about to on this death trap. *Panic mode: activated.*

I channel my inner director and shout at the top of my lungs, "NOLAN!" My thumb shoots up.

Thankfully, Nolan sees my signal and punches the boat into high gear before I die of embarrassment.

We take off in a flash, and I'm pretty sure I see my stomach *(and my dignity)* back on dry land sipping umbrella drinks and wishing me luck. It's all I can do to hold on. I'm bobbing up and down, thrashing wildly, and just one jolt away from flying to my death.

"Here comes the jump!" Ethan shouts, pointing ahead with childlike glee. He whoops and hollers like a true adrenaline junkie.

I spot the ramp through the waves just ahead of us. *Holy fuck!* The thing is taller than a freaking skyscraper.

"Fuckfuckfuckfuckfuck!"

I'm about to die. Today is the day this attention-obsessed lunatic kills me. I'd pictured my death being somewhat more civilized, like choking on caviar or being crushed by my tower of unread scripts. But no, I'm going to bite it in the freakin' Gulf of Mexico.

We hit the ramp.

We're airborne.

I scream.

He's cackling with glee.

We hang in the air. For a moment. Sheer. Frozen. Terror.

WHAM!

We crash back into the water with such force that I swear my uterus just high-fived my tonsils.

Ethan lets out a victory cry. "Holy shit! Did you see that?"

I don't respond. I'm doing a mental headcount of my limbs and internal organs. I'm not dead, and even better, my bikini is still on *(suck it, Gail!)*

Then it's as if Gail has some kind of supernatural, vengeful powers. A speedboat zooms by, kicking up a massive wake, and we go flying off the tube.

I'm underwater for an eternity—swirling currents have me upside down and disoriented. I have no idea which way is up. Thankfully, my life jacket pops me to the surface.

Ethan swims over, still clutching that damn phone connected with velcro to his wrist like a teen girl juggling three boyfriends.

"You okay?" he asks, and he actually looks concerned. It's almost enough to make me forgive him. Almost.

"Superduper," I gurgle, half the Gulf of Mexico expelling from my lungs.

"Gals, we did it! We conquered the tube of doom!" Ethan announces to his adoring audience. "Tune in tomorrow for another naughty or nice dare. This is your favorite holiday hunk, signing off!"

He ends the livestream, turns, and sees me glaring.

"Are you going to film my reaction every time you try to murder me?"

"Is that why you laid one on me earlier? Figured you'd better get your last kiss in before meeting your watery fate?"

"That little lip brush? Please. I was practicing CPR. Someone's gotta be ready to revive your sorry ass when one of these stunts backfires. Can't finish the movie without my leading douchebag, can I?"

"Aw, darlin'," he coos, swimming closer. "No need to make excuses. We both know you were finally admitting your burning desires."

"My only desire is to watch you drown," I answer, keeping my head above the surface.

Before he can respond, a fleet of jet skis races past, churning up a wake that sends waves crashing over us. Ethan's arms are around me in an instant, pulling me close as we bob in the water like awkward buoys. Our eyes lock...

And then he kisses me.

Holy mother of mistletoe.

His dynamite lips taste of salt water and sin.

My fingers dive into his wet hair, nails raking his scalp as the kiss turns ravenous. He groans into my mouth, the vibration shooting straight to my core. And *oh my fuck*, his lips. Ethan is doing this mouth-orgasm-inducing thing with his tongue that has me seeing stars. I can barely breathe, and I don't care. I want more.

I want his lips on my neck.

On my breasts.

In between my legs.

I'm drowning in him, and it feels so fucking good.

He grabs my ass, pulling me closer, as if he can't get enough either.

I wrap my legs around his waist, and the ache between my thighs grows. Especially when his hardening cock presses against my clit through the thin fabric of my bikini. My vagina twitches, begging for more. His length is pressing, rubbing, teasing me while waves rhythmically bob us up and down... up and down.

Is the water getting hotter? Do I see steam? I've lost all rational thought.

"Yes, harder," I murmur against his lips, our breaths mingling, hot and desperate.

I shamelessly grind against his shaft. I don't know how he's doing it, but he's stimulating my clit with a featherlike rapidness that is teasing me to the edge. But I need more than teasing. I want release.

"Harder," I demand.

"Fuck, yeah," he says in a low growl that sends shivers down my spine.

His grip intensifies, but his "clit rhythm" remains gentle. He's battling the waves and trying to connect with me where I need him. Yet, I yearn for more firmness. *Odd.*

"Adjust your dick and apply pressure."

"Are you really directing me right now?"

"Clearly, you need some guidance. Points for the fast flicking action, but where's the pressure? It's going to be dark before I come."

"The waves aren't making it easy to hold on to you."

"Okay, stop. Seriously. Ethan! Stop flicking my clit!"

"I'm not touching you," he says, his brows furrowing in confusion.

What the...

"Get it out!" I scream, flailing my arms and splashing. "It's touching my pussy!"

"Chase! Be still."

"The thing is trying to swim inside me! Oh God! Gross!"

Ethan grabs onto me, plunging his hand down my bikini bottoms.

"It's so slippery!" he yells, his fingers moving wildly as the mysterious creature wriggles and squirms. "Is that a—?"

"Goddammit! Get it!" I order.

Ethan's hand locks around the slimy intruder, and he yanks it out with a look of utter revulsion. As the creature surfaces, I'm greeted by the horrifying sight of an ugly, blunt-nosed fish with long whiskers. The aquatic pervert wears a smirk that says, *Was that as good for you as it was for me?*

The fish wriggles free from Ethan's grip and lunges toward me, its mouth opening and closing like it wants to give me a disgusting, unwanted kiss.

"Stay back, you clit-flicking fish!" I scream, splashing and thrashing frantically.

In my frenzy, I accidentally smack Ethan square in the face. "Ow! Fuck!" Ethan exclaims, rubbing his cheek.

I'm still flailing when I hear a boat engine approaching. In true Nolan fashion, he has materialized out of nowhere and looks supremely uncomfortable.

"Hey," Nolan says. "Are you two having ocean sex? Cuz I can leave."

I gape at him, my thoughts scattering like a flock of seagulls spotting a dropped hot dog. "What? No! There was a fish—and it—and then I—and Ethan—" I splutter.

Great. I've officially lost it.

Ethan, the gorgeous jerk, can't stop laughing. "Sorry about that, bro. Chase was just trying to shake off some affection from a catfish Casanova. Apparently, she's irresistible to all species."

I shoot him a glare, then swim to the boat without looking back. As I haul myself up, I form a two-step plan:

Step one: No more ocean, or Gulf, or whatever the fuck it's called.

Step two: Avoid Ethan Barrett and his almost orgasm-inducing lips.

CHAPTER TWELVE

CHASE

Who do I have to fuck to find the light switch?

It's two a.m. as I tiptoe across the chilly tile in my bare feet. I'm stumbling through the unfamiliar kitchen like a drunk raccoon. I'm thirsty, okay? Thirsty for water, I swear. That's the story I'm sticking to. Definitely not because Ethan's muscular arm was snuggling me in bed, stirring up all kinds of naughty thoughts that I shouldn't be having.

After our disastrous smooch-and-splash today, we've been dancing around each other like awkward prom dates. I pulled the classic "headache" card and dashed off to bed. And when he slid beside me under the sheets, I pulled off an epic Sleeping Beauty act.

Did hearing him breathe get me all hot and bothered? Absolutely. Did I want to strip down and climb on top of him? Hell yeah. Am I really this sexually desperate? Appears so.

My fingers finally find the switch on the wall and—

"Sweet baby Jesus!" I gulp out, staring down at an alligator. Bubble's beady eyes are fixed on me as if I'm a midnight snack. *Fantastic.*

I clap a hand over my mouth to muffle my scream. The last thing I need is to wake up the entire Barrett clan and have to explain why I'm having a standoff with their pet reptile in the middle of the night.

"Seriously!" I whisper-hiss. "I'd love just five minutes of not being scared shitless by things lurking around every corner. Fucking Florida!" I calmly approach the gator, cooing in what I hope is a soothing, please-don't-eat-me voice. "Can't sleep?"

Bubbles, unsurprisingly, says nothing. He doesn't move, which I count as a win.

"Want something? A snack?" I ask, inching towards the fridge like I'm defusing a bomb. I realize I have no idea what gators eat. Cold cuts? Sauerkraut? Cucumber sandwiches? I spot a canister marked "Bubbles' Treats" and grab it.

Please, God, don't let it be filled with human fingers. Knowing this family it wouldn't surprise me.

It's a small container that might be holding dog treats. I take a whiff. Whatever's in there sure as hell doesn't smell like puppy chow.

The scaly beast whips its head towards me, fixing me with a predatory stare that turns my blood to ice. I'm pretty confident I just shit myself.

"It's okay," I say in baby talk for some reason. *Am I talking like this for his benefit?*

"You want a treat?" I say, presenting the container. "Open wide, Bubbles!"

To my utter shock, he obeys. *Fuck me. Why would I tell a live alligator to open wide?* I gasp at the rows of yellowed, razor-sharp teeth pointed straight at me.

He's waiting... mouth gaping. *Hurry up, dummy, or he's gonna chomp on your leg.*

I pop the lid and gag. I see a dead freakin' frog.

"I bet Spielberg never had to be a reptile's personal chef," I sigh.

I reach for the frog but stop short. Bubbles eyes me suspiciously… as if *I* want to eat it myself. *I'm just guessing because I don't actually know what Jaws-Of-Life McGee over there is thinking.*

"Don't look at me like that," I snap. "I don't want to touch it, okay? Some of us didn't grow up in the swamp."

I'm trying to be cool, but my heart's racing. Predictably, Ethan's not here when I need him. He could control this stupid animal—keep me safe. He's protected me before—when my fingers were trembling—with his big, strong hands and his deep, blue comforting eyes.

Snap out of it, Chase! You're above his womanizing charms.

I grab a piece of chocolate cake from the fridge. "How about this? It's sweet, just like you." I waggle it enticingly, but Bubbles closes his mouth. *Tough crowd.*

"You know, sometimes we don't get what we want," I tell him. "I wanted to be in a cabin, alone, drinking wine and writing my next masterpiece. Instead, I'm in a crazy house where I'm bombarded with inappropriate thoughts and feelings—like wondering if Ethan's penis actually feels like a slimy, limp fish."

Oh God, did I just say that out loud? To an alligator?

"Don't you dare repeat that."

Bubbles takes a step forward, hungry, unimpressed, or maybe a little of both.

Was it my pep talk?

Is this gator judging my Ethan-centric thoughts?

Wait a minute. Can alligators sense sexual frustration?

"Fine," I groan, ditching the cake and holding up the Frog à la Mode tub. "I get it, you're hangry and conflicted. You understand how I feel, don't you? Wanting to kiss someone and also wanting to punch them in the face. But for you, it's biting their face off. Same difference, really."

I eyeball the lifeless frog, wondering how my life choices led me to this moment. Here, in the armpit of the Sunshine State, playing therapist to a scaly beast while holding Kermit the Frog's less fortunate cousin—this is rock bottom.

Slowly, I reach in and touch the slimy corpse. "Oh God, it feels worse than it smells," I gag.

The frog's leg is cold and clammy as I grip it with my fingers. I pinch my nose with my free hand and then dangle the carcass over Bubbles' waiting maw, acknowledging the sheer stupidity of hand-feeding an alligator in the dead of night. I let go, and he snaps his jaws shut with an ominous *CHOMP!*

Quickly, I wash my hands. Because, ew, frog cooties.

Good. That's done. Now back to me. What do I want? Orange Juice? Toast? Ethan? Ethan's abs. His chest. His rugged face with that cocky smile. I want the way he looks at me when he thinks I'm not paying attention. Yeah, I want *that*.

Why can't I stop thinking about him?

His lips.

That kiss.

Damn. My whole fucking body tingles at the memory.

"Bubbles, this is crazy, right?" I ask. "I mean, there's no way. He's an actor. He knows how gorgeous he is, and he uses it. Against me, against all women. If we hook up, it'll inflate his ego even more, and he'll be impossible to work with."

I groan, covering my face. "Directors do not sleep with the talent. Period. It complicates everything."

Even if it would be mind-blowingly, fan-freaking-tastic.

The creature is watching me with what I swear is sympathy. Or maybe he's just bored. It's hard to tell with reptiles. "You're a great listener. Has anyone ever told you that? You don't talk back, you never roll your eyes, and this may sound crazy, but I feel heard."

"Let's break this down. Banging Ethan—pros and cons. Pros: He's hot as hell. Like, unfairly attractive. It would probably be the best sex ever. I mean, you've felt his hands on your body."

"Cons: It could, no, it *would* wreck my career. We have half a movie to finish filming. Things would get weird on set, like super awkward. Plus, it'll make him even more of an arrogant jerk."

"Ugh. What am I supposed to do? I know you're cold-blooded, but you get it, right? The way Ethan makes your skin heat up every time he's near?"

Bubbles respects my thoughts with silence.

"Okay, I hear you. Shut it down. Slap on the chastity belt and lose the key. It's only a few more days. Eyes on the prize." I sigh. "You really are an emotional support alligator."

His giant mouth opens again, teeth so sharp they look like a freaking knife set.

"Got it, therapy session's over. Time for more snacks," I say, steeling myself. "Listen, big guy, *I'll* feed you another disgusting treat, and in return, *you* agree this conversation never happened. Deal?"

He stays still, which I choose to interpret as agreement. I open the fridge, and I see zero mysterious containers.

"Uh, we might have a problem here, big guy," I say.

He honest-to-God looks sad, and after all we've been through tonight, it breaks my heart a little.

"I can't... Where would I even find more?" I plead. "Come on, quit giving me that look... I'm not going outside. I'm in my pajamas, dude. They're silk!"

I swear he's giving me the stink eye.

As I weigh my chances of making it back to the bedroom alive, Ethan saunters in, wearing nothing but boxers and a tight white T-shirt that clings to his abs like a second skin. He looks like sex on a stick—deep fried in lust, dipped in sin, rolled in temptation, and powdered with the promise of pleasure.

"I gave him the frog," I blurt out.

Ethan stretches, all rippling muscles and golden skin. His eyes flick from me to Bubbles, and a knowing smirk plays at the corners of his mouth.

"He doesn't want a snack," Ethan says, voice husky with sleep.

"Excuse me?" I sputter. "I just touched a dead frog. Trust me, he *wanted* a snack!"

The king of assholes actually has the nerve to snicker. He leans over the counter, his arm brushing against mine, activating every nerve ending in my body. I'm tingling in places I didn't even know existed.

"Actually, Miss Gator Charmer," Ethan drawls, reaching for something behind the toaster. "He really wants..."

In one smooth motion that has no business being that sexy, Ethan tosses something towards Bubbles. The alligator's jaws clamp around it faster than I can blink.

"Feathers," Ethan finishes, looking so smug I could smack him.

I squint at the ratty flamingo stuffed animal now clutched in his mouth.

I hate it. I hate him.

"I hate Florida," I say instead.

"It hates you too, sweetheart. You two have irreconcilable differences."

Our eyes meet, and my breath hitches as his gaze drops to my lips. Suddenly, the kitchen feels like it's on fire. Or maybe that's just my self-control frying to a crisp.

Ethan inches closer, and I fight the urge to back up against the counter. Or, better yet, hop onto it and wrap my legs around his waist.

I clear my throat loudly and dramatically, then pretend to choke on my own spit, coughing and sputtering. "Wrong pipe," I wheeze, patting my chest and effectively breaking the tension.

"Why are you up?" he says bluntly.

"Plotting my escape. No, your demise. Yeah, that's it. I was planning on luring Bubbles into your room and—"

"Ooh, kinky." He winks. "But I think there's enough going on in our bed already."

Does he know? That I woke up clinging to him like he was my favorite teddy bear? A delicious shiver runs through me as I realize I'm not just wanting to be caught—I'm aching for it.

I can't help the nervous swipe of my tongue across my lips. Ethan's gaze locks on to the movement, his eyes showing unmistakable hunger. I lick my lips again, slowly, and he becomes a predator zeroing in on his prey. And damn, do I feel like letting myself get devoured. Repeatedly.

I gotta squash this, stat!

I avert my gaze, fixing my eyes on the floor. "Sorry, I've already decided. It's gonna be cold-blooded murder for you. Death by Bubbles. Right after I get myself a glass of water."

Ethan tilts my chin up, demanding my eyes meet his. I hold my breath, reeling from anticipation. *Is he going to kiss me right here, right now?* Without breaking eye contact, he reaches into the cabinet behind me, pulls out a glass, and fills it with sink water.

"Here ya go, Chase. But if you're feeling adventurous, I've got a few other methods in mind to quench your thirst."

I take a sip, trying to calm my heart that's pounding like a drum solo. My mind keeps flashing back to that kiss in the Gulf. His hold on me was so damn strong and confident. The taste of him mixed with sea salt...

My lady bits are chanting, *Ethan! Ethan! Ethan!* They've really developed a mind of their own lately.

"Why are you awake?" I ask, opting for a snarky comeback instead of doing something stupid like jumping his bones. "Having nightmares about underwater performance issues? Worried that limp fish dick syndrome might be contagious?"

He barks out a laugh. "Nah, I never have nightmares. I do dream, though, and tonight's fantasy was... inspiring."

"Oh?" I raise an eyebrow. "It was so *incredible,* it woke you up?"

"Actually, yeah. I dreamt about you."

"Shut up," I say instantly. "Really?"

"Really," he murmurs, his eyes darkening. "And we weren't wearing a lot of clothes."

I swallow hard, my mouth suddenly dry in spite of my recent drink. "You sure it was me? And not one of your co-stars?"

Ethan leans in, his lips brushing my ear as he whispers, "It's the kind of dream that's hard to explain. I'd have to show you."

"Is that so?" I ask dryly. *Ladies and gentlemen, Ethan Barrett, busting out "The Old Dream Seducer", technique #357.*

Ethan continues, "Come back to bed with me, and I'll tell you about it. You know you want to. I promise it'll be more fun than first-degree murder."

"No thanks, pretty boy," I say with a wave of my hand. "I'm going back to sleep. Stay on your side or else."

I brush past him, but Ethan catches my wrist, his tone shifting from playful to serious. "Chase. We need to talk about us, about the kiss."

I freeze. "There's nothing to talk about. A momentary lapse in judgment. It was a mistake."

"Was it?" Ethan challenges.

He steps so close that his body presses against mine, the heat of him radiating through my clothes. His hand cups my cheek, thumb gently stroking my skin. "Here's the truth. I can't stop thinking about you, Chase. You're driving me fucking insane."

His words slice through my defenses, burrowing deep into my core and igniting a desire I can't ignore. "Ethan," I breathe, not sure if it's a warning or a plea.

"I want to kiss you," Ethan says, his voice low and husky. "Your lips, the way you tasted, how you felt against me—it's all I can think about."

My heart races. The next thing out of my mouth surprises me. "Then why don't you?"

"Because if I start, I won't stop. Not until we're bare-ass naked and completely spent and you can't stop panting my name."

I suck in a quick breath. My body can't hide how much it craves those words. My breasts tighten. My clit tingles. There is not enough air in this goddamn room.

"This isn't a good idea," I manage to say, my body screaming for his touch.

"Tell me you don't want this," he growls, his anxious hands now on my hips. "Tell me no."

I should. I know I should. This is a disaster waiting to happen. A ticking time bomb ready to detonate. Every instinct is screaming at me to get out of here, to put as much distance between us as possible before it's too late.

But I'm tired of running. Tired of ignoring this electric connection we have. Exhausted from fighting how my body reacts to his touch. For once, I want the messy, dangerous choice—the one that could leave my heart in pieces.

"Kiss me," I command.

CHAPTER THIRTEEN

ETHAN

MY BRAIN'S SAYING, ***ABORT*** *mission!* while my dick's all, *You're cleared for launch!*

This is a terrible idea, man.

Don't lean in. Don't kiss her. Don't breathe in her scent.

And stop undressing her with your eyes. The problem is, my body is only hearing the last half of every sentence.

Her gaze never breaks from mine. It's steady, focused, like she's communicating directly through her stare. Her pink tongue sweeps across her lips, leaving a glistening trail—the allure of her mouth is offering promises I can't resist.

My heart's pounding, compelling me to act. Chase bites her lower lip, a tempting invitation. My thumb patiently traces the seam of her lush mouth. Finally, I hear it.

"Kiss me."

The authority in her voice obliterates my defenses. I'm powerless. I claim her mouth with a ferocity that steals her gasp, our kiss turning wild and consuming. Everything she's doing with those skillful lips and that sinful tongue has my senses spinning out of control.

"I want you naked," I growl. My hands move with purpose, pulling down the neckline of Chase's shirt to expose the creamy surface of her skin. I plant hot, open-mouthed kisses along her collarbone as my hand slips beneath the fabric, palming her breast with a possessive touch. She's soft and warm, her nipple hardening against my palm.

"Stop, wait. Wait!" she cries out, her breath catching in her throat.

I freeze, uncertainty flooding my features. "God, sorry. I uh, thought you wanted to—"

"No. I mean yes," Chase clarifies, her eyes darkened with desire. "But not here. Your parents could see us."

"Bedroom. Copy that."

In one fluid motion, I scoop her up, my large hands cupping the lush curves of her ass. Her lips find my neck, and the way she nibbles on my earlobe ignites my insides. Her tongue continues to tease before she sensually plunges it into my ear.

"Fuck!" I nearly drop her. A waterfall of sensations ripples through me. My grip on Chase's thighs falters as pure molten lust floods my system. Her breathy moan unearths something in me, the sound so insistent and needy.

Her legs—those sinful, mile-long legs—hug my waist like a vise, grinding her heat against me. The friction ignites sparks behind my eyelids. My cock strains painfully against her core, demanding attention.

"Sweetheart," I mutter. "If you keep that up, we're not making it to the bed."

"You get me to that bedroom now!" she commands.

Stumbling into my room, I grab the doorknob and carefully ease the door shut behind us, jamming a chair under the handle.

In the three and a half years I've known Chase, never once did I think I wanted this. We've butted heads more times than I can count, and there's the obvious reason she's off-limits: she's my boss.

But holding her now, in my arms, with passion pulsing through my veins, she's all I want. I've never craved anything more in my entire goddamn life.

"Bed. Now."

"With fucking pleasure," I growl devilishly. That bossy tone—the one that's always grated on me—feels different here.

I am so fucked.

The second Chase's ass hits the sheets, her hands are tugging at my shirt. I need to feel her skin against me. I reach behind, grab the collar, and rip it clean off.

"Oh my God, your body is fucking perfect," she breathes, her fingers trailing down my chiseled pecs and across my abs, leaving goosebumps of hunger with each touch.

"I showed you mine. Now show me yours."

She raises her arms above her head, signaling me to pull off her silk pajama top. I waste no time. Her exposed breasts—beautiful and full—perfectly match my greedy gaze.

"Jesus fuck, you're sexy," I groan, my eager hands already cupping her soft mounds. My thumbs graze over her hardened nipples. Chase's back arches, pushing her breasts toward me and intensifying my touch—a silent plea for more. I oblige, squeezing harder, reveling in the way her mouth falls open with a breathy moan.

I dip my head, my tongue darting out and lapping up her sweet flesh. *I want to worship every inch of her body.* "I could spend days sucking on these perky, rosy nipples," I murmur.

"Less talking, more orgasms," Chase demands.

"Okay, listen," I sigh, exasperated. "You gotta let me lead here. Equal partners, remember?"

"Ethan, if you want to be inside me when I come, you better get a condom on right now."

"You're the boss," I concede, grinning until—

Realization hits me. "Oh shit, do you have one?"

Chase's eyes widen. "No! Sex was *not* on my itinerary, especially with you."

Son of a bitch! My mind races as my body yearns to be sheathed deep inside her, pulsating and engorged so tightly I might black out and—

"Seriously, Ethan? Not a single condom in your room?

"Give me a second to think. My blood isn't exactly flowing to my brain right now."

My eyes scan the room, desperate for a solution. SpongeBob's eyes seem to mock me, saying, *Better luck next time.*

"Wait. My Pokémon cards!"

I spring up, my hand shooting under the bed to grab a yellow binder sporting a bright Pikachu emblem. With swift, precise movements, I riffle through the crystal-clear plastic sleeves, each card meticulously arranged by type, rarity, and personal significance. It's a collection that would make any enthusiast drool.

"Ethan, what the hell are you doing?"

"I stashed condoms in here. It's the only place I figured my mom wouldn't check," I say with unwavering concentration as I flip card after card. "Whenever I would explain stuff, like how to use the evolutionary stone to level up my Charmander, my mom would zone out. She couldn't stand these things—"

"I can see why."

Shut up, man! Stop talking about your mom.

And for fuck's sake, hurry! Between your SpongeBob sheets and Pokémon card collection, she's gonna change her mind.

But then Chase's fingers tug at my boxers, dipping beneath the waistband and brushing against my tip.

And I'm focused up—now that's what I call directing.

As I continue searching for a condom, her smooth hand starts exploring me. Her delicate fingers glide up and down my shaft, and then she gives my cock a firm squeeze.

My pulse skyrockets.

My dick throbs in her hand.

My brain's dizzy.

"Found one!" I exclaim, hastily pulling the condom from its sleeve, tearing the page out of the binder in my urgency.

Chase snatches the wrapper from my grip and smiles. She rips it open with her teeth—*what a savage!* Her eyes fix on mine as she slides the condom over my length with a confident, seductive motion.

God, I'm about to blow.

"My turn," I growl, shoving her back onto the bed firmly. My body hovers above hers as my hands and lips trailblaze a path down her neck, across her collarbone, and lower still. I'm enjoying every sigh and moan; obsessed with bringing her to the brink of ecstasy.

She spreads her legs, a welcome invitation. My mouth crashes onto hers once more, our tongues tangling in a heated dance as I position myself at her entrance. With agonizing slowness, I push in, feeling her walls stretch around me, her breath hitching against my lips.

"You all right?" I whisper.

"Fuck yes," she breathes. "Thank Poseidon, you don't have a limp fish dick."

"Sweetheart, I have a full-blown sea monster."

I smirk until she rocks her hips, encouraging me. I push deeper, inch by delicious inch, pumping in and out slowly and savoring every sensation.

She's so snug.

So hot.

So drenched.

It's a goddamn paradise.

"Oh my God, Ethan. You feel gooood," she says, moaning like an animal. I've never heard her make sounds like this. Breathy and low. Primal and raw. So... erotic.

I force myself to stay controlled. I'm able to prolong the moment by using steady rhythms, but Chase has other plans. She wraps her legs around my waist, pulling me in to the hilt with one swift motion. When she inhales sharply, her wispy gasp triggers a pulse throb all the way to the tip of my cock.

Fuck, I'm not going to last. I freeze. One more thrust, and I'll surrender to my climax.

"Why'd you stop?" she pants.

"Don't move," I warn, my voice straining from holding back. "I don't want to disappoint you."

I breathe deep, willing my body to calm down.

"Ethan, I'm so fucking close," she pants. "I want you to come with me." Her hands squeeze my ass, urging me on. "So move," she commands.

"Fuck, you're bossy," I groan.

With her green light, I immerse myself, thrusting deeply, relishing in the way her body grips mine. Chase's guttural moan fills the air, and I know we're both close.

"Oh hell yes... Chase, you feel amazing."

"You're so big, Ethan," she whimpers, her nails digging into my skin. "I love it. Give me more."

She pulls my hair, bringing my lips back to hers. "Kiss me," she demands, but I'm already there.

Our tongues enter a frenzied dance. I pick up the pace, my center snapping against hers with urgency. She arches her back, her legs tightening around me, drawing me impossibly deeper.

"Ethan, God yes, I'm nearly there," she whimpers into my ear with breathy moans. "Don't you fucking stop this time!"

My hips are relentless, meeting hers again and again—pushing and pushing. My old mattress springs cry out in protest.

Squeak. Squeak. Squeak.

I can feel the pressure of my own release tightening, blissfully ready to explode. But Chase's ragged breathing tells me she's still on the cusp. I need to bring her over the edge first, past the pinnacles of pleasure. I want to feel her shatter around me—to watch her come undone.

Squeakkkk. Squeakkkk. Squeakkkk!

"Shit, Ethan. Stop. It's too loud. Stop!" Chase pants, her eyes wide with concern.

"It's fine," I groan, my hips on a train that has long left the station.

"No, I don't want your family to hear," she insists, destroying our momentum.

"Jesus Christ," I mutter and stop. "You really *do* have to control everything, don't you?"

I reach my arm under her back. "Hold on tight."

Chase's arms and legs cinch around me. "Where are we—"

In a single, fluid movement, I pull us to the floor.

We land on the rug with a soft thud, still connected, our bodies molded together. My ass takes the brunt of the fall, a pain that quickly fades when I look up to Chase straddling me.

Exactly what I wanted.

I gently touch her cheek. "You're in charge. I don't come till you do."

A surprised look of satisfaction flickers across her face, a silent acknowledgment of the shift in power. She silently takes my hand and places it on her breast, gently squeezing her fingers over mine.

Chase begins to sway—slowly and deliberately. I watch, transfixed, as she moves.

Her body. Her eyes. Her breasts. Her rolling hips. Sweet Jesus, *she's beautiful.*

She tilts her head back, exhaling deeply, lost in the sensation of our bodies slowly moving as one. I ground myself, providing a steady foundation so she can use me as she pleases.

Her soul-baring stare... Fuck me, that stare. I've been on the receiving end of Chase's glances more times than I can count. I've seen her expression blaze with anger, roll with exasperation, even twinkle with hidden amusement. But this? This is something else. This is... everything.

I want to witness every flicker of emotion.

Every spark of desire.

I want to drown in the depths of her gaze.

She slides up my length, clenching me tightly, then slowly lowers down, releasing until she presses against my pubic bone. Each squeeze is more intense than the last, each movement more sensual and torturous as my cock begs for release. She has me vibrating with need, aching to give her so much more.

I breathe out the tension building within me. I gotta hold back, to let her guide us to the threshold of bliss.

"Pinch my nipples," she orders, and I obey, eliciting a gasp from her parted lips.

With both of my hands on her chest, I feel her heartbeat—its rhythm matching my own. Our bodies are in perfect sync.

Oh my God, do I want this. I want her to own me for her pleasure.

Chase's hair cascades around me as she leans down, overwhelming me with a searing kiss.

I've never had sex like this. Hot and heavy, yes, but slow and sensual? Never.

Her lips break from mine with a soft, lingering moan as she sits up tall, guiding my hands to her ass. She presses her palms to my stomach, and I swear her touch brands my skin. Her motions are precise and unhurried, rolling against me, her grip as tight as a glove.

Is this what it's like when two people who have a history come together, not just to fuck, but to make love? Because this is intimate as hell, intense on a whole other level.

It's not a territory I'm all that familiar with. My relationships, if you can even call them that, have always been pretty shallow. A few laughs, a good time, maybe a shared breakfast before we go our separate ways.

Chase and I working together is technically my longest relationship.

This isn't just about sex. She's exposing herself, letting me glimpse the real her. Behind the director's chair, beneath her tough exterior and razor-sharp wit.

And what I see? It's fucking beautiful.

I'm not just hungry for her body now; I'm starving for her trust, her openness, her vulnerability. I want every little detail that makes her who she is—the fierce, incredible woman who's finally letting me in, letting me see her true self.

Her eyes bore into mine, an unspoken connection sparking between us. She's staring at me... through me... into my soul.

What does she see?

Without a word, Chase tugs on the back of my head, guiding my lips to her tits. My mouth glides across her until I meet her pert nipple. My hand savors her right breast, and then I pull her left into my mouth, sucking hard and eliciting a breathy whisper.

"Yes. Harder."

She's got one hand buried in my hair, guiding me. As I feast on her, she plants her other hand on the floor and quickens her pace. She lifts herself until my dripping cock is almost entirely out of her, then slams back down in a dance of tortured exhilaration. My hard shaft is repeatedly pushed out, then teased back in by her slick, powerful pussy—over and over and over.

I submit fully to the exquisite new thrill she's orchestrating.

She tightens around me, her orgasm surging. Her body is buzzing as it edges, aching through the prolonged stimulation. It's the most fucking erotic thing ever, experiencing her waves of pleasure grip and let go.

"Oh, fuck, Ethan, yes, Ethan, Ethan!" she moans in my ear.

I hear my name from her lips, and I'm gone. My balls tighten and my orgasm explodes. My whole body bursts free in a blinding rush of euphoria. A wild, desperate groan escapes me. Overwhelming sensations course through my body, and I ride them out one by one, feeling like I've lost my damn mind.

Finally, the throttle releases. The throbbing up and down in my spine weakens, and I savor the last few ripples of ecstasy as she collapses on top of me. Our bodies stay locked in a fierce hold, unwilling to release each other.

I have no clue what Chase is thinking, but *that*... That was the most mind-blowing sex of my whole fucking life.

CHAPTER FOURTEEN

CHASE

Booming thunder rattles the windows. My eyes fly open. Disoriented, I blink at the unfamiliar room. *Why am I naked?*

Oh no.

I bolt upright. My heart pounds as I recognize the room. Ethan's bedroom. Ethan's *bed*. Ethan's... not here.

Chase, you stupid girl.

I scramble out of the SpongeBob sheets. *Where are my clothes?* I frantically look for my pajamas, but they're nowhere. I snatch up a discarded T-shirt from the floor—definitely Ethan's—and yank it over my head. His familiar, earthy scent goes straight to my core, making it all tingly as memories of last night come flooding in, raw and unfiltered.

What the hell was that between us?

His touch was like a wildfire. Ethan's hands on my skin, his lips discovering the secrets of my body. Everything was perfect. The way he filled me—that slow, exquisite build of pleasure—making my nerve endings sing. And after the build-up, I shattered in his arms. Never had I felt so desired, so utterly and passionately consumed.

Even now, my body craves his touch.

Goddammit! I know better than to let an actor in, to give them power over me. It's Directing 101. When the project wraps, they move on, leaving you to pick up the shattered pieces of your heart. But yesterday, with Ethan, I lowered my defenses. One mind-blowing encounter, and I've jeopardized everything, giving him parts of me I never intended to share.

And where is Ethan now? Not the fuck here. Why would he be? To him, I'm just another conquest, nothing more. He's probably hiding out at his mom's store to avoid the awkward morning-after conversation.

I have to get out of here before I screw things up even more. I should check into a hotel. *Shit.* Why does a part of me want to stay? To see how this plays out? No! I can't risk letting my guard down with Ethan any more than I already have.

KRA-KOWW!

I jump at the crack of thunder. At the same moment, the bedroom door swings open.

Ethan stands there in boxers and a T-shirt, hair tousled, holding a tray of food. My stomach does a little happy dance, and it's not because I'm craving breakfast.

"Oh, you're awake."

"Yeah," I croak. "The storm."

He crosses to the bed, setting down the tray. "I thought you might be hungry, ya know, after our evening together. I know I am."

Is he seriously blushing right now?

"My specialty—key lime pancakes with fresh-squeezed orange juice. And coffee, but I don't know how you like it, so I brought sugar and cream just in case."

Oh hell. He made me breakfast? This is not good.

"Ethan, about last night," I begin, steeling myself for the *let's pretend this never happened* speech.

But he cuts me off, reaching out to gently cradle my face in his hand. His touch is so tender that it makes my chest ache.

"How about we stay in this moment a little while longer? Let's just put a time-out on that conversation for now," he suggests, his voice smooth and inviting. "We've got the house to ourselves today."

"Everyone's gone?"

"Yup. At work." His grin widens. "We can enjoy the day together. Push reality back a bit."

A break—

From responsibility...

From consequences...

From the voice in my head screaming, *this is a colossal mistake.*

I grasp at the only lifeline I can think of. "We can't. What about the subscriber challenge for today?"

Ethan responds by holding up his phone to the rain-lashed window. The camera clicks, and he starts dictating, "It's stormy outside, so here's the deal: I dare you to gift a Cherish Channel subscription to a friend. If we hit 100,000 new subs today, we'll dance in the thunderstorm. Let's make it happen! #CherishChallenge."

He taps the screen. "Posted! Now, how about you take a few bites and join me in the shower?"

"Are you telling me what to do?"

Ethan responds by standing up and peeling off his shirt. *Oh, sweet Lord have mercy.*

"Not yet," he says, his voice low and husky.

I watch him stride to the bathroom, my gaze drinking in every inch of his stupidly perfect body as if I'm dying of thirst. He pivots, flashing that cocky smirk that has me battling the urge to kiss him and then promptly knee him in the junk. His thumbs hook into the waistband of his boxers, and suddenly they're gone. He stands there, bare-assed and beautiful, the light behind him outlining his form like some kind of asshole angel.

His hard dick demands attention.

Ethan turns on the water and steps into the shower, leaving the door open.

He's got this "come hither" act down, that's for sure. I see why he's banged half of Hollywood—this routine works. But it's not supposed to work on me. Sure, breakfast was sweet. And yeah, that shower invite is tempting as hell...

But no. I'm too fucking smart for this.

Aren't I?

Once is like, *Oopsies, my bad, your dick just slipped right in there.* But twice? That's on me.

I shove a few pancake bites in my mouth, trying to ignore how flavorful they taste. The fluffy texture is exquisite with the zing of the lime. Abs like that *and* he can cook?

My stomach growls, reminding me just how hungry I am after last night's... activities. I chug the orange juice, feeling the sugar rush sing through my veins.

A deep groan echoes from the bathroom, and either my imagination or my memories run wild. Ethan's in there—naked and dripping, water cascading down his chiseled chest. He's stripped down and waiting, like a dirty gift that's already been opened.

You know what? *Fuck it.* Let's see what happens.

My heart races. This feels so reckless. So daring. So wrong, but in the most delicious way possible. I stumble toward the bathroom, stripping off the borrowed shirt as I go.

I enter the steam-filled room with a rolling inferno of emotions. My internal firestorm is far outweighing the actual temperature of the misty warmth. With a deep breath, I pull back the shower curtain and step inside.

Ethan's reaction to my naked body sends a thrill straight through me. Before I can say a word, he comes to me, his lips crashing against mine in a sizzling, electrifying kiss.

Oh God. The world melts away. All I feel is the exquisite sensation of his mouth. Heads tilting. Lips on lips. Tongues sucking and savoring every sweet second. I'm lightheaded with lust.

Ethan's powerful arm snakes around my waist, effortlessly pulling me flush against him. He skillfully grinds his thick erection against me, causing all attention to go to my center. I crave the way this man makes me feel.

My clit throbs, desperate for the same mind-blowing ecstasy he gave me less than twenty-four hours ago. Hungry for more, I take control. My hands slide around to grab his ass—and oh damn, what a fine ass it is. Firm and sculpted. I'm greedy for it. I squeeze harder, feeling his cock pulse against my folds.

"Not this time, sweetheart. It's my turn to be in charge," he demands, breaking our kiss.

I hear the dominance in his voice, and... I don't hate it.

The realization hits me like a thunderbolt. I've spent a lifetime keeping everyone at a safe distance—never letting anyone behind my carefully built walls. Am I actually ready to let someone in? And not just *someone*. Ethan. The man who's seen me at my most demanding and difficult.

How can he look at me like I'm something precious?

This is definitely new territory for me. Instead of fighting for control, I find myself surrendering to the safety I feel in his arms.

Ethan presses my back against the cool tile. His searing lips glide like embers down my neck and along my collarbone, lingering on my breasts. He hungrily sucks my nipple into his mouth.

"Think you're a director now?" I manage to gasp out.

Ethan's lips curl into a wicked smile. "You'll like me in charge. You're already begging for my touch."

I swallow hard, fighting the temptation to press myself against him. "Begging? You must be high. I don't beg, I command."

"Your nipples betray you. You want this as badly as I do. Maybe more."

"It's biological. Don't read too much into it. I'm just curious how far you'll go to convince me."

He drops to his knees, and I gasp as he exhales a warm breath onto my aching center. The shower water pelts against his back, creating a shield that protects my sensitive clit from the relentless spray.

"Your mouth can deny it, but your body doesn't lie. Come on, baby. Let me see how much you're dripping for me."

His strong hands spread my legs, and then—oh fuck—his tongue drags slowly across my clit. My back arches compulsively off the steamy bathroom tiles.

"Oh my God! Ethan, yes," I pant, nodding frantically.

"Lift up," he demands, and I comply instinctively, tilting my hips and offering all of me to his giving mouth.

Ethan gently hooks one of my legs over his shoulder, and I brace myself against the slick shower wall. I try to stay upright as his tongue goes to work, but dizzying waves of euphoria wash over me. Each steady stroke brings me higher, closer to the edge of blissful oblivion.

"I'm addicted to your pussy. You taste like heaven and hell all wrapped into one."

His words make me crumble. Little earthquakes rock my core. I'm trembling, torn between the urge to let go and the need to make this last forever. I've been wound too tight for too long. It feels so good. The only thing I can do is chase this orgasm rising inside of me like a tide.

I'm pulsing with life.

Like I've just taken the first full breath of fresh air after living in a work cave for years.

Ethan's breathing grows ragged, and I glance down. He's stroking himself as he drives me to my release. I'm so turned on by it. I moan my approval, cueing him to press his mouth harder against me. His tongue swishes my clit with such force that my fingers claw into his hair.

Hottest. Experience. Ever.

"Yes, Ethan yes! I'm... I'm..." I can't get the words out before my thighs start to tremble. White heat flashes behind my eyes, and my entire body convulses as I come.

Fast. Hard. On Ethan's face.

My muscles, stomach, and limbs quake with the pleasure that ripples through my body.

Too soon, Ethan's mouth releases me. He groans loudly as he comes. His heavy breathing lightly tickles my clit before he rests his head against my hip. We're both panting, spent and sated.

So much for keeping my distance.

***

YOU KNOW THIS IS not a competition, right? Don't take it so seriously," Ethan says as he watches me furiously pipe frosting onto a Christmas cookie.

"Everything is a competition, especially Christmas."

We're in the kitchen, surrounded by the warm scent of freshly baked cookies, and Ethan is all smiles and laughter. His casual demeanor is unsettling, considering that less than an hour ago, he was feasting on me—drawing out an orgasm so intense that I'm still seeing stars.

"Oh wow, that is... I'm just gonna say it. It's terrible," Ethan quips, eyeing my frosted cookie critically. "What's that even supposed to be?"

"It's a stocking full of presents, obviously."

"It looks like a penis. And not a good one—all crooked and half-hard."

"No, it's not!" I protest, though now that he's said it, I can't unsee the phallic shape.

"The Cherish Channel would not approve," Ethan jokes, waggling his eyebrows.

I burst out laughing. "No, they would not. I can save it. I'll add a little green frosting and look! A souvenir."

"Of what?"

"Your limp fish dick," I say with a smirk, licking frosting from my finger.

"You seemed pretty content with my mighty sea snake last night," he says, smiling, but then his eyes darken and smolder with desire.

An awkward silence falls between us. Why does he have to be so temping? This isn't how it's supposed to be. He's an actor, playing a role. None of this is genuine. It's his game, a well-practiced charm offensive that he's mastered for the camera and countless women before me.

I can't let myself fall for it.

I look away and focus on my cookie. "You're overestimating the impact of your flaccid jellyfish. I barely felt a sting."

"Sweetheart, you can't bullshit a bullshitter," Ethan says with a chuckle, then changes the subject. "Talk to me, tell me something, anything. How do you celebrate the holidays?"

I tense up. "Normal stuff."

"Come on, give me more than that. Growing up, did you leave milk and cookies for Santa? I bet you bossed your parents around like a mini director to make sure they built your Barbie Dreamhouse to perfection."

"We didn't do the whole Santa thing."

"Okay, no Santa. But how about the tree? I can totally picture a little Chase managing the ornament placement."

"Can we just focus on the cookies?" I cut him off, my tone harsher than I intended.

Ethan's face falls slightly.

I hate that I notice.

I hate that I care.

"Hey, I'm not trying to pry," he says softly, his eyes searching mine. "I just... I want to learn more about you, Chase. There's so much I don't know."

I sigh, my shoulders sagging under the weight of his honesty. I get that we're stuck together till Christmas, but what's his angle here? Why the sudden interest?

"Can we not... Please?" I beg.

I don't do backstory. I don't do vulnerability. And I sure as hell don't spill my tragic childhood over dick-shaped sugar cookies.

In my line of work, I've learned to keep my guard up and my emotions in check. I've earned my title as the Ice Queen of Romance. I can make America swoon with my movies, but that doesn't mean I'm buying into the whole "love conquers all" nonsense.

Because here's the thing: Love isn't always pretty. It's seldom made of fairy tales and happily ever afters. I've seen firsthand what "epic love" can do to a person. How it can take a vibrant, charming man like my dad and reduce him to a shell of his former self, numbing his sorrows with whiskey and neglecting his only daughter.

My parents' love story was the stuff of movies—a chance meeting at a laundromat, a whirlwind courtship, a picture-perfect life. But when my mom died, she took a piece of my dad with her. And I was left with a man who could barely remember to keep the lights on, let alone make sure there were presents under the tree on Christmas morning.

Love is just another way to lose yourself. I've seen the damage it does, watching my father drown in a love that left him empty. Some people might call it tragic. I see it as a warning.

Ethan's eyes are on me, warm and knowing in a way that makes my skin prickle. I hate it. His presence is a reminder of everything I'm trying not to feel.

For a while, we frost cookies in silence. The only sounds are spatulas scraping against bowls and the occasional clink of a sprinkle shaker.

"You know, it's kind of ironic," Ethan says. "You love the idea of Christmas in your movies, but you clearly hate Christmas."

The words sting. My hands freeze mid-frost, the cookie suddenly blurs in front of me. "I don't hate Christmas." I admit too honestly. "My dad wasn't really... great at it. He... wasn't around much. Let's just say he preferred a liquid dinner to family dinner."

I force myself to keep frosting, to focus on the mindless activity. Anything to avoid looking at him.

"That sounds... tough."

There's no pity in his voice—just understanding. And that's way worse. Pity I can handle. Sympathy I can shut down. But genuine concern? That threatens to split me wide open.

"It's not a big deal. I had the Cherish Channel." A real smile tugs at my lips, surprising me. "Every December, I'd curl up on the couch with store-bought sugar cookies and watch their holiday marathon. Twenty-four hours of perfect families, magical moments, and guaranteed happy endings."

"And now you create that magic for others." It's not a question.

How does he do that? How does he cut straight through my bullshit to the truth I've buried under years of careful control?

"Someone's gotta do it," I say, shrugging casually. "And I'm pretty good at making people believe in the fantasy, even if it's just for ninety minutes."

"Is that all it is to you? A fantasy?"

He moves closer, his arm brushing mine, and electricity shoots through my body. The air between us feels heavy with everything I'm terrified to want.

I open my mouth to respond, when—

DING!

Our phones chime simultaneously, and I've never been more grateful for an interruption.

"Looks like we hit our daily subscriber goal," I say, checking the app.

"Chase, babe! I'm gonna need more excitement than that. We crossed five hundred thousand. We're halfway there! Woo!"

Ethan pulls me in tight, peppering my face with fast kisses that make me laugh. Then he stops, a playful smile on his face. "You know what that means? Time to get wet again."

***

THE SKY'S DUMPING BUCKETS. Gusts of wind slap us with misty high-fives. The ground beneath us? It's a soggy, squishy mess. We're huddled under the house stilts, our own little hideout in this crapstorm. *Not my idea of fun.*

"How about *you* dance in the rain?" I say. "And I'll film it."

Ethan grins, already pulling out his phone. "You're not afraid of a little water, are you?"

"Ethan, no, wait, let's talk about this."

I try to grab the phone from him, but it's too late. He's already hit the *Go Live* button.

"In Florida, it doesn't snow for Christmas, but we have something better. We call it the Holiday Downpour," Ethan declares with a grin. "Let's all dance like our hearts are open and anything is possible."

With that, he breaks into a cheesy rendition of "We Wish You a Merry Christmas," running into the monsoon as he livestreams.

"You look ridiculous!" I yell after him, trying not to laugh.

He rushes to me, takes my hand, and tugs me into the spray. A surprised squeal escapes me as the cold water hits. Ethan laughs, continuing to sing, and despite my reservations, I end up singing along.

"Look, she does know the words!" Ethan crows triumphantly.

Now we're both dancing like idiots in the water. I can't stop smiling.

Me. Him. Us.

The moment is absurd. I embrace it.

I belt out the lyrics obnoxiously, even louder than Ethan. Then I twirl, letting the rain kiss my cheeks, and something magical happens. A weight lifts from my shoulders and a deep tension within me releases. I'm somehow being washed clean by the Florida showers.

"We love you, Ethan Addicts! We hope you're having just as much fun for the holidays," Ethan says to the camera, wrapping up the livestream. "See you tomorrow."

"What are you doing? The fans—"

"They've seen enough. This moment's just for us," Ethan says.

I don't question his sincerity. Instead, I find myself yielding... trusting... free-falling. Because this isn't the suave performer I've directed in countless scenes. This is Ethan, raw and real, showing me what's behind the charm and easy smiles. His heart is in every spontaneous gesture, every vulnerable look. And for the first time, I'm not calling "cut" to stop myself from feeling too much.

He captures my wrist, and we start to dance. The cold barely registers, not with his arm wrapped around me, his touch searing through my wet shirt. I shift closer, drawn to him instinctively, my heart hammering louder than the storm.

We fall into an easy rhythm, and with every sway, every shared breath, the space between us crackles with invisible electricity. The spray, once an intruder, now feels like a cocoon, wrapping us in a world of our own making. Two people slow dancing in a downpour.

Ethan tilts my face to his, and then he kisses me so hard it nearly lifts me off the ground. I kiss him right back. The sensation vibrates through my whole body, electrifying every nerve ending. My hands fist in his shirt then slide under it, desperate for skin-on-skin contact.

His steady palms claim my hips, lifting me like I'm weightless. I wrap my legs around him possessively, and he transports me out of the rain—to our intimate sanctuary under the house. He pins me to one of the stilts. I yank off my sopping wet shirt and carelessly throw it to the ground.

Somehow, his mouth is already on my jaw, making his way to my ear. I've got one arm around his shoulders for balance, the other tugging at his shirt. It needs to come off... now. His shirt joins mine on the ground, landing in a puddle with a wet splat.

Our skin slides against each other, slick with precipitation and desire. Ethan shifts his hips, pressing me harder against the house stilt. I can feel the unmistakable firmness of his cock, hard and insistent against me, and I arch into him, craving more.

I have no idea what the fuck I'm doing. But I can't seem to keep this from happening.

CHAPTER FIFTEEN

CHASE

HANG ME LIKE A stocking on a stripper pole. I have got to be around people today. Ethan deserves that "ladies' man" title—his hands have some kind of magic sex glue, because once they're on you, you do not want them to come off.

I'm keeping my distance, and by "distance," I mean just a pheromone's waft away. Ethan's loading box after box of decorations onto a double-decker pontoon boat. All the boats in the harbor share a similar decorative theme—half-working strings of lights, inflatable flamingos, and enough plastic palm leaf garlands to make a low-budget luau.

It's gaudy as hell, but I can appreciate the commitment. The Cherish Channel would never fork over the funds to create a spectacle like this.

Ethan's tight T-shirt and jeans hug his body like they're afraid to let go *(tell me about it)*, and there's a Santa hat tucked into his back pocket. He looks like he's starring in a XXX-Mas special, and my body is all, *Santa, I've been very, very bad.*

My face blushes.

My heart quickens.

I force myself to look away, but not before my tongue pays tribute, darting out to lick my lips.

"Chase, hun, you are in for such a treat tonight," Darla chirps, breaking me from my Ethan-induced trance. "The holiday boat parade is my favorite every year. We start with a little Mardi Gras celebration, throw in some Christmas flair, and wa-lah! We got our-selves a party on the waves!"

"Then I'm bringing the eggnog margaritas, Darla!" I practically sing it, for fuck's sake. Oh yeah, all the sex is definitely going to my brain.

"Do you enjoy yourself out on the water?" Doug asks, sporting an alligator-themed Christmas shirt that's so hideous, even a thrift store would reject it.

Before I answer, Ethan chimes in. "Chase likes the ride if she's at the helm." He throws me a wink.

"You're right, I do like to be on top... of things," I reply. "Problem is, Ethan can't keep up." I wink back with a surge of satisfaction.

That's right, buddy. This director can play dirty too.

Darla fans herself dramatically with a plastic flamingo. "I thought I was having a hot flash, honey, but nuh-uh. It's the sparks flying between the both of you!" She dissolves into a fit of giggles. "You two get any hotter, and we won't need these Christmas lights!"

"You know me," Ethan says. "I'm always a big fan of fireworks. Especially when it comes to lighting Chase's fuse."

I'm locked and loaded, ready with a snappy retort involving bottle rockets and certain body parts, when Ethan grabs me, pulling me in for a kiss that makes my toes curl in my sandals.

He has lit my fuse.

And it's burning hot.

Suddenly I want to be anywhere but in this crowd. For a hot second, I wonder if this boat has a bedroom. Or hell, I saw some port-a-potties when we were walking down the dock...

Get a grip, vajayjay!

Okay, enough. I need to focus on work. This isn't some tropical getaway. It's a job. Even if that job currently involves being pressed against abs that could slice through steel.

I pull away from the kiss, trying to ignore how his lips chase after mine. "I've been doing the math for our subscriber goal," I say, my voice embarrassingly breathy. "And I was thinking—"

"Bah. We'll deal with it later. Let loose and have some fun decorating. Ya know, be part of the Christmas festivities."

"We've only got five days left. Sure we're on track, but we can't afford to lose focus."

"It's always work with you. Fine." Ethan sighs. "Mama, can you start decorating without us? Chase and I got a work thing."

Darla's eyes twinkle. "If that's what you're gonna call it, fine by me. Just don't forget to hang your stockings with care, if you catch my drift. Ya know, wrap up that present extra tight... Unless you're hankerin' for a special little delivery." She sighs dreamily.

As soon as we're out of earshot, I hiss, "Your mom thinks we're leaving to go have sex, doesn't she?"

"Yup."

"Tell her we're not. I don't want her thinking we're getting freaky. It's embarrassing."

"You want me to lie to my mom, before Christmas?"

"Either that, or we are not having sex anymore," I say, crossing my arms over my chest.

Ethan leans in close, his breath hot against my ear. "I know you love my cock. But if you think you can live without it, be my guest."

And there's that damn charm. I find it as infuriating as I do exhilarating.

Ethan grabs my hand, practically dragging me down the boardwalk. The weathered planks creak under our feet, and the smell of salt water fills the air. Seashell garlands with twinkling blue and green lights decorate the railings. It's "Florida festive." Not what I'm used to, but it's growing on me.

"Where are we going?" I ask, pushing aside the thought of how perfectly our fingers fit together.

"To get our subscribers for the day so you'll relax and have some fun."

"What about the dare jar?"

"It's all up here," he says, pointing to his head.

I grab him and plant a kiss on his goofy grin. I can't control it. He's adorable, and his laid-back vibe is rubbing off on me *(and now other things are too)*. When he finally pulls away, we're both breathing hard. A nearby palm tree, wrapped in golden lights, seems to sway from the intensity.

"After this is over, I need more of that," Ethan groans.

I somehow manage to find my snark. "You want it, you gotta earn it. I don't give my Christmas cookies away for free."

Ethan smirks. "Time to put those directing skills to work, boss." He presses the *Go Live* button on his phone and hands it to me. Suddenly we're streaming to thousands of eager fans.

"Hey, Ethan Addicts!" he greets the camera. "Today we're granting Christmas wishes in real time. If you're local, come on down to the boardwalk. And if you're on the livestream, reach out and tell me your wish. Just keep it PG-13, folks. This isn't *Miracle on 69th Street*."

He winks at the lens. "You gotta help me out because Chase said she won't kiss me until we hit our quota today. I'm dying of thirst over here! Let's grow those Cherish Channel subscribers!"

Watching him work his magic on screen, something within me shifts. This is Ethan in his element—charming, genuine, and connecting effortlessly with people. For once, I don't want to critique or micromanage him. Instead, I see possibilities unfolding naturally and spontaneously. Perhaps our dynamic doesn't have to be all sharp edges and power struggles. Maybe there's room for both of us to shine, blending his natural charisma with my vision.

What if I don't have to choose between being respected and being happy?

Ethan pulls off his shirt—his physique, tanned and tone, is on full display. *Yowsa!* He grabs the Santa hat from his back pocket and puts it on.

Sweet baby Jesus in a manger. He's the King of Christmas and the king of my fantasies.

Seeing how much the livestream is blowing up, he's the king of a lot of women's fantasies—apparently every woman on the planet. Fan after fan approaches Ethan, and when I glance at the phone, very provocative comments are flooding the chat.

Damn ladies! It's enough to make an OnlyFans model blush. Nothing PG-13 about these wishes.

It's the reminder I need—to tread lightly. To be realistic. To *not* fall into the fantasy myself.

This is a fun fling, nothing more. Guys like Ethan don't end up with girls like me. They want the red-carpet-ready babes, the models with perfect teeth and Instagram-filtered lives. Not some Type-A control freak who guards her feelings like a maximum-security prison.

Ethan is a Hollywood playboy. He loves the attention more than anything or anyone. I, on the other hand, am not used to any of it. Not the public displays of affection, and certainly not Ethan being sweet to me. The snarky, annoying Ethan I know how to handle. This caring, adoring Ethan is messing with my head.

I'm just here for the sex... Shit. Subscribers! I mean subscribers.

Mere minutes later, Ethan's drawn a crowd. "Who has a wish for me to grant? And no, I can't make it snow in Florida. I'm magical, but I'm no wizard."

A pack of teenage girls giggle and raise their hands. "Will you do a TikTok with us?"

"Your Christmas wish is my command," Ethan says with a grin. "But fair warning, I only have one dance move, which I call the Drunken Reindeer."

I hold the camera, filming as they teach Ethan the dance. He's surprisingly good, picking up the moves quickly. It's all over in two minutes. The girls squeal and thank him profusely.

A teen in the group approaches me, her eyes wide with envy. "You're so lucky you're dating Ethan. Is he a good kisser?"

"He's the best," I blurt out.

Ethan's grin widens. He pulls me into a photo with the girls, his hand clasping my waist possessively. Dangerous butterflies gather in my stomach as he moves his thumb sensually over my hip. If he's trying to start a fire down there, mission accomplished.

"Next dare," I announce, forcing myself to step away.

For the next hour, Ethan fulfills wish after wish as our subscriber numbers steadily climb. He's recording personalized video messages, snapping pics for husbands to surprise their wives, signing Christmas cards, and even singing carols.

At one point, he starts juggling ornaments, which goes about as well as you'd expect. One slightly banged-up nutcracker and several broken ornaments later, he gallantly gives up.

My favorite wish comes next. Ethan begins acting out famous scenes from our movies with fans. I'm shocked when I see him remembering his lines perfectly. Then I hear women recite back lines that I've written, word for word, and unshed tears fill my eyes. Their reactions show me they love it as much as I do. I can feel how much my movies have touched them. I've brought them the warmth of Christmas, just as I'd hoped. My heart cries out with purpose and joy.

One fan even gets a kiss on the cheek, which definitely doesn't make me jealous. Not at all. I'm not imagining pushing her headfirst off the pier. Nope.

Ethan charms everyone around him, and I'm in awe. He's so good at this, and it's not an easy job. To read someone—know how to meet them where they're at in an instant. To match their expectations and bless them with a moment. Seeing him with his fans is kind of... magical. It's got the warm, fuzzy feels of Santa, but like if Santa was a hot, flirty sex god in tight jeans.

A group of little old ladies holding grocery bags approaches me. "Can we go next?"

"Of course," I say, calling out to Ethan. "These lovely gals are coming up."

Ethan beckons them over. "Hello there, lovelies. Enlighten me... What's your Christmas wish?"

The most innocent-looking lady of the bunch, possibly a retired kindergarten teacher, says, "We want you to be a human sundae. Extra whipped cream, if you know what I mean."

I almost drop the phone.

Suddenly the seniors are pulling out different sundae toppings from their bags—hot fudge, caramel, and a spray can of Reddi-wip. I half expect one of them to pull out edible underwear.

Ethan smirks into the phone. "Okay, this is pretty crazy, but since it's Christmas, I'll do it. I have one condition. Only if my gal licks it off."

The roaring crowd loves it as much as I hate it.

"No, no, no," I protest, but Ethan's already extending his arms, welcoming the gooey mess.

"Ladies, get pouring!"

The not-so-sweet seniors whoop and cheer, drizzling an excess of pure sin onto Ethan's broad, muscular chest. The caramel flows down in golden, molten streams, tracing every hard line and curve of his pecs like a lover's fingertips—like *my* fingertips. I can't deny it's a tantalizing invitation.

Hellz yeah, except for all the bystanders. Hard pass.

My eyes are hypnotized by the hot fudge as it slides down his torso. The sweet, slow lava oozes, thick and dark—a wicked contrast against his tanned skin. It travels its way across the valley of his rippled abs—a slow, sensual tease that causes my breath to hitch and my pulse quicken. The sight of it, decadent and dirty, makes my tongue tingle.

Then comes the whipped cream, sprayed generously from the can, forming soft, fluffy mounds on each nipple, just begging to be licked. It melts slightly against the heat of his skin, a creamy temptation that has me biting my lip and squirming with anticipation.

God, this is embarrassing. Who does this in public? Where's the shame, people?

But still, the combination of the sinful toppings on his rock-hard body is fucking criminal. It's a feast for the senses, a playful, erotic promise that has me aching to let my guard down and taste him. Ethan turns to me, his eyes dancing with challenge, a dare testing my resolve.

The crowd cheers. Ethan looks like the world's sexiest human sweet treat. My face is hotter than a blowtorch. If I blush any harder, I'm going to burst into flames.

Ethan walks up to me, takes the phone, and gives it to a grandmotherly figure to keep filming.

"Okay baby, time to eat your sundae. C'mon. Don't do it for me. Do it for the subs."

A tug-of-war brews inside me between my self-respect—my carefully crafted director rep—and the immediate pressure to play the part. I scan the mass of people, thinking about all the subs we still need. He's right. I asked for this. Not *this* exactly, but this fake relationship, and whatever comes with it.

I watch the fudge and caramel combo dripping down those abs. Decision made. I smile like I'm not mortified and aroused beyond comprehension.

"You're gonna like this a lot more than me," I whisper to Ethan before shouting, "Let's make this a Christmas to remember!"

I take a deep breath and flick my tongue to his nipple for a little taste test. Then, I begin a long, slow lick from his abs all the way up to his collarbone. Mmm, yummy!

The crowd bursts into cheers and whistles. My face is beet red, and my silly smile takes over my cheeks. I'm feeling ridiculous, wild, daring, and invigorated all at once.

Amidst the excited praises and screams, one of the grannies shouts, "Get it, girl! Now lick those abs like a lollipop!"

"You heard her," Ethan says. "You coming back for seconds?"

Before I respond, Ethan's arm snakes around my waist, pulling me flush against him. I gasp. I'm colliding with his sticky chest, my hands instinctively coming up to brace against his shoulders.

Then his lips are on mine, sweet and sugary like a candy shop exploded in his mouth. The kiss is soft yet demanding, his stubble rough against my skin. I'm talking make-you-for-get-your-own-name kind of kissing. The kind that makes you wonder if you've been doing it wrong your whole life.

It shouldn't feel this wonderful. It's aggravating. I pull him closer, and—

My phone buzzes angrily in my pocket, shattering the moment. I jerk away from Ethan, flushed and breathing hard. The caller ID flashes "Wiley & Riley," my bosses, and reality comes crashing back.

"I have to take this," I tell him, putting distance between us.

"Chase Pemberton," I answer, trying to sound professional, despite my sticky, goopy clothes and the fact that I was just exploring Ethan's tonsils.

"Excellent work, Chase!" Wiley's voice crackles through the speaker. "The content you're producing is pure gold. Stay on track. You're halfway there."

I blink. Content? What content?

Then it clicks.

They think I'm the mastermind behind all the viral dares.

Stunts that were entirely Ethan's ideas.

I almost spill the truth, but then I remember the massive debt from film school and the tiny apartment I can barely afford. I need this job, or I'll end up directing feel-good ads for adult diapers.

A twinge of guilt hits me, but I squash it.

"Thank you," I say smoothly. "I am producing results, aren't I?"

Riley chimes in, "Quite. And then some. Keep this up, Chase, and those ten films are all yours. And as promised, you'll have your pick of any cast member you want... that we can afford."

My heart leaps. This is it—exactly what I wanted. It's everything that I've been working for.

"We've even started taking meetings with other directors who are willing to work with Ethan," Wiley adds. "You know, in case he decides to play hardball with his contract."

The implications of that statement hit me like a bucket of ice water. Other directors? Working with Ethan? My Ethan?

I shake my head. Not *my* Ethan. Just... Ethan.

"Plus, we found some extra cash in the couch cushions for your 'Shamrock Shenanigans' parade scene."

"Great," I manage.

"Maintain the effort," Wiley says. "We'll see you back in LA after the holidays—*if* you hit that million-subscriber mark."

The call ends. I stare at my phone.

"Everything okay?" Ethan asks.

"Couldn't be better. The network says we're killing it and to keep up the good work."

"Fantastic news, babe!"

Ethan pulls me in for another kiss, and I'm filled with regretful longing. I swallow the guilt like a shot of black coffee—bitter, hot, and burning its way down to my stomach.

CHAPTER SIXTEEN

ETHAN

DID YOU BRING ME here to feed me to the sharks?" Chase asks, eyeing the water warily.

"Nah, sweetheart. The sharks wouldn't dare come near you. They're too afraid."

We're alone on the speedboat, watching the sun sink below the horizon, casting its last golden rays across the gulf. The boat rocks gently, and I use it as an excuse to snuggle up to Chase. She lets me hold her, and we quietly take in the view. The scene is like something from one of our romance movies. Just us, the sound of waves, and the day's fading light.

But this isn't a scripted scene with perfect lighting and calculated camera angles. This is as real as it gets, and I'm done playing the charming lead. I want more.

Being home has filled holes in me I didn't know existed. Yeah, I still have an image to maintain—fans are always watching. But here, I can breathe. In Florida, I'm a guy who helps with his mom's craft store and laughs at his dad's bad jokes. I can take my boat out at sunset and remember who I was before Hollywood changed me. This is the real me—the version Chase has been seeing.

She's different here too. Away from expectations, her sharp edges soften. I see it every day —how she gets swept up in my mom's wild family traditions, how her phone stays forgotten in her bag. I'm seeing moments when raw joy breaks through before she can lock it down again.

But fuck, I'm in dangerous territory. While I'm imagining a future where this isn't just a PR stunt, Chase is building walls faster than I can tear them down. Every time she lets herself be vulnerable, panic follows. When she truly smiles—those real ones that hit me straight in the chest—fear immediately darkens her eyes. She's opening up, sure, but like someone waiting for the ground to disappear beneath her feet.

How do I prove that this could be more than a holiday fling?

"The sunset is beautiful, but it's got nothing on you, babe."

"You see, this is why you need me to write your lines," she quips. "Your flirting game is... lacking."

I move in, my lips gently grazing her neck, and when her breath falters, I know she can't deny the magnetic attraction between us. "The way your body responds, darlin', I'd say you're into me."

Chase stiffens and pulls away. "Oh, you're mistaken, pretty boy. My body's just scared of being thrown overboard and sinking into the dark abyss. Do you not remember the last time we were on this boat? You strapped me to a pool floatie and launched me forty feet in the air."

"You mean the day you kissed me?"

"Oh, that day..." Chase taps her chin, feigning deep thought. "I don't remember you, but I do remember Fernando, the clit-flicking fish prince. It's so sad because he's still trapped in a fish body by an evil sea witch with anger-management issues."

"Right, let me guess. One kiss from you will turn him human?"

"Bingo!" She snaps her fingers. "Then we'll live happily ever after in an underwater sex dungeon, where he gives me orgasms daily. Twice on Sundays."

And there it is again. Our little back-and-forth, like a well-rehearsed dance. Keeping me at arms length.

She shuffles over and sits on the starboard side of the boat, her gaze fixed on the fresh evening sky and its shimmering stars. Off in the distance, a flotilla of boats covered in decorations and sparkling lights bobs along, getting in position for the Christmas parade. My mom's giant flamingo topper towers above the rest.

"So why aren't we boating with your family?" Chase asks. "Aren't we supposed to be *in* the parade?"

"Well, I thought for your first time, it might be more fun to watch it instead. Just us. No family. No fans."

"Can I be honest? When we were decorating today, I felt like I was giving a makeover to a garbage barge. All those janky cords and lights. I was sure it was going to look like a floating flea market. But I have to admit, at night, with all the boats lit up, it's not completely hideous."

"That is some high praise there, sweetheart. Careful, now. People will think you're falling in love with Florida."

"There's more of a chance of me falling in love with you."

Our eyes meet, and we're lost in each other for a moment. But then her lips curve into that smirk I know so well, and I brace for impact.

"Which means absolutely zero chance."

Well, that hurts more than a bee sting to the dick.

My typical arsenal of charming one-liners and smooth moves has evaporated, turning me into a fumbling idiot. I don't want to fall into the same old player routine. Not with Chase.

I wish she could acknowledge the man behind the heartthrob mask. The guy who gets so anxious before each take that he sweats through his fitted T-shirts. The man who spends hours in the shower rehearsing lines, until his fingers are prunier than a 90-year-old's ass. I need her to realize that I'm an actor who genuinely aspires to be taken seriously, especially by her.

When Chase looks at me, I know she thinks what everyone else does—Ethan Barrett, Hollywood's charmer, a leading man with plenty of style but lacking substance. To most women, I'm a fantasy come to life, a walking, talking embodiment of their wildest dreams.

A passing thrill.

To bang and forget.

I'm just a fuck on their bucket list.

Turns out, shaking off a persona you've honed for years isn't easy. I don't fault Chase for seeing me that way. But it's not the real me... not anymore. And I need her to understand that.

I notice her shoulders tremble slightly, and I spring into action. I reach into the picnic basket I'd stashed earlier and pull out a soft blanket.

"Here," I say, my voice coming out huskier than intended.

"Thanks. I wore this stupid dress because I thought we were riding on the SS Holiday Disco Barge," she grumbles, wrapping the blanket around her shoulders.

I'm relieved she's covering up, because that dress is testing every bit of my self-control. It's a knockout green, with a neckline that accentuates her cleavage and a skirt that's teasing my imagination.

My fingers itch to reach beneath it and feel her soft skin, to coax her sweet moans back into my ear.

But I want to give even more than that. I want to tell her how incredible she is. How her talent leaves me in awe every day. How her fierceness and vision inspire me to become a better actor, a better man.

I take a seat next to her, trying to appear casual, but every muscle in my body tenses. My usual charm is nowhere to be found, leaving me unsure of how to act without my go-to moves.

"So," I manage, clearing my throat with a chuckle. "Who's the genius that decided leading ladies in Cherish Channel movies have to wear dresses for parades? Seems a bit impractical for December, don't you think?"

"That was me," Chase admits with a sigh. "But I had no clue they were freezing their tits off. I'm totally changing that for my future movies. So, get ready to act like you're hot for parkas and snowsuits."

I let out a laugh, but it's cut short by a deep, bellowing horn that pierces the night air. Chase jumps, instinctively gripping my arm.

"What the hell was that?"

"That, sweetheart, is the start of the Marco Island Christmas Boat Parade."

Right on cue, the first boats round the bend, lit up like Vegas on New Year's Eve. The cheers from the shoreline crowds fill the air, with the enthusiastic ringing of cowbells adding to the excitement. We're far enough away that we're surrounded by darkness, fully taking in the spectacle.

"That's... actually pretty incredible," she admits, her eyes fixed on the show.

You're incredible, I long to say, but I'm not quite ready to face another rejection just yet.

I take the champagne and flutes out of the picnic basket, popping the cork with a flourish before handing her a flute.

"Ooh, very suave," she says, eyebrow arched. "Now I see why the women are lining up to be your rotating arm candy."

It's confirmed. She still thinks I'm a douchebag ladies' man.

And now, I'm paying the price for living up to that shallow image. I've had my share of ladies. Actresses, models, fans who wanted a taste of the "King of Christmas." I played the part, reciting Chase's scripted lines as foreplay and making their holiday rom-com dreams a reality. But none of them ever wanted *me*.

"Okay, I gotta know," Chase says. "Where do I rank on the Ethan Barrett Starlet Scale? Am I a solid 7? Or have I reached the coveted 8.5?"

Ouch. Is that really all she thinks she is to me? The idea of Chase being just another quick fling has me ready to hurl myself into the bay.

I take a deep breath, looking her straight in the eye. "Chase, you're not like the rest. You play in a whole different league."

"Oh please. I'm being serious. Don't give me your heartthrob lines. We both know I'm not your usual type."

Something snaps inside me. How can this brilliant, hilarious, insanely talented woman not see how amazing she is?

I set my glass down, turning to face her head-on. "That's right. You're not my usual type. You are something else entirely."

She tries to cut in, but I can't control myself. Words just tumble out like I've cracked open some kinda emotional floodgate.

"You're whip-smart and funny as hell, and yeah, you make me crazy. Sometimes I don't know whether to argue with you or shut you up with a kiss. You challenge me, and you call me on my bullshit, and make me want to be better. That's not something I'm used to. I really like that about you."

I tuck a strand of hair behind her ear, happy to use it as an excuse to touch her.

"So no, you're not my woman of the week, Chase," I continue, my heart pounding. "I don't know what this is, but you're the woman I can't stop thinking about, the one I want to impress, the one I..."

The weight of my realization hits me like a sudden plot twist. *She's the person I can't picture my life without.*

Chase stares at me, her expression unreadable. The silence stretches between us, filled only by the gentle lapping of waves against the boat and the distant sounds of the parade.

I'm laid bare, raw as hell. It's like I'm out here, treading water in a churning sea, just waiting. And she's either gonna toss me a lifeline or let the abyss claim me.

Come on, Chase. Say something. Anything.

She clears her throat, her voice dry. "Wow... I'm going to steal those lines for my next script. Maybe you're better at wooing than I thought."

Words aren't getting through, so I switch to action. I softly cradle her mesmerizing face in my hand. "Chase," I whisper, bringing our lips so close we're almost touching. "I want you. I need you. Please."

That single word—please—ignites an inferno between us. Her mouth comes to me with a hunger that sends my senses reeling. She battles for dominance, and I gladly surrender, letting her shatter my defenses.

Her hand reaches over, bold and unapologetic, palming my fast-growing hard-on through my pants. A groan escapes me, swallowed by her relentless kiss.

She offers a gentle squeeze, and my hips instinctively move towards her, craving more.

Her fingers trace the length of me, triggering shockwaves of pleasure.

I'm pulsing.

Throbbing.

Every nerve ending aching with need that only she can satisfy.

She breaks away, her mouth charting a blazing course down my jaw, my neck, her breath hot and ragged against my skin.

"Chase, you drive me out of my goddamn mind."

She meets my gaze, her eyes dark and predatory with a wicked smile. "Good," she whispers, her hand still stroking me.

In a torturously slow teasing motion, she bunches up the skirt of her dress around her hips and slides her leg over my lap. Her fingers nimbly release the button of my pants as she lingers above me, allowing just enough space for me to slide my pants down to my knees.

"You might have had your share of women," she murmurs, her voice a sultry whisper, "but I'm the one you'll never forget."

She grasps my rock-hard cock in her hands, steadying herself on my lap, and my body tingles with want. I hastily dive into the wicker basket and grab an entire strip of condoms. *I was hoping the evening would go this way.*

"Quite presumptuous of you, don't ya think?"

"Not sure if you know, but I grant Christmas wishes. And I guessed what yours might be."

"Maybe you really are magic." She sets the condoms aside with a smirk. "For later."

I bask in her wetness as she nestles my shaft between her legs, rubbing against the fabric of her see-through panties, the flimsy barrier driving me wild with anticipation.

"You're so damn wet."

"I'm drenched for you, Ethan."

She moves against me, slow and deliberate, a sweet torture that has me gripping her hips, my fingers digging into her soft flesh.

Her lips part, and the subtle gasp that escapes sends a shiver of anticipation down my spine.

Chase tugs down the top of her dress, guiding my head and pressing my face firmly against her breasts. My stubble grazes her silky skin as I lick and kiss my way to her nipples. I suck hard, anxious to hear that sweet moan of hers again.

She rocks her hips more forcefully, and I can tell she's climbing faster than expected. I reach around from behind and yank her lacy underwear to the side. I take two of my fingers and soak them in her wetness before plunging them inside her. She gasps at the sensation.

"Mmm, Ethan, that feels so good."

"Tell me what you want."

"More. More!"

I finger fuck her pussy, and she rides my fingers hard. I'm pushing so deep, and she's grinding with purpose. She's right there, and I sense her walls tremble. Her slick muscles squeeze around me, and suddenly I'm sucking so hard on her breasts I'm marking her.

I want her to know that she was mine, even if just for tonight.

"What are you... doing to me... I'm—" Her moans crescendo, pitching higher and higher—like a melody of need.

Her muscles lock tight around my fingers as her orgasm takes control, ripples of pleasure cascading over her. Until she finally goes limp, collapsing on top of me. I can feel her heart racing against mine, her breath choppy. Knowing I'm the man who got her to this peak... It's deeply satisfying.

I long for more. So much more. But at the very least, I can give her this.

"Are you done, baby?" I whisper, still sliding my fingers in and out of her, savoring the feel of her velvety walls.

Chase hazily murmurs, "Fuck me hard," before diving her tongue into my ear. The euphoric feeling unleashes a rush of pleasure to all the right places.

Holy hell. She knows that sends me right to the edge.

I hastily grab the condom and roll it on, stroking myself with a rough, eager touch. I want to give her every fucking inch I've got. To bury my cock so deep in her that she'll feel me for days.

"You got a position in mind?"

Her eyes meet mine. "Take charge, Ethan. Take me how you want me."

I almost detonate right then and there.

In a swift, dominant motion, I lay her down on the boat, pressing up against her entrance. "Brace yourself, babe," I rasp, my voice barely recognizable. "It's gonna be fast and intense. Once I'm inside you, I won't stop until you're screaming my name."

I drive into her with a powerful thrust, a groan ripping from my chest as her tightness envelops me. Instantly, I'm pumping feverishly, my thickness filling her completely, every inch of me claiming her. I'm out of control, head spinning, hips grinding shamelessly into her with wild abandon. The boat rocks beneath us, swaying in time with our frantic rhythm.

"Fuck, Chase. You feel incredible."

"So do you... God, Ethan, you're so deep."

Her nails dig into my shoulders—sharp pinches of pleasure that spur me on. Her hips rise to meet each of my thrusts, urging me deeper, harder. The sounds of slaps, skin on skin, grow louder, more desperate, echoing across the water.

Insistent. Raw. Urgent.

"Fucking yes, Ethan! Yes!"

Her breath hitches as I hit a spot deep inside her, that special spot that makes her cry out, her body trembling around me. She's getting close, and I can feel her pussy tightening, her muscles clenching.

I need to be the only one who makes her lose control like this.

I want her to crave me, to feel like I'm the air she breathes. I have to be the only one who satisfies her, the one who knows exactly how to touch her.

I have to ruin her for anyone else.

"Yes, Ethan. Like that. Just like that."

She quivers, and suddenly both our bodies are tingling, vibrating, circling around nirvana—pleading with us to fully succumb to the pleasure.

"You're so fucking perfect, Chase," I growl, the words escaping my lips like a secret.

She is. Unlike any other woman, perfect. The word repeats in my head with each forceful plunge.

Perfect, perfect, perfect.

"Come for me, Chase. Say my name."

Her body tenses, her inner muscles clamping down on me. "Ethan... I'm close. So close."

I capture her mouth in a searing kiss. "Let go, baby. Let me hear you scream," I growl.

And she does. Her climax ignites, her body quivering as she's screaming my name. The sight of her coming undone beneath me, the sound of my name on her lips, sends me over the edge. With a final, fierce thrust, I explode, my body convulsing as I pour myself into her.

As we lay there, panting and spent, I press my forehead to hers. "You're fucking perfect."

CHAPTER SEVENTEEN

ETHAN

"Howdy, darlin's!" I flash a wink at the camera, the gateway to my legions of fans. "Today we're soaking up the sun and the fun at the Barrett Family Jingle Beach Games!"

Behind me, the whole fam is going nuts with cheers. Well, almost everyone. Chase, in her cute, awkward way, misses the cue and shouts a late "Woo!" that makes me want to laugh and smother her with kisses.

"Chase sweetheart, could you grab a dare from the jar and read it out loud?"

She grabs a green slip and says, "Sand-Trapped Merman?"

"Wowie, that's a good one. If we hit 100 thousand subscribers, this handsome fella—*me*—will get buried in the sand up to my neck. Then my brother Nolan here can have his fun."

"Hi, I'm Nolan. I'm his brother," Nolan states flatly, as if I didn't just say that verbatim.

"His job is to mold me into a truly embarrassing merman. He'll be sculpting a skimpy outfit on me with the largest breasts you've ever seen. Meanwhile, my lovely assistant Chase will tease my hair into an Ursula-worthy makeover, complete with a hideous seaweed wig. Subscribe now to the Cherish Channel to see if I transform into the mermaid of your dreams... or a warty frogfish with an underbite."

"Yahoo! Let the games begin!" Mom squeals as I end the livestream.

With business done, I can get back to my favorite family holiday tradition. Every year, we gather on this slice of paradise for some good old-fashioned competition. And trust me, we Barretts are serious about our fun.

We're decked out in our beach finest—shorts, T-shirts, and bare feet. The weather couldn't be better. Maybe it's all this amazing sex I'm having, but the sand is like powder between my toes, the sky is a flawless blue, and the sun's warmth is just right.

Most days, Chase dresses like she's headed to a funeral—all black, all the time. But today, she's switched things up... She's lighter, more radiant. She's wearing a breezy tank top in a soft pastel pink, paired with frayed denim shorts that tease with the slightest peek of her ass cheek. The glimpse of her bright-red bikini string under her shirt has me eager to play a game of *Peek-a-Boob*.

Her hair's down today, and it's a bit of a frizzy mess thanks to the humidity. But it's a gorgeous disaster. Dad always says he's got beer goggles for Mama because she's beautiful every second. Now, I get it. It's not only the way she looks—it's the way she makes me feel. Every time I look at her, I see something new, something incredible.

I've never felt this way about anyone.

I can't take my eyes off her.

Whoa there. Shut 'er down and stay focused, buddy. It's game day.

"This year, I done outdid myself," Mom announces. "I cooked up a prize that'll leave ya speechless. Feast your eyes on the Yuletide Flamingo Flickers!"

She presents a pair of obscene pink flip-flops that are a hate crime against fashion, cluttered with flamingos, bows, and tasteless tinsel. And thanks to those obnoxious blinking lights crammed between the toe straps, the winner will definitely *shine*.

Chase starts snickering, but I quickly cut her off.

"Laugh all you want. You're not even in the running."

"Oh Ethan. I have zero interest in the family prize. But destroying you, that's a game I'll play to win. You just lit a fire inside me."

I tilt my head. "A fire that I plan on feeling inside you later tonight."

"Always so cocky, aren't you Barrett?"

I plant a quick kiss on her lips before whispering, "There you go again, thinking about my cock."

"Alright, you two turtledoves, that's enough!" Mom hollers. "No canoodling with the competition. It's every man for himself in these games."

Dad jumps in, looking at Chase. "Ethan's been the reigning champ for three years. We'd be thrilled if you could knock him off his pedestal. Do whatever it takes."

Chase sends a playful wink my way, purring, "With pleasure." The way her tongue caresses that last word sends a jolt straight through me.

Dude, seriously, concentrate!

First up: Frosty the Sandman Sculpt-Off. The goal? Build a snowman out of sand and decorate it with seashells, dead wood, and whatever other beachy bits we can scavenge. Chase was in so much awe that she Googled it, and yeah, it's a real thing.

The catch? We only get twenty minutes.

Mom yells, "Go," and Chase is instantly in the zone. I'm knee-deep in sand. My hands move like sand-sculpting ninjas.

Chase is a few feet away, tongue poking out slightly as she concentrates. It's her directing face but beach-ified. Hair dancing in the breeze. Sand-dusted legs. It hits... different.

My hands are molding my tubby sandman, but my mind is stuck on last night on the boat. I laid it all out there for her, raw and honest in a way I'd never done with anyone. And Chase? She brushed it off with a laugh.

Oof. I'm still cringing.

"Ten minutes left!" Mom shouts.

A rush of panic grips me. Time is running out. And I don't mean the game... I mean us. Our Christmas vacation is almost over. In a few days, we'll return to L.A., back like we never left, and whatever this is between Chase and me will be... who knows?

I quickly arrange a row of small shells to form Frosty's face, stealing glances at Chase. She's smiling, lost in the moment, clearly not on the same emotional rollercoaster. Obviously not feeling what I am, because for me...

I'm falling for her, hard and fast.

"Are you ready to be outshone by an actual artist," Chase says smugly.

"Ha. How about you surrender, and I won't say I told you so?" I chuckle.

"Not today, pretty boy. You're about to get schooled. I'm turning this lumpy potato into a work of art."

She throws me a wink that makes my heart do a little flip.

Why did I go and make things so complicated? This woman's job is literally to yell "Cut!" on my life. She's the director, calling the shots and deciding when a scene—or a moment—is over.

How can I go back to normal? Acting is one thing, but pretending my heart doesn't race every time she calls "Action!" is another.

I've gone and screwed myself, in the most cliché Hollywood way. I've seen fellow actors blur lines with film producers and execs, and they usually crash and burn. Which means this most definitely ends with my career in the toilet, probably landing a gig in commercials for erectile dysfunction meds—if I'm lucky.

Side effects may include a recurring kicking sensation to your emotional groin while spontaneously bursting into tears.

"Five minutes!"

Crap. Five minutes till it's game over. NO! Five days left in Florida. Only five days?!

I watch Chase frantically trying to give her sandman a seaweed toupee. It's hilarious. The look of pure joy on her face makes my soul sing. And I realize something.

I'd gladly hawk dick pills for the rest of my life if it meant seeing that smile every day.

"Time's up!" Dad calls out.

I sneak a peek at Chase's sandman—more blobfish than snowman. It's not bad, maybe even adorable if you squint, but my sand-sculpting genius stands as a granular masterpiece. I've given him a strong chin and a six-pack made of seashells that are making seagulls swoon mid-flight.

"Wow, Ethan, that's amazing," Chase says. "Seriously, you should totally get a picture for social media. Toss me your phone."

Victory surges through me like I've just bagged an Oscar or, more realistically, like I've found that sweet parking spot in Hollywood on a Friday night. I grin, hands on my hips, and strike a pose next to my pudgy snowman.

Chase backs up, framing the shot.

"Can you take a step to the left?" she directs. "Almost, scoochie a little more... Okay, one more baby step."

And then, because I'm a fool who's too busy channeling my inner Zoolander "Blue Steel," I step right onto my carefully crafted creation. Within seconds, my snowman crumbles, reducing it to a sad, damp pile of sand.

I whirl around to confront Chase, who's wearing an angelic expression that's so mock innocent, a blind man could see through it. But with those flirty, twinkling eyes, no way can I be mad.

"You little cheater," I accuse. "You're gonna pay for that!"

Before she can react, I lunge forward and scoop her up, tossing her over my shoulder like a sack of presents. She shrieks with laughter as I charge towards the ocean.

"No, Stop! I don't want to get wet!" Chase squeals, pounding her fists ineffectually against my back.

"Do you promise to play nice and stop with the tricks?" I demand, wading deeper into the cool water.

"Yes!" she gasps between giggles. "I promise!"

I ease her gently into the calf-deep water, but her hands stay firmly on my shoulders like I'm her anchor. She tilts her chin up, and I'm drowning in those eyes.

Time slows, the world narrows, and it's just us—toes in sand with the ocean lapping against our legs. The sound of the waves and my family's laughter on the beach becomes background noise. It's

Chase and me, standing in the shallows, on the brink of... something.

What if I told her?

What if I was completely honest and held nothing back.

Hey Chase, I'm falling hard for you. Let's give this a shot when we're back in L.A.?

Before I can bare my soul, Chase's face sparkles with mischief. Quick as a flash, she holds up her hand, revealing crossed fingers.

"Fooled ya, sucker! I cheat to win. Race ya back!"

She sprints out of the ocean, leaving me floundering in her wake. I'm so baffled by this intriguing woman. One minute she's ice, the next she's fire. All in or all out—no in-between. Today, she's clearly chosen "all in" on our little competition.

I've got to come out on top, show her I can match her stride for stride. Maybe if I prove myself her equal, she'll finally hear what my heart's been screaming.

The next few games turn into a fierce competition of cleverness and charm. She won the snowman-building round, but I crushed her dreams (and the ball) in beach volleyball.

The Reindeer Ring Toss had us neck and neck until she pulled out her secret weapon. Chase flashed her tits, and I missed my last throw by a mile.

She was on her way to surefire victory in "Candy Cane Fishing." As she reeled in what should have been her winning catch, I struck. My hand found her ass, giving it a firm squeeze. Her startled yelp was music to my ears as she lost her balance.

I'm not above fighting dirty. After all, she started it.

The Polar Express Sprint—the final showdown. We're lined up on the sandy shore, adrenaline pumping and our game faces on.

The finish line taunts us from waaay down the beach. Nolan, our supposed impartial judge, stands ready.

I scan the faces of my family, searching for a hint of support.

"Chase, sweetie," Mom says, her voice syrupy sweet, "you've played your little heart out today, haven't you? We are all rooting for you."

"Mama?" I protest. "What about me? Your flesh and blood?"

"Ethan, hun, give it a rest. No one wants you winning again. Besides, I think you've met your match."

"Don't worry, son," Dad chimes in. "You have our love. But I must admit, I'll enjoy seeing you finish second."

My last hope is my brother. I spot him down the shore, arms spread wide. *Perfect.* I flash him our secret twin signal for "Bro, I need you."

Nolan hollers back, "Go Chase!"

Chase bumps my shoulder, her grin wicked. "Sorry, not sorry, but I guess they like me more."

"I hate to disappoint everyone," I declare, "but those flip-flops are mine!"

Mom raises her arms, ready to start. "Racers, line up!"

Chase and I stand side-by side, our toes pressed into the sandy ground. In the distance, Nolan waves to signal he's ready.

I stare Chase down, taking one last chance to trash talk her. "No shame in losing to the king, newbie. I'm the champ. Fast, experienced, and unbeatable in the sand."

"Maybe speed isn't the key. Strategy is."

"It's running—that's all about speed."

Determination sets in. My heart races. Muscles primed and ready. Let's do this.

"On your mark," Mom calls out. "Get set..."

"Prepare to cry into your pillow tonight, darlin'. Losing is gonna be a tough pill to swallow."

Chase leans close and whispers in my ear, "Oh I'll swallow alright, when I let you fuck my mouth tonight."

"GO!"

Her words hit me like a hurricane, and she's off.

Sand flies, her legs pumping, tearing up the beach. My brain's spinning, feet suddenly useless. I stumble forward, still dazed, and face-plant into the warm sand, getting a mouthful of Marco Island's finest.

I scramble to my feet, spitting out grit, but Chase is halfway down the sandy stretch. She crosses the finish line, arms raised in triumph, a solid three seconds ahead of my second-place finish.

My family of backstabbers cheers her victory.

I sweep her into my arms and kiss her, knowing without a doubt that she's the prize I truly want.

***

THE DAMP SAND MOLDS to our feet, cool and velvety, as Chase and I walk along the shore. Our fingers are entwined, swinging gently back and forth, a silent expression of our affection. With each step, a shiver runs up my spine. I wonder if it's the rhythm of the waves or Chase's magnetic presence causing this sensation.

Our third wheel—Bubbles—waddles beside us on his leash. He eyes a seagull like it's the last hot dog at a Fourth of July barbecue.

"Bubbles, no," I mutter, giving his leash a tug.

He shoots me a look that says, *You're not my real dad*, but thankfully decides the bird isn't on today's menu.

I am constantly drawn to Chase, my eyes taking in both her physical beauty and the subtle changes in her expression. She's relaxed, happy... comfortable in her own skin. I'm getting to see the woman behind the director's chair, the Chase, who isn't afraid to be a little silly and a little vulnerable.

Am I the only person who sees this softer side of her?

But I can't shake the feeling that once this trip is over, I'll be nothing but a passing moment in her life.

"I see you side-eyeing my flamingo flip-flops," Chase teases, catching me staring. "Don't hate the player, hate the game."

"Player?" I scoff. "You're a dirty, dirty cheater. Filthy promises were made. I expect you to keep them."

"Oh, I meant what I said," she quips with a smirk before turning her gaze back to the water. "Ethan, look! Dolphins!" Chase shouts, her eyes lighting up with childlike wonder.

I pull her close, her back against my chest, and wrap my arms firmly around her waist. Resting my head on her shoulder, we watch two dolphins play together, jumping in and out of the waves.

I hold her tight, the moment expressing what words cannot. I'm hoping she can sense the depth of my feelings through my embrace.

"Come on, lovebugs. It's picture time!" My mom's voice cuts through the ocean sound, and our time is up.

We trudge up the sandy shore to join the family. My mom is jumping with excitement. "Okay, Barrett family! Who's ready for this year's photo theme?"

We give a halfhearted cheer, and I nudge Chase to join in.

Mom's not satisfied. "Y'all can do better than that. Who wants to hear this year's theme?"

Chase, bless her heart, really gets into it this time, cheering the loudest, which makes my mom smile.

"Dougie darlin', drum roll, please," Mom says.

Dad obliges, performing high-spirited tapping on his belly.

"This year," Mom announces with flair, "we will be… an '80s glam metal band!"

I stifle a groan.

"I've got costumes and wigs and blow-up guitars. Go get dressed!"

Chase shifts into director mode. "Darla, I'd be glad to snap the photo. Just share your vision with me, and I'll bring it to life."

Mom waves her off. "We've got a camera timer for that, hun. Besides, you can't take the picture. I want you to be in it."

"Oh no, I couldn't impose on your family Christmas card photo," Chase protests.

"Sweetie, you were the inspiration! There was a whole other theme chosen, but when I saw your hair, it hit me!" Mom beams at Chase. "I didn't get you a wig 'cause you're already good to go."

I let out a snort-chuckle. Chase's frizz-bomb hair has grown wilder and wilder throughout the day. It's looking especially windswept from our beach walk, so yeah, rockstar perfection.

Mom addresses me. "You, mister, you're a curly redhead today. And I better see matching red lipstick."

"You got it, Mama," I say, knowing full well I'm about to regret this.

Right as I'm getting ready to "spiffy up," I notice Chase looking overwhelmed. "You okay?"

She nods, a bit too quickly. "Yeah, uh, yes, totally fine." Then she adds with a shrug, "Guess I better go try to shimmy into this spandex. Hopefully I can rid myself of the sand that's been living rent-free in my butt crack."

I can tell something's off—her eyes are clouded and her smile isn't genuine. I've learned that when she's like this, her walls are up and there's no getting past them. She hates it when I pry, no matter how much I want her to trust me.

But does she trust anyone, really?

So many times I've seen her on set, fixing things that weren't her job. When problems pop up, she's the first to jump in. She's the last to leave, making sure everything is perfectly in place.

I may jokingly call her a control freak, but now I'm wondering if there's more to it.

What if it's not about control? Maybe she believes she can't ever trust anyone else and that she has to take care of everything herself.

How can I show her that she can rely on me?

A short while later, my family stands in front of a Christmas tree set up and decorated along the beachfront. The sun is starting to set, and the timing couldn't be more perfect. It's a stunning backdrop for our photo.

Mom applies extra makeup to all of us, glamming us up so we get her vision just right. She, of course, looks like Dee Snider. Her bleach-blonde hair is teased out so high, I'm afraid a gust of wind might send her flying.

"Now everyone hold your blow-up guitars," Mom instructs. "Except you, Doug. How 'bout you hold Bubbles like he's a guitar? Ain't that funny?"

We all strike our best rock 'n' roll poses as Mom sets the timer on the camera. "Okay, family, say 'Candy canes'!"

We repeat the phrase in unison, and with a click, the moment is immortalized forever. Mom runs over to check the photo then squeals with delight.

DING!

My phone chirps, and a pit forms in my stomach as I check the notification. *Shit.* This isn't good.

"Oh, man. We didn't reach our subscriber quota for today," I say, trying to keep my voice light.

Chase's head whips around. "Wait, what? Are you sure?" She fumbles for her phone, her eyes growing wide as she checks the numbers. "We only got half?!"

I can see the unease building in her eyes. "Trust me. It'll be okay. I'm gonna go live real quick and tell the fans what happened."

"Sure," Chase says, nodding in a daze.

I turn the camera away from her and start my livestream. "Hey, Ethan Addicts, sorry to report that we missed our goal for today. That means you don't get to see me looking like a whacked-out merman and I don't have to rinse sand out of my ass for three days. Your loss, but my win."

As I scan the comments, I spot a familiar name pop up. Gail, my self-proclaimed number-one fan and president of the Ethan Addicts fan club. She's requesting to join the livestream.

My finger hovers over the *Accept* button. *Might help lighten the mood?*

I press the button, and suddenly Gail's face joins mine in the split-screen frame. She's draped in a deep-purple satin robe that highlights her bright-red hair. Full makeup, of course, and she's angled the camera just so, giving everyone watching the live a generous view of her cleavage.

"Oh hey, Gail," I say, aiming for casual while my brain screams, *Abort! Abort!*

Gail's face lights up. "Ethan, baby!" she coos. "You look absolutely scrumptious today. That tan is *everything*."

I force a laugh, suddenly very aware of Chase's presence just off-camera. "Thanks, Gail. It's that Florida sun working its magic."

Gail shifts closer to the camera, offering a view that would make a Victoria's Secret model embarrassed. "I was about to take a nice, long bubble bath. While thinking of you, of course, you naughty boy. Care to join me?"

I'm about to stammer out a response, when Chase's face appears in the frame, her smile sharp as a razor. "Sorry, Gail, but Ethan's bath time is booked solid. Maybe try again in, oh, never?"

Gail's eyes narrow, her simpering smile morphing into something closer to a snarl. "Well hello, *Chase*. I didn't realize you were there. Though I suppose I should have. You're always there, aren't you?"

"Occupational hazard of being Ethan's girlfriend," Chase replies sweetly. "You know how it is... Oh, wait—you don't."

The comments section explodes into chaos, Team Gail and Team Chase fans fighting like they're in a virtual wrestling ring. The viewer count skyrockets.

Gail sneers. "Why don't you take a hint and realize that everyone is bored with your so-called 'relationship.' That's why you didn't hit your subscriber goal. It's pathetic."

Chase grabs the phone. "Or maybe, Gail, you're salty because the only action you get is from your vibrator."

Shit. Did she just say that?

Gail's face turns as red as her hair, resembling a tomato in a microwave that's about to explode. "Excuse me?" she sputters, her eyes flashing. "I'll have you know that I have a very active love life."

"You wish," Chase scoffs. "The most thrilling thing you'll do tonight is dry humping your Ethan body pillow."

I clear my throat, trying to slice through the tension. "Ladies, let's not—"

But they're not listening to me. They're too busy glaring at each other through their screens.

"You don't know the first thing about what Ethan needs," Gail hisses.

"And you do?" Chase fires back. "Because you've watched his movies a hundred times and have a shrine in your closet?"

"I do not have a shrine!" Gail protests, but her eyes dart to the side, and I have a sinking feeling that she's lying.

"Okay, that's enough," I say, finally finding my voice. "Gail, thank you for joining us, but I think it's time to—"

"No, Ethan," Gail interrupts, her voice suddenly sweet. "You shouldn't defend her. We all know she's using you to boost her career."

Chase lets out a laugh that sounds more like a growl. "Using him? Ha! That's rich coming from you, Miss 'I Run a Fan Club Just to Get Close to Ethan.'"

I grab back my phone. "Alright," I say firmly. "Gail, thanks for joining, but we've got to go. Chase and I have... uh... lines to practice."

"But Ethan—" Gail starts to protest.

"That's a wrap on this livestream. Thanks for being here, Ethan Addicts!" I press down hard on the *End Stream* button.

Silence crashes over us.

Chase is a statue of rage beside me, jaw clenched and eyes blazing.

Fuck! That was a disaster of epic proportions. Rule number one of social media: Don't pick fights on the internet.

CHAPTER EIGHTEEN

CHASE

I NOW KNOW WHY he's called the King of Christmas—because Ethan's dick is magic.

Last night, after everyone had gone to bed, I made good on my promise. Giving blowjobs isn't usually my favorite thing—like, why have a dick in your mouth when you could be devouring a burrito? But holy fucking shit, Ethan's love wand is next-level. I took my time, teasing him to the edge and then pulling away, savoring his cock like it was the last lollipop on Earth.

My tongue teased his engorged tip, licking until he begged for release. I drew out strange, wonderful sounds from his core—guttural moans of pleasure mixed with soft whimpers and sharp, surprised exhales. I reveled in making his entire body tense and tremble. It was such a fucking turn-on to know that I was the one causing his exquisite torture, his delicious undoing.

It felt so dirty and selfish to wield all that power over him—to control how and when he breathed, to make his muscles strain at my command. And just when he thought I couldn't squeeze out any more dirty fun, I opened wider and deep-throated his giant throbbing length until he was screaming uncontrollably into his pillow, "Fuck, Chase. Fuck!" He came so hard down my throat that I'm still grinning like the Grinch when he steals Christmas.

I've never done anything so filthy and fantastic.

And I'm craving a replay.

Those poor SpongeBob sheets have seen some things the past few days, and I'm not sure they'll ever recover.

I thought Ethan was spent after the experience. The way he lay there, his arm draped over his eyes—his whole body relishing the moment. I kissed him goodnight and snuggled up to him, ready to drift off.

"Not a chance, darlin'." He chuckled, propping himself up on one elbow. "Sleep? We're not even close to the finish line. Not until you're throughly satisfied."

The mere memory of his words has my clit pulsing, eager to obey.

Ethan camped out down there like he was at a cozy cabin retreat, giving my lady garden a luxurious, never-ending spa day. The slow, deliberate flicks of his tongue on my sweet spot, how he groaned against my pussy, and the million vibrations coursing through me...

He was unhinged, driven to prove how masterfully he could command my body. And he's right. My whole being molded to his hands, formed to his touch, and surrendered completely to his will.

And fuck me, don't even get me started on the orgasms, because they kept coming and coming. They didn't just leave my thighs quivering. No, even my soul trembled like a goddamn jackhammer.

Ethan can summon climaxes—the man is the Pied Piper of pussy.

It's a dance of desire and dominance.

And that scares the ever-loving shit out of me.

But I can't go there right now. Time to quiet the buzzing in my lady bits and get these merch orders filled.

Darla's craft store is so packed with fans today, there's a line out the door. I wish I could stop thinking about you-know-who, but everything I touch in here is covered in Ethan's face, the very same face I sat on last night.

I shove another Chathan shirt into a box. Nolan's voice drones on in the background, a monotonous hum about labeling and address verification. We have over a thousand online orders to fill, and the last hour has been a long, mind-numbing loop.

"...and then we double-check the zip code to ensure—"

"Right, because checking once is for amateurs," I mutter, no longer hiding my sarcasm. Meanwhile, my traitorous gaze is playing a twisted game of hide and seek. It drifts across the crowded store, magnetically drawn to the one person I'm trying desperately to ignore.

Ethan.

He's in his element, a golden retriever in human form, all easy smiles and effortless charm. He's like a one-man boy band—taking selfies and signing autographs. Everyone within a ten-foot radius is falling head over heels for him.

Flirtation is his superpower, activated by the merest hint of a grin. The man oozes charm as if he's been honing this skill since birth. And that's the problem—this comes far too naturally to him. His effortless allure? It's nothing more than a carefully crafted performance.

Ethan glances over, catching me staring. He winks, and I swallow hard. There's no stopping the warmth spreading through my chest like wildfire.

The way he looks at me. The things he says. He's so convincing, it almost feels real.

Stop it, Chase! This is nothing more than a fake relationship with benefits. A carefully orchestrated PR stunt to boost our subscriber count. Casual sex is how we LA people operate. No big deal, just killing time between livestreams.

But seriously? How did I go from wanting to superglue Ethan's lips shut to wanting them wide open and all over me? Hooking up? Never crossed my mind.

Fine, I'll come clean. Maybe I've had a dirty thought or two *(or ten)* about him over the years. But I'd rather eat glass than admit that out loud.

It doesn't matter anyway. It's not like we're gonna live happily ever after. He'll go back to chasing supermodels and Hollywood 'it' girls.

What if I did desire something genuine? To be treasured and adored by him, not just another conquest. To be the only name tattooed on his heart. To be each other's... person.

The truth is, Ethan isn't relationship material, even if I did want that.

As if he can hear my thoughts, Ethan saunters over and pulls me in for a kiss so intense it leaves me lightheaded. His mouth is warm against mine, his arms strong and secure around my waist. The store erupts in a chorus of "awws" and for once I don't shy away from the attention.

"Isn't my girlfriend adorable?" Ethan asks the crowd.

Another performance for the public. He knows exactly how to make it feel sincere, because it's his job to convince all women to believe in the fantasy... Apparently that includes me.

He's a much better actor than I give him credit for.

I paste on a smile, playing my part. "Are you just kissing me to get out of helping with orders?"

Ethan smirks. "Is it that obvious?"

I'm about to respond when Darla's chipper voice cuts through the air. "Ladies, we got a brand-new batch of Chathan shirts in flamingo pink! If you buy yours now, Ethan and Chase will sign them!"

I gotta hand it to Darla. That woman pounces on trends faster than a cat on a mouse.

The crowd surges forward like they're racing to an all-you-can-eat hottie buffet, but Ethan's focus is on me. He holds me tight, his fingers tracing the gentle features of my face, and it makes my heart flutter.

"Hey," I whisper. "We need to talk about Gail."

Ethan's gaze doesn't falter. "What about her?" he says. "The online meltdown thing? Meh, it's fine."

"You've seen it? And you're not worried?"

He shrugs. "It'll blow over, Chase. Fans get upset, they vent, they move on. It's the circle of celebrity life."

"This is serious. Look at what she's posting!" I shove my phone at him, scrolling through Gail's "Ethan Addicts" fan page feed.

Wake up, Ethan Addicts! Your beloved star and his stone-cold director are nothing but Hollywood smoke and mirrors. #CHATHANisFake

Calling for a boycott: Forget the countdown to Christmas. This year, let's all #CountdownToCHATHANBreakup

Betting pool: How long before that shady witch Chase dumps Ethan? I'm betting on Christmas Eve for maximum drama. #CHATHANisOver

Ethan's smile finally wavers. "Ouch. But hey, give yourself some credit. She's implying you're doing the dumping and not me. That's something, right?"

I ignore his attempt at humor. "There's more. Look at this thread she started, breaking down every interaction we've had on camera. She's got screenshots, body language analysis, the works."

"Wow... When Gail commits to something, she really commits."

"This isn't funny," I snap. "We didn't hit our subscriber goal yesterday, and today's looking even worse. All our hard work could go down the drain because I told her the only action she gets is from her vibrator and her creepy Ethan-shaped body pillow."

"You played the jealous girlfriend part pretty well. If I didn't know better, I'd think you were actually jealous."

Ethan falls silent for a moment, his gaze shifting from the phone to my face, those eyes of his searching, probing. Like he wants to tell me something, but the words fail him.

Darla's spunky voice interrupts. "Ethan! Chase! The shirts are ready for signing. We've got a line of fans waiting. Y'all better get a move on!"

"Coming, Mama!" His mouth finds mine, gentle but insistent. "Stop worrying about the subscribers. I've got this—I've got you."

We work our way to the autograph table together, hands entwined. For the first time in my career, the lines between fiction and reality are blurring. This whole thing is spiraling out of control. I'm losing grip on what's real and what's part of the act.

I've always been the one behind the scenes, the one calling the shots. But with Ethan, I feel like I am no longer in command. And that fucking terrifies me.

Unlike the movies I write, I have no idea how this story ends.

***

"**THIS IS MY HOUSE.** I have to defend it!" Ethan declares, striking a heroic pose.

I'm perched on the edge of the couch next to Darla, watching the Barrett men act out scenes from *Home Alone*. Apparently, this is another cherished family tradition.

Doug and Nolan are playing the *Wet Bandits*, chasing Ethan around the living room performing the movie's pranks. They're slipping, sliding, and fake-punching with the coordination of drunken sorority girls playing a game of Twister blindfolded.

Darla squeals and claps her hands when Nolan takes a dramatic tumble, pretending to be smacked in the face. The whole scene is utterly ridiculous and my cheeks ache from laughing.

I haven't smiled this much since... well, *ever*.

Somehow, the Barretts managed to sneak past my defenses, winning me over with their joy and endless love. It's surprising how genuine my fake boyfriend's family feels—as if I truly belong with them.

"I gotta get home to Kevin!" Darla leaps up, shouting the line with more gusto than a cheerleader captain. "I'll do whatever it takes!"

The movie always seemed like pure nonsense to me. What kind of mom forgets her kid and then flies halfway around the world to get back to him? The *Darla* type, that's who.

The bandits finally corner Ethan, which is my cue. I've been given the prestigious role of the creepy old neighbor.

Armed with a throw pillow instead of a snow shovel, I sneak up behind Doug and Nolan.

WHACK! WHACK!

My pillow connects, and they collapse to the ground like they've been hit with tranquilizer darts.

Well played, gents.

Ethan whirls around. "My hero!" he exclaims, giving me a big, theatrical kiss.

I can taste the hint of peppermint from the candy canes he's been munching on all night. His lips are so fucking juicy. I can't resist pulling him closer, deepening the kiss.

This is fake, this is fake, this is fucking fake, I chant internally, battling against the riot my nerves are staging. My skin sizzles like I've been struck by lightning, every cell crying out for more.

It's no big deal. He's enjoying a bit of fun, and so am I.

"Hey, that's not how the movie goes," I protest weakly.

A devilish grin appears on his face. "Right, cuz that'd be weird, huh? My bad. Back to one!"

I think "Kevin" is going to kiss me again, but instead he turns to the others, waving his arms like an overzealous traffic cop. "From the top, people! The director said she wants to see more authenticity. That means less improv from you, Dad."

Doug pops up from the floor, looking way too excited for a grown man playing make-believe. "Great notes, Chase. I'd like a do-over for my hair-on-fire scene. I felt like I was phoning it in."

"Alright, boys," Darla chirps. "You keep defending the house. Chase and I are gonna whip up some sugar, spice, and nicey-nice in the kitchen."

I trail after her, still buzzing from that kiss. I bet she's seen enough tonsil hockey to qualify as a referee by now. Just another Tuesday when your son is America's favorite man candy, leaving a trail of swooning women in his wake.

The second we're in the doorway, Darla is a whirlwind of activity, whipping out bowls and ingredients. "So, Chase, what do you cook up for the holidays?"

I freeze, feeling like I've been asked to perform brain surgery with a spork. "Oh, um... my family doesn't really have special recipes. We didn't celebrate much when I was growing up."

"Well, butter my biscuit and call me Sally! We're gonna fix that faster than you can say 'food porn!'"

She whips out a recipe box that looks like it survived the sixties, stuffed with cards in more colors than a bag of Skittles. She selects one and hands it to me with a flourish. "Ethan loves this. It's his favorite. My nanna's special rum cake."

She leans in close, her voice dropping to a conspiratorial whisper. "Don't tell a soul, but the secret is the eggs. Always double 'em up. That's what gives it that nice gooey pudding texture."

She acts like she's just handed me her entire VHS collection of Jane Fonda exercise tapes and is trusting me to not loan them out. I nod solemnly.

As we gather ingredients, Darla narrates the complete Barrett family history, complete with footnotes and a dramatic reenactment. "Now, Nanna Clark was sweeter than pie, but this recipe? It's from Nanna Wilson. That old battle-axe had a tongue sharper than a porcupine's backside and a heart colder than a witch's tit. Tough as nails, that one. Kinda like you, sweet pea. But ya know, ain't her fault. She had a real hard life, and that changes a person."

I blink, not sure if I should be flattered or offended. Am I the bitter old broad or the witch with the droopy frozen tatas?

Is this what it would have been like?

Would my own mother have shared secret family recipes passed down through generations? Would she have pulled me close, her eyes sparkling with joy as she shared something special, like Darla does? Would our kitchen have been filled with the scent of vanilla and love instead of takeout and silence?

Darla hands over a festive apron covered in flamingos, giggling about Ethan's attempt to 'improve' the recipe with a heavy pour of rum. But I'm trapped in that treacherous zone between past and present, where memories I've spent years evading are suddenly nipping at my heels.

My mother's absence is an open wound, painstakingly covered with professional success, personal achievements, and a firm policy of keeping others at bay. But here's Darla, humming Christmas carols and teaching me family secrets like I belong here. As if I'm worthy of being someone's daughter. It hurts. Oh God, it hurts. Like pressing on a bruise you forgot you had.

"So, what can I do to help?"

"You measure, I'll pour."

"Sounds good," I agree, relieved to have a task to focus on.

As we work, Darla chatters away. "Lordy, I'm tickled you're here! Having another gal in the house is a treat. I love my boys, but I've always wanted a daughter. Don't you tell 'em, but I've also been prayin' for some grandbaby girls. Then you came along." She winks.

Guilt washes over me like a tidal wave. I suddenly understand why Ethan insisted we lie to his parents. It would crush his mom, knowing our relationship is as fake as the plastic Christmas palm tree in their living room.

Elbow-deep in eggy batter, the words slip out before I realize it. "So, I'm guessing Ethan's brought home his fair share of holiday arm candy?"

"Shucks, hun, you're the first girl Ethan's ever had us meet. Don't take this the wrong way, but I was kinda surprised it was you."

I nearly drop the egg I'm holding. "Never?"

"I swear on my mama's sweet tea, I ain't lyin'."

My brain's still buffering from that bombshell when Darla launches an attack on the bundt pan with enough cooking spray to lubricate a jet engine.

"That boy of mine, he calls every week, regular as rain. We do this FaceTime game night on Sundays. But ever since he started working with you? He's been more uptight than a nun in a cucumber patch. We helped him practice his lines instead of our usual shenanigans."

I'm flabbergasted. *Ethan? Rehearsing lines? Yeah, right.* Memorizing is against his religion. He's more likely to give up sex.

"That boy wanted to impress you somethin' fierce," Darla continues, oblivious to my befuddled expression. "He would go on and on about how he couldn't believe someone as talented as you chose him. Like you were in a different league in Hollywood. You make him feel special."

"You're shitting me," I blurt out.

"I shit you not, buttercup." Darla grins. "I think Ethan's got a bit of that, what's it called, imposter syndrome when it comes to you."

She takes the bowl and dumps the mixture into the pan. My mind's running in place, like it's on a hamster wheel, trying to process this info dump. Ethan? Mr. *I'm God's Gift to Cinema*, having self-doubt? No way.

"I see why he was so torn up now," Darla says with a knowing smile. "That boy has love written all over his face. He's just like his daddy. He can't hide it."

Before I can respond—or have the panic attack that's bubbling up faster than this cake batter—she changes subjects. "Alrighty, time for the fun part. Watch and learn, sugar."

She swipes a finger through the creamy mix and pops it into her mouth with a full-bodied moan. "Now you try," she commands.

I take a lick. Holy mother of mouthgasms. How can sugar and eggs hit so hard?

"Damn, that's good," I admit, wondering if it's impolite to dive face-first into the bowl.

"Wait till we drown this sucker in boozy glaze. You'll be seeing God and calling him *Daddy*."

She shoves the three and a half metric tons of calories into the oven. "While that's baking, I got you a little something."

Darla leads me to the dining room and settles me at the table, presenting me with a beautifully wrapped package.

"Really, this isn't necessary. You shouldn't get me anything."

"Technically, I didn't 'get' it. I made this for you."

I open the gift, revealing a handcrafted seashell frame with a picture inside. The photograph features the entire Barrett clan and me dressed in full 80s rock glory—posing on the sand and making ridiculous faces. It's simultaneously the most absurd and endearing thing I've ever seen.

"You hold a special place in Ethan's heart," Darla says softly, "and that makes you incredibly important to me. You're part of the family now."

I want to... cry? Scream? Go back in time? *I don't know.*

Darla pulls me into a hug that threatens to squeeze the cynicism right out of me. As I sit there, enveloped in her warmth and the scent of rum cake, I feel something inside me start to crumble.

After she finally releases me, I can't stop staring at the image, a lump forming in my throat the size of my emotional baggage.

"Maybe next year we can dress up as Dolly Parton through the decades," I say, surprising myself.

Her face lights up, a blazing supernova of pure joy. "You wanna plan the photo with me? Now that's a dream come true!"

My stomach sinks with an anchor of regret.

What am I doing?

This isn't real. I'm not part of this family.

Hell, I'm not even Ethan's girlfriend.

I don't belong here.

CHAPTER NINETEEN

ETHAN

'Tis the season to wear a candy cane sock on your junk.

I'm sprawled out on my bed in a, let's say strategic position. I've been looking forward to getting my favorite director back in the sheets all day, hoping she's down for some holiday fun. The door flies open, and Chase barges in. Her eyes are frenzied, distress all over her face. My playful demeanor vanishes, and I'm fully alert.

"Where are the fucking keys?" she demands, her voice tight with desperation. "I need to get out of here."

She's trashing my room faster than a reality TV show makeover.

I sit up, totally confused. "Whoa, whoa. You need me to drive you somewhere?"

"No! I just need to be gone."

I give my candy cane one last sorrowful glance then quickly throw on some pants and a shirt. She's going through my things like a whirlwind, and I'm totally lost, but I join her anyway.

Whatever her reasons, I need to help her.

I start riffling through my pockets as Chase spots the keys on my desk. "There!"

She lunges and accidentally knocks over the challenge jar of dare slips. Red and green papers scatter everywhere, exploding across the floor like confetti. Her eyes dart from paper to paper, and she freezes. *Uh-oh.*

I watch her face change—her eyes widen as the pieces fall into place. Confusion overtakes the panic, followed by a moment of realization, and then, finally, pure rage.

"Kiss an alligator, kiss an alligator... These all say the same thing." Her eyes snap to mine, blazing. "You set me up. You LIED to me. You knew!"

I hold up my hands, trying to calm her. "Of course I knew. It was my idea."

"I thought Nolan wrote them!"

"What's the big deal?" I ask, genuinely confused. "You're not an actor, Chase. We needed an authentic reaction. You, more than anyone, should understand."

I reach for her, needing to console, to explain, but she pulls away like my touch is fire.

"Chase, it was about the fans. Nothing more."

"Oh my God," she whispers, and I see tears forming in her eyes. "Of course, the fans. I'm such an idiot. I thought—" She cuts herself off, shaking her head and wiping away tears.

Then she bolts out of the room.

"Wait. I'm coming with you!" I yell, grabbing my shoes and chasing after her.

The front door slams, the sound echoing through the house like a gunshot. My heart's racing—a wild drumbeat in my chest.

I rush outside just as Chase flings open the driver's side door of the Mustang. She's a tornado in human form, all wild energy and chaos. I jump into the passenger side, my hand still clutching my shoes.

"Chase, what the—"

The rest of my sentence is lost as she guns the engine. The force slams me back against the seat. We peel out of the driveway with a screech that wakes up the entire neighborhood.

"Jesus Christ!" I yelp, scrambling for the seat belt. My fingers feel clumsy, useless. We're already hitting forty in a twenty-five zone, the speedometer climbing like it's trying to reach orbit.

"Chase, slow down! What's going on?"

"I can't breathe," she gasps. Her eyes are manic, pinballing between the road and the dashboard. "How do you get this damn top down?"

My pulse is racing, matching the car's insane acceleration, but I force myself to focus. "Here," I say, reaching for the console. My hands are shaking so badly that I almost hit the wrong button. "I've got it. Just... Just watch the road, okay?"

I'm a mess of jangled nerves, my eyes darting between her white-knuckled grip on the steering wheel and the blur of houses whipping past us. Sixty-five mph.

The convertible top starts to retract, painfully slow. Wind blasts through the car, messing up my hair and drowning out my ragged breaths. But Chase doesn't calm down. If anything, she looks even more frantic, like a caged animal desperate to escape.

She turns sharply onto a road, taking the corner too fast. I swear I feel the car lift onto two wheels. My stomach lurches, and I dig my fingers into the leather seat hard enough to leave permanent indentations. Gravel sprays from beneath the tires, pinging against the undercarriage like gunfire.

Please, don't let us die tonight.

"Why does your family have to be so nice?" she demands suddenly.

I blink, thrown by the question. "I... What? What does my family have to do with this?"

But Chase isn't listening. She's muttering under her breath, words I can barely catch over the roar of the wind and the engine. "Can't do this... not real... don't belong..."

"Chase," I say calmly, despite the fact that we're now doing ninety down this treacherous gravel road. "Whatever it is, we can figure it out. Just... please, slow down."

"I was okay with my childhood of shitty Christmases because I convinced myself that it was normal," she says, her words sharp and bitter. "That no one has a *real* Christmas. That everyone was as disappointed as me."

I'm trying to listen, I really am, but my attention is split between her words and the haze of the world outside. With every sentence, Chase presses harder on the gas. It's like her foot is synced to her mouth—the faster she talks, the faster we go.

My stomach does a backflip as we hit 100 mph.

"But not your family," she continues. "No, they're so into fucking Christmas, you're the goddamn Griswolds. And your mom, she's so loving, like really loving. She's not pretending one fucking bit. And when I told her that I wanted to help plan next year's family Christmas photo, she hugged me. She was so fucking happy."

My brain struggles to keep up. "Why did you tell her you were coming for Christmas next year?"

"I have no idea!" Chase yells. "We're fuck buddies! We're not a real couple."

Her words sting, but the fear coursing through me pushes the pain aside. "I think we're both real enough to die if you don't ease up," I say, watching the speedometer climb to 115.

Chase doesn't ease up. She punches it to a heart-stopping 145 mph, and the outside world becomes a dizzying blur. Palm trees morph into green smears, road signs are unreadable blips, and beachfront condos grow into focus at an alarming rate. The Marco Island Bridge, once looming in the distance, is now a concrete monster charging towards us.

The car swerves slightly, and my heart lodges in my throat. My mouth is dry, and I can hear my pulse pounding in my ears. A terrifying thought crosses my mind.

"You're not going to drive us off that bridge, are you?"

She doesn't answer. Instead, Chase erupts into a full-blown rant, her words spilling out so fast I can't process them.

"Of course you had the picture-perfect Christmas growing up! Try losing your mom at eight. Merry fucking Christmas, right? Santa brought me grief and a dad who became a shitty alcoholic. And me? I was the kid stuck loving a ghost. Because that's what he was—looked like my dad, but hollow inside. Just... fucking empty."

I want to reach out, to comfort her, but one wrong move and we're roadkill.

She's hysterical now, screaming. "But you? Your life's a Goddamn movie on the Cherish Channel. Family that actually gives a shit, parents who adore you. You get to live in fairytale land, Mr. King of Fucking Christmas."

Shit. Maybe the truth will make her hit the brakes.

"You don't have a clue about my life," I shout through the howling wind. "This whole King of Christmas shtick? I don't do it for the shits and giggles. It's a fucking lifeline."

Chase's foot eases off the gas slightly. But it's enough to let me breathe.

"You want to know why I agreed to this insane fake dating plan? It's not just about my job, it's for my mom's store. The pandemic nearly destroyed everything. My parents were on the verge of losing their house. You mock all the merch, but my career is what saved my family from financial ruin."

At last, the car slows to a mere eighty-five mph.

I swallow hard. "The truth is... I'm stuck being the King of Christmas... whether I want to be or not."

"Ethan, I-I had no idea." Her death grip finally eases as she blinks at the speedometer. "Christ, I'm driving like a damn lunatic. I'm sorry. I didn't mean to scare you."

"Can you stop the car?" I ask, desperate to hold her. "Please, Chase. Let's figure this out together."

Too late.

Red and blue lights explode in the rearview mirror.

The siren screams to life.

Busted.

"Fuck," Chase breathes, pulling over.

The car rolls to a stop, and I'm caught between relief that we're alive and dread at what comes next. I extend my hand instinctively, but she flinches away.

"Let me handle the talking," I say, hoping to use my hometown hero status to clear things up.

A middle-aged officer with a balding head and a beer belly approaches the driver's side. "Evening, folks," he drawls. "Care to explain the rush?"

Before I can open my mouth, Chase jumps in. "Officer, I apologize for the speed, but we're in the middle of a code-red PR crisis. Hollywood emergency, not your typical swamp stuff."

Insulting the officer. Great plan.

"Sorry, Officer. She's from California. One of those yoga-pants-wearing, green-juice-sipping, paper-straw-drinking, eco-warrior types who doesn't know any better," I say, trying to lighten the mood. "The holidays have her a little high-strung."

Chase whips her head around to glare at me. If looks could crush, I'd be dust.

"High-strung? You mean you think I'm crazy. I open up, share my feelings. I tell you how suffocated I feel by your family, and you're—"

"Are you serious?" I snap, my patience running thin. "You almost killed us. That's a whole new level of crazy—and yes, I'm comparing this to the crazy you give me on set every day."

The officer flashes his light into our faces, and his eyes widen. "Well I'll be, it's Chathan! Your mom sold me a shirt for Christmas. My wife's a huge fan. That's so neat how you come up with those movie ideas together."

Chase bristles at his words. "Give him all the credit for that atrocious shirt, but those are my movies. I'm his boss. He works for me."

"Yeah, I'm the guy she orders around nonstop. My reward is getting blamed for all her problems when things don't work out exactly like she wants."

"Excuse me?" Chase's voice rises an octave. "You only get blamed when it's your fault. Which is all the fucking time!"

That's it. I open the car door, stepping out into the cool night air. The breeze does nothing to cool the fire in my veins. "I don't have to listen to this shit," I growl.

The officer's voice takes on a warning tone. "Sir, you need to stay in your vehicle."

But Chase stomps right behind me, meeting me in front of the car. Her voice is now a near-shriek. "I never should have trusted you to take over the subscriber campaign. It was too important. Now look where we are! We missed another goal today."

Her words set something off in me. All the pent-up frustration I've been holding back for years rushes out like a volcano erupting. "Every time something goes wrong, whenever there's a hiccup or a screw-up, who's the first person you look at? Me. Every damn time, it's me. And I'm sick of it. I'm not a punching bag for your fucking failures and frustrations!"

Chase steps closer, her eyes flashing dangerously. "Excuse me?"

I don't back down. My heart's pounding, but I can't hold back anymore. "How about you take a good, hard look in the mirror? Because the problem isn't just with me. It's with you too. You don't trust anyone. You never let people in, and refuse to rely on anyone but yourself. That's why you're alone. You push everyone away because you can't let go of control for even a second."

"This isn't about trust. It's about competence," Chase spits back. "Something you're sadly lacking, along with talent."

Her words twist like a knife in my gut.

"You're nothing but a talentless fuckboy with a pretty face. I made you the 'King of Christmas.' So enjoy your fame and the endless parade of one-night stands while it lasts. It's all you'll ever be good for."

Something inside me snaps. "Ice queen to your fucking core," I snarl. "Or should I call you by your other on-set nickname? Bitch."

SMACK!

The sharp sound of Chase's hand meeting my cheek cuts through the night air. The sting radiates across my face, a small twinge compared to the pain in my chest. We stand there, breaths ragged, the weight of our words lingering between us like a toxic mist.

What have we done?

The officer clears his throat. "Right. Chathan, you're both under arrest. Hands behind your backs."

***

JAIL CELL, THREE DAYS before Christmas? There's a plot twist I didn't see coming.

Christmas in the slammer wasn't on my vision board. Then again, nothing about this trip has gone as planned. I squirm on this rock-hard bench, my ass going numb. The stench in here is a blend of stale sweat and harsh lemon disinfectant, enough to make anyone feel sick. Or maybe it's the guilt twisting me up inside.

I glance at Chase, perched on the other bench. She's facing away, arms wrapped tight, her body language screaming, *Keep away*. I notice the tiny tremor in her shoulders. She's crying. Silently, but definitely crying.

I'm to blame for this. The words I hurled at her earlier are echoing in my ears, each one feeling like another nail in the coffin of the fragile trust we'd started to establish.

"Ice queen." "Bitch."

God, I'm such an asshole.

But then her words cut through my self-loathing, feeling as brutal as when she first said them.

"Talentless fuckboy... Nothing but a pretty face..."

No. I'm not letting myself dive down that rabbit hole of insecurities. Not now. Not when Chase is crumbling right in front of me.

I'm still processing what she said, especially the anguish in her voice when she talked about her mother's death. After all these years of working together, I never knew Chase was hiding such deep wounds. While I was living in a bubble of unconditional love, she was learning to survive on her own.

Chase built herself up from nothing. She had no safety net or family support when things went wrong. It was just her against the world, fighting for success step by difficult step. I can't imagine not having the constant encouragement of my family to cushion every fall.

Something primitive stirs in my chest. The need to hold her, to somehow pour twenty years of missed love into one embrace. I want to be her soft landing, her safe harbor, her whatever-the-hell she needs, whenever she needs it.

I want to be everything the world never gave her.

Not because she needs to be saved, but because everyone deserves someone who will catch them when they fall.

If only I knew how to tell her that without making things worse.

Only one way to find out, dumbass.

"Chase, I—"

"Don't." Her voice is raw, as if it's been ripped to shreds by broken glass. "Just... don't, Ethan."

She finally turns to face me, and the pain in her eyes nearly knocks me off the bench. There's anger there, sure, but beneath it... God, there's so much hurt. Hurt that I caused. Hurt that goes way deeper than our petty squabbles on set. I watch as she discreetly wipes away another tear, and a weight presses down on my chest.

"I'm sorry," I whisper, knowing it's not enough. Not by a long shot. "I didn't mean—"

She cuts me off, her gaze piercing. "Yes, you did. You've wanted to say those things for a long time."

She's not wrong. Yeah, I've had those thoughts. I've nursed my resentment, fed it with every criticism, every demanding note, every impossibly long filming day with her. But now, seeing the toll it's taken on both of us, I want...

Christ, I don't even know what I want. To understand her? To make things right? To be the kind of partner—on screen and off—that she deserves?

But as I see her shrink back, hiding behind her walls I helped strengthen, I'm scared it might be too late.

Have I pushed her too far?

Is there any coming back from this?

I take a deep breath, bracing myself. "Look, we've got time to kill in this fancy suite. Might as well lay it all out there." I lock eyes with her, refusing to look away. "I've always wondered. What was it that I did when we first started working together that made you hate me?"

She uncrosses her arms, her shoulders sagging slightly. "I don't hate you, Ethan," she says, her voice barely above a whisper. "You just... You made my job so much harder with all your bullshit on set."

"I thought I was keeping things fun. Our movies are meant to be lighthearted, you know? A little improv adds to the vibe."

"It also adds hours to our shoots and increases the budget," Chase counters weakly, as if the very memory is exhausting. "So then I have to cut back on other scenes and endure constant lectures from the network executives."

My heart sinks, and shame floods through me. "I'm an idiot. I should have realized how it affected everything," I mutter, more to myself than to her. "I... I didn't know. Never saw it that way. I'm sorry, Chase. Really."

Chase's expression softens a little. "It's not your job to know. It's mine."

"I bet you're sorry you ever hired me, huh?" The words come out more vulnerable than I intended.

"No, of course not," Chase says, surprising me. She pauses, and I can see her carefully choosing her next words. "I might have reconsidered had I known we'd be at each other's throats every day on set. My stomach has more ulcers than there are freckles on your perfect tushy."

A laugh bursts out of me, unexpectedly. Chase's lips curve into a small smile, and for a beat, we're both at ease.

She sighs. "And I'm sorry too. For the things I said, for pushing you so hard without explaining why. Ethan, you're more than a pretty face and perfect abs. But let's be clear, those features are ridiculously and unfairly incredible."

I flash her a grin at the praise, and then we sit in silence for a moment, letting the significance of our apologies sink in.

"Why do you push me so hard? Why bother?"

Chase looks at me, and the intensity in her gaze takes my breath away.

"Because I see what you could be. There was something in your audition that just... Wow. Raw talent, depth, everything. I've been trying to bring back that Ethan ever since. But all I get is the heart-throb, the charmer. You're so much more than that. You just won't let yourself be seen."

I clear my throat, suddenly feeling exposed. "I didn't think anyone noticed," I admit quietly. "It's easier to be the charming goofball. Safer."

Chase says softly, "I get it. It's terrifying to let people see the *real* you. But with me, I want you to know you don't have to hide."

Our eyes lock, and for a long moment, neither of us speaks. I stand up to pace the small cell, my nerves suddenly on edge.

"This... This thing between us," I start, the words feeling clumsy on my tongue. "I don't know what it is, but—"

"Oh my God, Ethan, it's nothing," she interrupts, her voice sharp, her expression hardening. "We slept together. We're not falling for each other."

"Why not? Chase, I like you. Really like you. And I think... I think you might like me too."

She scoffs, but it sounds forced. "You like your fan club and your women of the week. And I'm not judging, but let's not pretend this is something it's not."

I feel a surge of frustration, not at Chase but at the image I've cultivated for so long. "That's just sex," I say soberly. "You think any of those women made me see a future like my parents have? No way. They want to fuck the King of Christmas. Your creation. Not me."

She goes quiet. Chase starts to say something then stops. It's clear she's torn and doesn't trust me. And I'm struggling to find a way to get her there.

"Chase," I say, my voice steady and sure as I step closer. "I've given you a million reasons to doubt me. My reputation, the tabloids, the never-ending line of women—I know. But that's not who I am anymore. That's not the man I want to be."

"Ethan, we can't—"

"Why not?" I interrupt, sitting next to her. "I know you feel it too. This connection between us. It's not only physical. It's way more than that."

She shakes her head, but it's easy to see she's wrestling with herself. "It's complicated. We work together. There's too much at stake."

"I know this campaign didn't hit the mark," I say, attempting to find common ground. "But it's not over yet. I understand you're upset, but—"

"Upset?" Chase's voice rises. "I'm way more than upset. If we lose our jobs, you'll be fine. You'll land another acting gig. You have family, your friends—people who care about you." Her voice cracks on the last words, and it breaks my heart. "This job, these movies—it's all I have. I've sacrificed everything for it."

"There are people trying to care for you," I argue softly. "Let them in."

"No."

"What do you mean, no? You can't control how other people feel about you."

Her eyes flash to mine, sharp enough to draw blood. "The hell I can't. I've spent my whole life controlling exactly who gets close.

I don't let things in that can hurt me. Not disappointment. Not distraction." Her voice catches. "And especially not you."

"You don't mean that." I lean forward, desperate to get past her defenses. "I know you're scared, but—"

"This is over." Her words slice through me like a blade. "I need my life back. Before you made me want things I can't have. Before you made me feel—" She swallows hard. "Just stop pretending to care. Your fake concern hurts worse than when you hated me."

I slide closer, my hand hovering over hers. For the first time in my life, I'm fucking terrified of saying the wrong thing. Every script, every smooth line, and every charming response—useless. I want her to direct me in this scene and tell me how to fix this.

Our hands finally connect, and her eyes fill with tears. Before I can think, I pull her into my arms. For one perfect moment, she melts against me, and I think maybe—just maybe—I've gotten through to her.

Then she's gone, retreating to the far corner of our cell and leaving me cold.

"No. I trusted your promises that you had everything under control. You were either lying or delusional. It doesn't matter which." She wraps her arms around herself. "I should have known better. Trusting you was a mistake. I'll fix this myself. I'm done talking."

She turns away, but not before I see tears spilling down her cheeks. *Fuck.* She's right—I failed her. Made promises I didn't keep, too caught up in my own cockiness to take her fears seriously. Every time she voiced her concerns about the subscribers dwindling, I brushed them off with a smile. I already have other acting opportunities coming in, but Chase stands to lose everything she's worked for.

Her controlled breathing echoes through our cell, each careful breath a knife to my chest. Watching her pull further away, convincing herself she's better off alone—knowing I caused it—it's destroying me. Because this woman, this beautiful, fierce, broken woman, is everything I never knew I needed.

And I'm losing her because I couldn't deliver on the one promise that mattered.

CHAPTER TWENTY

CHASE

"Ethan! Is it true your whole relationship is fake?" a paparazzo shouts.

The police station door clangs shut behind us. Instant chaos. A mob swarms. Camera flashes explode. Voices roar from every direction. My heart hammers against my ribs. It's hard to breathe. I can't think.

The madness has me aching to crawl back into that cell, even after a night of choking on tears and painful silence.

Ethan's powerful arm tightens around me, and I don't shake him off. His body is a fortress against the increasingly hostile crowd. Aggressive shouting and shoving bombard us as we fight our way through the swell of the mob.

More questions—a jumble of curiosity, accusations, and vicious slander.

"Why were you arrested?"

"Chase! Tell us. Is he blackmailing you?"

"Are you dating each other just to promote your new movie?"

A burly man lunges, but Ethan deftly maneuvers us out of the way, his reflexes lightning fast. With each move, his muscled chest presses against my back, and despite the adrenaline surging through my veins, I find myself leaning into him, craving his touch.

The crowd inches closer. Microphones jab at my face. Cameras click rapid-fire. I'm drowning in noise and light and bodies. And then I hear a female voice that makes my blood run cold.

"Ethan, she forced you into this relationship, didn't she?"

My stomach lurches. Thorn in my fucking life, fan club president psycho hose beast from hell, Gail.

Her eyes burn with hate, and she's clutching a sign with our mugshots on it. Ethan looks like a handsome rascal who got caught stealing hearts (and maybe a few wallets), while I look like I stuck my head in an airplane engine. On purpose.

Ethan's grip tightens.

Possessive. Protective. Real.

The steady thrum of his heartbeat presses into me. How can he be so calm?

Gail shoves her camera in my face and snarls, "We all know the truth. You used your director status to force Ethan to sleep with you. Admit it!"

I open my mouth, ready to defend myself, but Ethan speaks first, his voice deep and firm.

"We have no comment on our private relationship."

The questions keep coming.

"Ethan, have you sworn off dating popstars?"

I want to hide.

"Chase, are you a childless cat lady?"

Preferably in a hole.

"Who came up with the name Chathan?"

On Mars.

I am safe with Ethan. There's madness swirling around us, yet somehow he has this ability to make me feel like everything's okay. But it's definitely *not* okay. We're in the middle of a paparazzi shitstorm. Wait, did I just see a "Team Ethan" T-shirt?

I spot Nolan outside the crowd, waving us toward the red Mustang like we're about to pull off the ultimate heist. Ethan guides me into the back seat, his hand lingering on the small of my back. Instead of claiming the front seat, he slides in beside me, staying close, as if sensing my fear and refusing to let more than two inches come between us."

The door slams. Nolan guns it. I'm thrown against the seat as we peel out, the world outside the windows becoming a blur. Behind us, a swarm of cars. Predators chasing prey.

I gulp in air, lungs burning. When did I stop breathing?

"How did they know we were there?"

Nolan's eyes meet mine in the rearview mirror. "That crazy redhead lady, probably. She's been everywhere. Taking pictures. Stalking the store. Showed up at our house last night when you guys didn't come home." He grips the steering wheel tighter, weaving through traffic. "Mom nearly unleashed Bubbles on her."

Anxiety washes over me. I pull out my phone, fingers shaking. The Ethan Addicts page loads. My breath catches. Pics of us everywhere. Walking. Talking. Some of it shot through the Barrett house's windows. There may not be nude photos, but I still feel exposed seeing our private moments splashed across the internet like some twisted peep show.

Nolan continues, "Bro, I don't care what your guys' relationship is—real, fake, or performance art gone horribly wrong—but this is not cool."

"How screwed are we?" Ethan's words come out clipped.

His thumb gently strokes my knuckles, our fingers entwined.

When did we start holding hands?

Nolan's words fall like hammer blows. "Paparazzi is swarming the house. Mom's being harassed at the store. It's a circus out there."

"Nolan, I'm sorry. This is my fault," I say.

Ethan locks eyes with me, his gaze intense. "No, it's my fault, and I'll take care of it."

"How?" The word comes out sharper than I intend, dripping with skepticism.

"I don't know. But we will figure it out together."

He kisses my hand, and a sinking feeling settles in my stomach, unrelated to Nolan's NASCAR driving. I do not deserve this—Ethan's support, his unwavering presence beside me. This mess is my doing, a disaster I created. Deep down, I know I've done something far worse. And the truth always comes out...

Guilt weighs heavy on my shoulders. I want to come clean before it's too late—to explain the ten-movie contract, to confess I took credit for his social media campaign. I'm overwhelmed by the urge to admit that I'm the ungrateful, self-sabotaging moron with an ego the size of the Rockefeller Center Christmas tree, not him.

I should open up completely.

And then maybe we can figure this out together. If I let Ethan in.

"Hold on," Nolan warns as he speeds through a yellow light.

Ethan's arm wraps around my waist, pulling me flush against him as Nolan takes a sharp turn. I feel every hard plane of his body, his chest rising and falling with each breath. My heart races, and despite the speed of the car, it's all Ethan.

Nolan jerks a hard right down an alley. Seconds later, he cuts across three lanes of traffic, tires screeching in protest. A gleaming high-rise condo comes into view with a discreet entrance to an underground parking garage. The vehicle groans as it veers down the ramp, until finally, we lurch to a stop. I realize I'm practically in Ethan's lap, my hands gripping his biceps tightly.

"Nobody fucks with my family," Nolan says, channeling his inner Vin Diesel.

Who is this guy? How can this be the same Nolan who sweats nervously through gaudy tropical shirts? One minute, he's showboating as the most fabulous dancing drag queen I've ever seen, and the next he's driving like he's trying out for *The Fast and the Furious: Miami Drift*?

Nolan turns around, tossing a set of keys to Ethan. "Go to my place. Hide out. I'll keep the paparazzi off your tail, but fix this." He pauses then adds with unexpected firmness, "Seriously, tomorrow's Christmas Eve. Don't let this ruin our Christmas."

"Understood, bro. Thanks for your help."

Ethan exits the Mustang and offers me a hand. My feet have barely touched the ground when Nolan slams on the gas, the car's tires shrieking against asphalt as he tears out of the parking garage. The smell of burning rubber lingers in the air, and the filmmaker in me can't help but admire the scene. I may have to hire him as a stunt car driver in my next movie.

If there is a next movie.

Ethan ushers me to the elevator, staying close, his hand wrapped around mine. He doesn't let go, not even for a second.

***

WE STEP INTO NOLAN'S twelfth-floor apartment. I'm immediately blown away. It's nothing like the cozy, knickknack-filled Barrett family home. This place is legit. Picture bachelor pad meets tech mogul—all clean lines, modern design, and tasteful furnishings. Now, imagine a wall of windows, ten times larger than normal windows, that let in gobs of natural light and, more importantly, offer an expansive view that leaves me awestruck.

I practically float to the balcony, irresistibly drawn by the jaw-dropping, panoramic Gulf vista stretched out before me. "I thought Nolan lived with your parents?"

"Why would you think that?"

"Because he's staying in the bedroom next to yours."

"We always stay in our old rooms for Christmas. It's tradition."

Of course it is. Another wholesome Barrett family tradition that's so pure it pulls at my heartstrings.

"Nolan left home before I did. Right out of college, he got snatched up as a data analyst for some big tech company in Silicon Valley. He was totally killing it there. When the pandemic hit, they let him work from home. So, he came back to help our folks and missed it so much, he decided to stay. Still works his analyst gig from here and helps Mom part-time at the store."

My chest tightens as it sinks in. Both Barrett brothers, incredibly successful, unwaveringly devoted to their family. I didn't know. The guilt burrows into my mind. This family is so united, endlessly loving and supportive of one another. And here I am, an intruder. The one who created all of this drama. And for what?

My career?

I must look as distraught as I feel because his arms are suddenly around me. I welcome his embrace, greedily drawing in the comfort, despite the guilty voice in my head.

"Don't worry," he murmurs. "We'll sort this out."

His phone chimes. "It's my mom," he says, glancing at it before answering the FaceTime call.

Darla's concerned face fills the screen. "Ethan, sweetie, y'all okay?"

"Hangin' in there, Mama."

"Let me get a look at Chase," Darla demands.

I paste on what I hope is a convincing smile.

"Oh, thank goodness, hun. I was worried to bits about you being in that jail cell."

"We were both there," Ethan interjects.

"Yes, but you're not some pretty little thing that needs protecting." Darla says and then quickly adds, "Not that a tough cookie like you can't handle herself, Chase. Still, who knows what kind of ruffians they have in there."

I pause, not sure how to respond, when Doug's face suddenly crowds into the frame. "Okay, you two," he says, his tone serious. "Time to fess up. Are you fakin' it like they're saying on the news?"

My heart plummets. I can't do this anymore. I can't keep lying to these people who've shown me nothing but kindness. They deserve to know, even if it means losing everything I've worked for.

Ethan takes his phone back, angling it away from me. "It's real," he says firmly. "Gail, my fan club president, has hated Chase ever since we got together. She's behind the rumors."

I stare at him, dumbfounded. Why is he lying? Why is he digging us deeper into this hole? I want to grab the stupid phone and spill the truth. But I'm speechless.

"Ooh, I knew she was a freaky one when she turned up at our door last night," Darla says.

I'm so exhausted. I'm tired of pretending, worn down by this whole charade. If I just take the fall and bare my soul right now—

My phone buzzes in my pocket, the screen lighting up with an incoming call. The caller ID reads *Wiley and Riley*.

Oh, fuck.

"Sorry, but I have to take this. The network is calling."

At the same moment, Ethan's phone chirps. "It's my agent. I'll call you back. Love you both."

He ends the FaceTime with his parents. Then, without warning, Ethan pulls me in for a kiss so nuclear that my mind melts and my legs almost give out. A soft, needy moan escapes my lips before I can stop it. My phone's ringing sounds are distant compared to the roaring in my ears and the feeling of his hard body pressed against mine.

He shifts away, still cradling my head in his hands. His piercing eyes fix on mine. "I'm here," he says gently. "We got this."

Is he right?

Could we make this work?

RIINNGGG!

Is that what Ethan really wants?

Do I?

RIINNGGG!

No time to untangle the mess of my thoughts; the network is waiting.

I steady my breath as I step out onto the balcony, the Gulf breeze doing little to cool the heat in my cheeks. With a calm exhale, I answer the call. "Chase Pemberton."

Riley's angry voice crackles through the speaker. "Jail? Cherish Channel associates do *not* get incarcerated in penal institutions."

"We thought you had this under control," Wiley says.

"I did—I do. All press is good press, right?"

"No," Riley snaps. "This is bad. We are not the Spice Network. We are in critical damage control."

I wince, bracing myself for the axe about to fall. Instinctively, I look to Ethan for comfort, but he's pacing, deep in conversation on his own call. Our eyes meet briefly, and I'm startled. A hurt look flashes across his face before he turns away.

Oh shit. What's happening? What's his agent saying?

"Well, Ms. Pemberton? Can you handle it or not?"

Dammit. I should have been listening. "I'm sorry, you cut out," I lie. "Say that again."

Wiley's voice turns stern. "We've had to tap into our reserves to hire a Florida PR firm who swear they can make the public forget about your recent... activities. They've already started planning a Christmas Eve livestream event in Marco Island. You have twenty-four hours to work together and make this happen. Do not disappoint. We anticipate crowds, we expect buzz, and there better be stellar performances."

"And a happy ending!" Riley adds.

"Our directing offer with you still stands," Wiley says, "*if* you hit that million."

"Ensure you do!" they finish in unison.

"Yes, I'm truly sorry," I stammer. "I will give it 110 percent. I promise I won't let you down."

"We'll be there in person to be sure of that," Riley says ominously as the line goes dead.

"Fuck me in the fucking fuckhole!" I sag against the balcony railing, both enraged and defeated.

Ethan's still on the phone, so I take a moment to collect myself. He finishes his call just as I step inside. Immediately, I'm confronted with the full force of his anger.

"You're firing me?!"

"What? No—well yeah, I was, but that was before—"

"Before you tricked me into boosting your career?" he says, cutting me off. "What the hell, Chase? My agent found out about your little scheme. A ten-movie deal *without your leading man*!"

The disappointment in his eyes cuts deeper than his rage.

"This whole time I'm trying to get you to trust me, but you were going to dump me after we hit a million subscribers? You're the one who can't be trusted!"

I match his outrage. "Drop the innocent act—you wouldn't have lifted a finger if I'd told you the truth. And you should be fucking thanking me. I secured both our futures. You get to keep your perfect little King of Christmas title where everything's easy and you don't have to make hard choices."

"I don't understand how you could do this. How can you pass me off to another director? We're the magic, Chase. You and me," Ethan insists softly.

"No, we're not. Remember how it is when we're on set? We don't work well together."

"Seriously? Look what we've achieved. Sure, it's stressful sometimes. But the spark of our movies only happens because we push each other."

His raw vulnerability threatens to shatter my determination.

"This vacation has been a wild ride of emotions, and every single one of them pointed to one truth: we are incredible together. I've never experienced anything like it with anyone else. It's something extraordinary. Can't you see it? Why are you denying this pull between us?"

His voice, passionate and pleading, is a wrecking ball to my heart, each word pounding into me, demolishing who I am and what I stand for.

It's too much.

Too intense.

Too scary.

I clench my eyes tight, the past rushing in, a tidal wave of memories. Suddenly, I'm that little girl again, watching my father crumble, promising myself I'd never let love consume me like that. Never give someone the power to leave me in ruins.

I take a deep breath, strengthening my resolve. It's time to walk away and protect myself.

My face hardens. "We're both getting a good opportunity. Let's not get in the way of each other's goals."

"That's what I am? In the way?"

The pain in his voice, the agony etched on his face—it's all I can do not to fall apart. But I need him to stop this pursuit. I hold his gaze, even as every piece of me is breaking.

"You're in my way. Every. Fucking. Day." The words are like poison, but I force them out.

"So that's your plan? Fire me and find another pretty face?"

"Exactly. Someone who listens and doesn't give me so much god-damn grief." The moment the sentence leaves my mouth, I wish I could take it back. "Ethan, I didn't mean—"

He silences me, cold and unforgiving. "Understood. You want us finished? Fine. But I'm not letting my fans down. From day one, you didn't hide that you don't give a damn about them, but I do. I won't let you ruin anyone else's Christmas."

The Ethan I know—the guy who's always full of warmth and happiness—is gone, replaced by a cold stranger. "So, what's the solution, boss? How are *you* gonna fix this?"

"I'm going to do what I always do," I say, my voice steadier than I feel. "Write the unrealistic ending that everyone wants. And this time, you better perform it word for word."

He lets out a bitter laugh. "Why am I not surprised? Fine. You win, like always." He runs a hand through his hair, eyes dark with resentment. "I'll be your puppet. Send the damn script. But you're staying here. Away from me and my family. I'll have Nolan bring your things."

And then, he's gone—the door slamming behind him. A trembling gasp gives way to uncontrollable weeping. The tears come hot and fast. I sink to the floor, my cheeks flooded with emotion.

I had to let him go. This is control. This is my choice.

CHAPTER TWENTY ONE

ETHAN

I DRAG MY SORRY ass onto set, my usual swagger replaced by a defeated shuffle. One glance at my reflection in a nearby trailer window confirms it—I look like shit. A sleepless night has a way of doing that, especially when it's filled with replays of fights and what-ifs.

The familiar buzz of the movie set hits me like a hangover, all noise and chaos. Marco Island's quaint downtown park has been swallowed whole by the beast of Hollywood. Where's the cozy little gazebo? The peaceful walking paths? Gone. My two worlds have collided in a mess of wires, spotlights, and fake snow.

My kingdom, they say. *Yeah, right. Some king I am.* Today, this crown feels more like an anchor, dragging me down with the weight of a million expectations.

Crew members chirp out happy hellos as I pass. I paste on a smile and wave back, hoping no one can tell how close I am to losing it. I navigate through a sea of white chairs prepared for tonight's crowd, all facing a stage resembling a winter wonderland.

Then I see her.

Chase is a beacon of control in the chaos, dressed in all black, clipboard at the ready, headset firmly in place. Her presence pulls at me like a tractor beam.

"Hey, Picasso with the glue gun! Yeah, you. The snowflakes go on the left side of the arch. Camera left, not your left. Fix it."

Her voice slices through the noise, sharp and commanding. She's in full director mode, barking orders like a five-star general, and damn if it doesn't get my heart pumping.

I can't tear my eyes away, even as yesterday's fight gnaws at my guts. Yes, she shut me down and labeled me a "problem"—but that just makes me want to seize her gently, look her in the eye, and demand she admit that this is not an act between us.

This is real.

We're real.

Or we could be if she'd let us.

"I need the crane set up here behind the audience. That way we'll get the full panorama in the wide shot," she yells.

God, why is she so sexy when she's in command? I want to kiss that stern look right off her face. Pretend that icy conversation yesterday never happened.

But there's no more avoiding it. Time for an Emmy-worthy performance of "Everything's Just Dandy in Ethan-land."

"Morning, sweetheart," I say, the endearment slipping out before I can stop it. "I guess Santa's elves have been getting a real workout with the boss lady."

Chase's eyes meet mine with a hint of yearning, but they swiftly change to a more detached demeanor. "You're late."

I hold up the script. "Blame this masterpiece of yours. I was up all night decoding it. I have notes."

"Ethan, I don't have time for this. You agreed to say the words as written."

"That was before I saw the crazy shit you wrote into it. A fake engagement? Seriously? What's next, a sham pregnancy? Alien abduction?"

"Keep your voice down," she snaps, her eyes darting around nervously.

"It's all just a game to you. Another scene to direct. But this isn't a movie, Chase—this is my life we're talking about."

Her assistant Taylor appears as if summoned, tablet in hand and looking frazzled. "Chase, Frank is looking for you."

"Who?"

"The drone guy. Something about the opening shot." She spots me and her professional smile kicks in. "Oh! Ethan. Hair and make-up want you in twenty."

"Sure thing, Taylor. Nice to see you got sucked into this mess. What do you think of Florida?"

"It's like breathing soup," she says flatly.

Chase starts to leave. "Tell Frank I'll be right there."

"Whoa, hold up," I say, catching her elbow. "We need to talk about this scene."

"Let go," she snaps, wrenching her arm free with a sharp twist and taking a step back. "This is exactly what I was afraid of. I have an entire production to manage. You are not the only person who matters here."

"Yes, you've made it very clear how low I am on your priority list," I say with unmistakable hurt. "But we're going to discuss this script and—"

Out of nowhere, Chase's arms are around my neck and she's kissing me. My thoughts explode like fireworks. Instinct kicks in, and I'm bringing her to me, deepening the kiss. It's everything I've been craving, everything I was terrified I'd never have again.

She breaks away, breathless, and for a second I think maybe, just maybe—

"Don't look now," she whispers urgently, "but Gail's filming us."

Clarity smacks me in the face when I hear Gail's shrill voice. "Your fans deserve better than this, Ethan. You can't hide the truth. Chase, I will not rest until they fire you!"

Protective anger surges. I yell to a nearby security guard, "Get that woman off this set, NOW!"

I grab Chase's hand, her fingers trembling in mine, and lead her toward my trailer. I fling the door open and guide her in, kicking it firmly shut.

The sudden silence engulfs us. I turn to face her, my heart racing and lips still tingling. For a moment, hope flutters in my chest. But the guarded look in her eyes kills it.

"You alright?"

Chase nods, finally peering back at me. "I'm fine. It's fine. Sorry about the kiss. I couldn't think of anything else."

"Emergency makeouts are my specialty. It's written in my contract."

She doesn't laugh. Instead, her face goes serious. "We can't have any more bad press, Ethan. We only have 800k subscribers. Both our jobs are on the line."

"But a fake engagement? That's your big idea?" The words come out harsh. "You want me to pop the question on live TV?"

"I'm giving the fans what they want. The love story ends happily ever after."

I scoff. "How will more lies fix this?"

"Until we hit a million, we keep up the act. And you can stop judging me. I'm not the only one being dishonest." she fires back. "You brought your parents into this. I told you to be honest from the start."

Well, crap. She's right.

I misled my family... at first. But my feelings for her? That part isn't a lie, not anymore.

"You said not to ruin anyone's Christmas," she continues. "I'm making sure that doesn't happen. We'll have a whirlwind engagement, followed by a very public breakup in L.A., and then you can return to your revolving door of starlets."

I wince. "Damn, Chase. Don't sugarcoat it or anything."

Beneath the sarcasm, I'm fucking shattered. Does she honestly believe I'm still that guy—Hollywood's favorite playboy? A man incapable of depth or commitment? Can't she see how she's reshaped my world—redefined my priorities? Because of her, I've caught a glimpse of a future that I want more than anything.

"Ethan, please," she says, her shaky tone threatening to break me. "Do your job and let me do mine. This is hard enough."

I take a step toward her, my heart pounding against my ribcage. "This might have started as a lie, but it's become the most real thing in my life. I'm asking you—no, begging you—don't shut down the possibility of 'us' before we even see where it could go."

I catch the glimmer of tears forming. I reach out, desperate to pull her close, to make her understand. But she steps back, putting miles between us with that single movement.

"Weren't you listening? I've already written our ending. Fake engagement. Public breakup. The end."

She disappears into the tiny bathroom, the door clicking shut with a finality that makes my stomach drop. The flimsy barrier might as well be made of tissue paper for all the privacy it offers. I hear her muffled sniffles, each one ripping out a piece of my heart.

"Ethan, you need to leave. You're late for wardrobe." Her voice comes out strained and raw.

I rake my fingers through my hair, pacing the trailer like a ticking time bomb. This is fucking insane. All of it. From the charade we're putting on, to the genuine emotions I can't shake, right down to this ridiculous on-camera proposal.

And yet...

I pick up the script, flipping the pages. Chase's handwriting is all over it, neat little notes in the margins. Always the perfectionist, even when she's crafting the most complicated lie.

She's not wrong—it's a happily-ever-after ending for everyone... except us.

And it will destroy both our careers if we mess it up.

What's the use? She's made her choice, and no impassioned plea will change her mind now. She'll stick to her script no matter how I feel.

Swallowing the lump in my throat, I turn away without another word. My feet carry me to the exit, each step feeling like I'm sinking into concrete. I'm not just leaving the trailer but also the foolish hope I'd been clinging to.

***

"ACTION!" CHASE'S VOICE CUTS through the air.

Game face: Activated. Charm: Turned up to full blast.

I'm waiting on stage when the camera's light goes red. "Hey, beautiful people. Ethan Barrett here, your friendly neighborhood King of Christmas. Wait till you hear what I've got planned."

Dancers spin around me in their Santa outfits, a holiday tornado of red and white.

"I'm personally inviting you to the huge livestream event before the premiere of my new movie, *Fa La La Love*."

On cue, fake snow starts to fall. It catches in my eyelashes, but I don't miss a beat.

"Trust me, you won't want to miss this live event—musical performances, behind-the-scenes sneak peeks, and... a big moment for me. I'm going to ask the love of my life, Chase Pemberton, a very special question. And hopefully, she'll make my Christmas wish come true." I toss in a wink, pushing aside the tightness in my chest at those words.

Staring into the camera, I carefully avoid Chase's gaze. I'm a consummate professional—an actor who can summon the emotions demanded by the scene while ruthlessly suppressing my own. No doubt my future therapist will sail off on a yacht named after me from this soul-crushing experience.

"Be sure to subscribe, because it's all happening tonight, only on the Cherish Channel." I hit my ending pose, and the dancers surround me with jazz hands.

"Cut!" Chase yells. "Moving on!"

I stride over to her, eager to see if she liked my take. I still crave her approval. *God, I'm a sucker.* Our eyes lock briefly before she turns, addressing Taylor, her ever-efficient right hand.

"Please tell Ethan that he's on break but needs to stand by," Chase says, face buried in her clipboard.

Taylor acknowledges me with an expression of *I'm so sorry* and *please don't make this difficult.*

I smirk and say, "Please inform Director Pemberton that I'll be a good little boy. No wandering off set, no sneaking cookies from craft services, and there will be no thinking on my part whatsoever. I'll perform the script exactly as written."

That earns me an eye roll from Chase. I'll take it.

As I'm exiting the stage, a flustered guy intercepts me. "Hey, I'm Mike, the prop master," he says, all business. "Quick question: Does your wardrobe tonight have pockets?"

"Yeah, we can both be glad they vetoed the sexy Santa Speedo idea." My attempt at humor falls flat, as Mike doesn't even crack a smile.

He holds out a small ring box. "Think this'll fit in your pocket? Or should I hunt down a smaller box?"

Mike hands it to me, and the ring inside is... one-of-a-kind. The garish design seems to be inspired by a disco ball, featuring an uneven hodgepodge of rejected gemstones.

When I hold it up to the light, the jewels sparkle so intensely that it's almost blinding. It's not Chase's style, not that it matters. If I were to choose, I would go with something understated yet elegant—a solitaire in white gold with clean lines. Classic, strong, and timeless. Just like her.

The thought catches me off guard, and I almost drop the gaudy rock.

Why am I acting like this is an actual proposal?

Whatever sparks we had are now tightly sealed off.

"Any chance you could hold on to that until after this number?" Mike asks, already retreating. "I have to drag that 500-pound sleigh onto the stage."

"Sure, man," I respond, but he's already gone.

I slide into one of the audience chairs, my gaze locked on the engagement ring as if it's the key to everything. "This day cannot be over soon enough," I say, snapping the box shut.

I'm startled by my dad's voice, who pats me on the back and plops down next to me. "Would you look at this? You Hollywood people sure go all out, don'tcha son?"

"Hey Dad, what—"

Chase's deafening voice from her megaphone interrupts. "Let's run the 'Santa Baby' dance number from the top! And Santa, either nail your blocking this time, or you're fired. No more mistakes, understood?"

"Wow," Dad says, eyebrows raised. "She's a fierce little thing, ain't she?"

Fierce doesn't even scratch the surface. That woman is a force of nature, a whirlwind of creativity and passion. And me? I'm the guy who got swept up in her storm, spinning out of control, not able to—hell, not wanting to—break free.

"Where's Mom?" I ask, trying to change the subject.

"At the store. She's barely keeping up with all your fans," Dad replies. "Your event's bringing in lots of new folks with money to burn."

I should step up and offer to help, but the idea of facing a crowd of zealous fans, all expecting to see the happy couple... Yeah, that's more than I can handle right now.

Dad must sense my hesitation because he adds, "Nolan's there. Your mama's fine. She sent me down here to check on you." He pauses, and I feel him studying my face. "She's got it in her head that you're gonna propose to Chase tonight."

The velvet case suddenly feels like it's burning a hole in my pocket. I pull it out, holding it up like some kind of evidence. "So I'm told."

Dad opens the box and studies the tacky diamond. His expression says it all. "Hmmm," he muses. "That's something... not something Chase would like."

"That's what I said..." *Oh shit! I said that out loud.* "I mean, when I bought it. Um, that is to say, when she picked it out... We agreed that—"

"Son," Dad says gently, cutting me off and placing a hand on my shoulder. "Now's as good a time as any to stop with the lies."

"You know? When did you find out?"

"Pretty much the second you said you were bringing Chase home for Christmas."

"So why did you let us pretend?"

"You're a grown man, Ethan. I assumed you had your reasons."

A laugh escapes me, hollow and brittle. "I have no idea what the hell I'm doing, Dad."

"Kid, that's the way love goes."

Unbelievable... My dad casually drops the L-bomb like it's no big deal. *Love.* Here I am, caught up in this cyclone of emotions, trying to understand all my twisted-up feelings, and my father nails it with one word.

"I let her down."

"I'm sure you did," Dad says plainly. "And you will again, and then you'll figure it out. That's the nature of relationships."

"But how the hell can Chase trust me when I keep screwing up?" I run a frustrated hand through my hair. "She's been let down her whole life. She doesn't trust anyone."

"You plant your ass down and don't budge. Every time you take a tumble, you get back up and keep at it. Let her know you're sticking around, no matter what."

As his words rattle around in my brain, I fixate on Chase. Goddamn, she's incredible. The sheer intensity radiating from her, the passionate drive that fuels her every move—it's like watching lightning strike in slow motion.

And I know, deep in my bones, that this is why I'm so completely, utterly gone for her.

"Son..." Dad's voice pulls me back. "Ever notice the common theme in all your movies?"

"Let me think—happily ever after?" I say sarcastically.

"In every single one of 'em, the girl gets scared and runs off 'cause she's too afraid of getting hurt by love."

I nod slowly, still unsure where he's going.

"Since the girl you love is the very same girl who wrote those movies, who do ya think she's been writing about this whole time?"

My heart jumps. It all clicks into place. All those scripts Chase has written, filled with characters wrestling with love and fear and the terrifying prospect of opening their hearts—they weren't just stories. They were her, laying her soul bare on the page, grappling with her own fears of falling in love.

I look back at Chase, seeing her with fresh eyes. The way she dives into her work, the defenses she's built...

"Holy shit," I breathe. "She's pushing me away because I'm scaling those walls. She's freaking out because she's actually letting me in."

"I reckon so. But as your mama says, a little shove ain't the same as getting kicked out the door."

"I don't know if I can be the man she deserves," I admit, voicing the fear that's been gnawing at me. "I've never been that person before. To any woman."

Dad squeezes my shoulder. "I get it, son. It's downright scary. But there's only two options. Show up trying every day, or walk away... What's it gonna be?"

CHAPTER TWENTY TWO

ETHAN

Live television is on another level, and I'm crushing it.

"987,211... 212... 216..." I announce, my eyes fixed on the colossal digital countdown clock on the stage. "We're so close, folks! Just a few more, and we'll hit a million!"

The words leave my mouth, but I barely hear them. My heart's pulsing so intensely I can feel it in my teeth. The crowd, the lights, the adrenaline—it's exhilarating.

The network execs told Chase to put on a big event, and man, did she ever. Not to jinx it, but everything's been flawless. The stage is electric, every performance topping the last. I would sweep her off her feet, kiss her, and tell her how incredible she is, but that's not in the script.

She made damn sure to cut out any kissing when I fake propose to her at the end.

I raise my mic. "We're only halfway into our show, so use this commercial break to call your nanna, your auntie, your dry cleaner—heck, even your ex if you're bold enough—and ask them to subscribe!" I wink at the camera. "And stick around because you won't want to miss the moment when I ask the love of my life, Chase Pemberton, a very important question."

Her voice cuts through the buzz. "And we are clear for commercial!"

I turn, hoping to catch her eye, but she's already barking orders at the crew. "Set up for the 'Santa Baby' dance number. We have three minutes. Everyone to your marks!"

Taylor appears at my side. "Chase says you're doing great." She hands me a water bottle along with a paper. "And she asked me to give you this."

I take a drink and glance down at the page. Written in letters so big you can see them from space, she has scrawled: *STICK TO THE SCRIPT!*

I let out a chuckle. "Assure her not to worry. No spontaneity, no deviation. Pinky swear."

I say it as a joke, but I mean it.

Mid-gulp, I spot the Barrett clan. Mom is waving so enthusiastically she could be an air traffic controller. Dad is giving me not one, but two thumbs-up. And Nolan? He's perfecting his "I'd rather be anywhere else" face, complete with an eyebrow twitch that seems to say, "I support you, but I'm also considering the sweet release of death." I laugh.

My eyes dart back to the subscriber counter. *Damn.* The numbers are crawling up, each new subscriber coming in at a snail's pace. It'll be tight, but I've got this sense—we're gonna make it.

Only minutes stand between now and me asking Chase to marry me on live television. She thinks this is all for show, but I'm planning something bigger.

This proposal? Step one.

Operation Win Chase's Heart: Initiated.

Once we're back in Los Angeles, I'm going to sweep her off her feet. We'll film together for months, finishing *Shamrock Shenanigans*. It'll be the perfect opportunity to prove to her I'm not some shallow playboy. I'll be there every morning with her favorite tea. I'll stay late to help her review dailies. I'll listen to her ideas, support her vision, and prove that I'm the man she can depend on.

Not just on set, but in life.

What we have isn't some Hollywood fling. It's that once-in-a-lifetime bond, the kind she writes into her movies. I'll wait, fight, and do whatever it takes till she admits she's as crazy about me as I am for her.

Her grand breakup scheme once we're home? *Yeah, that's not happening.*

"Thirty seconds. On your marks!" Chase's commanding tone makes my whole body perk up.

God, I love how this woman takes charge.

Our eyes lock, and for a split second, the rest of the world can go fuck itself. It's just us.

"Ethan, you're live in 3, 2…"

I step back into the spotlight, and the crowd lets out a massive cheer. Their energy surges through me, electrifying every nerve. I see their outstretched hands, and I want to crowd-surf their wave of adoration. But nah, I promised the woman I love to stay on my best behavior.

"You may call me the King of Christmas," I say, a grin spreading across my face. "But there's someone who rules the North Pole with more magic than I could ever muster." I pause, letting the anticipation build. "You know who I'm talking about—Santa Claus."

On cue, the music starts and dancers flood the stage. Santa gets wheeled out on his sled to the sultry tones of "Santa Baby." I half expect him to break into an Elvis-style hip shake. Now that would be entertaining.

I slip offstage, mentally rehearsing the next segment's lines, when I'm ambushed by the Perpetual Saints of Frowning—Ms. Riley and Mr. Wiley, Cherish Channel's notoriously stiff CEOs.

Ms. Riley, a bundle of tweed and disapproval, stands with her frail frame swallowed by an oversized blazer. Her hair is pulled back so tightly that her eyebrows are practically on the back of her head. Beside her, Mr. Wiley, a walking raisin with glasses, has jowls so droopy they could double as a neck pillow. His sunken eyes peer through thick, horn-rimmed glasses.

"Mr. Barrett," Ms. Riley's voice creaks out. "Your little... performance, seems to be drawing attention."

Wow. This is literally the biggest compliment she's ever given me.

Mr. Wiley's eyes narrow behind his glasses. "Yes, quite the spectacle. Though I doubt if allocating resources to this endeavor will be money well spent. For your sake, I hope it is."

Talk about friendly fire in a hostile environment. I feel a twinge of guilt for all the times I stirred up trouble on set and Chase had to fight with these soul-sucking fossils for our productions.

My expression stays neutral. "Glad you're enjoying the show."

Ms. Riley's lips purse into a thin line. "Enjoyment is irrelevant, Mr. Barrett. What's important are results. Numbers. Subscribers."

"Speaking of which," Mr. Wiley interjects, "we've made some practical decisions regarding your future projects."

My heart races. This does not sound good.

"We've never let an actor direct their own film," Ms. Riley continues, her voice devoid of any enthusiasm. "It's a frivolous allocation of budget."

Mr. Wiley nods, his bald head gleaming under the stage lights. "However, Miss Pemberton made a rather... impassioned argument on your behalf."

I blink, struggling to process this information. "She did?"

"Yes," Ms. Riley says, her tone implying Chase's passion was more of a nuisance than a benefit. "She seems to believe you'd make a... skilled director."

"She also credited you with the idea for the social media stunts," Mr. Wiley adds, adjusting his glasses. "Why anyone would squander their time on such trivial matters is beyond me."

My mind is reeling. Did Chase really fight for me? Maybe winning her heart won't be as tough as I imagined.

"Effective immediately, however," Ms. Riley interjects, her voice sharp and cold, "Miss Pemberton no longer wants you two working together. She'll be assigned to a different project, as your collaboration has reached its natural conclusion."

The fluttering in my stomach plummets like a broken elevator. I bite my lip, desperately willing my face not to betray me.

Mr. Wiley nods solemnly. "Yes, we've already selected a new director to complete *Shamrock Shenanigans*. Time waits for no one, Mr. Barrett."

Wait, what? Our Saint Patrick's Day rom-com with two months of shooting left? The one I was counting on to win Chase back?

Gone.

Just like that.

"But it's her script. She doesn't want to oversee it?" I ask.

"She deems this separation is best to advance both your careers," Ms. Riley says. "Ms. Pemberton was quite insistent upon it."

Mr. Wiley adds, "Details later. Time is currency, Mr. Barrett. Don't squander it. Now back to work."

With that, they shuffle away, leaving me stunned and disoriented. My gaze shifts to Chase, drawn to her like a magnet. She's across the stage, locked onto her monitor, completely in her element. The sight of her, so close yet impossibly far away, makes my chest ache.

It's already over.

She's closed the door on me.

Making it impossible for me to change her mind.

Taylor's voice disrupts my spiraling thoughts. "Ethan, we have press interviews lined up right after the broadcast. No time for a wardrobe change."

"What about Chase?" I ask, a sense of unease growing in my gut.

Taylor's phone rings, and I overhear a conversation that shatters what's left of me. Chase is leaving. Tonight. For her cabin.

I don't wait for Taylor's call to end. "She's not staying here for Christmas?"

"Shit. You weren't supposed to find out," she admits, looking guilty.

"Taylor, please. What's going on?"

"Fine, but you didn't hear it from me. Chase is taking off as soon as the show ends. I've got a car waiting."

Fuck. Fuck. Fuck! She's running.

The stage lights dim, and suddenly Chase's face fills the giant screen. My breath catches in my throat. She's so goddamn beautiful it hurts.

"Ethan Barrett. Where do I start?" Her voice is soft, almost shy. It's a side of her I rarely see, and it makes my stomach clench.

"What the hell is this?" I mutter.

"She filmed this interview earlier today." Taylor's whisper hardly registers.

On screen, Chase continues, a hint of a smile playing at her lips. "He drives me absolutely crazy. He's always cracking jokes at the most inappropriate times, and his ability to push me to do outrageous stunts is, well... I guess you've all seen, haven't you?"

The audience bursts into laughter as clips from our past livestreams play. There we are kissing Brutus the alligator, braving that insane polar plunge, and our inflatable raft soaring through the air before crashing spectacularly into the water. I can't help but grin.

But something's off. This Chase... She's different. It's like seeing behind the curtain, the unedited director's cut of the woman she keeps hidden. Has she been this good at acting the whole time? *Is that why it's so easy for her to walk away? Has everything been an act?*

"Ethan has this... this infuriating ability to find joy in everything. He can make me laugh when all I want to do is scream or cry. He's sunshine in my world that's been serious for far too long."

My smile fades. There's a rawness in her voice that hits me deep. This isn't the Chase I'm used to seeing.

"If I'm doubting myself, he's the first one to remind me of what I'm capable of. He's so encouraging."

She pauses, her gaze drifting off-camera for a moment. I know that look. She's searching for the right words, and suddenly I realize—this isn't scripted. This is Chase, stripped bare.

She's talking to me.

"He makes me brave," Chase continues, her voice thick. "There's this constant push to be better, not only behind the camera but within myself. My defenses, my masks—they all disappear when we're together. Ethan accepts me. The real, messy, imperfect me." She inhales shakily. "That's why my heart belongs to him."

Did she just say...?

"Okay, man, it's almost time." Mike's voice permeates the fog in my brain. He's holding out the ring holder like it might explode. "Go slow pulling the ring out of the case. The band is a little slippery since I just had it polished. Can't be too careful when you're broadcasting live."

I nod, only half-hearing him. My eyes are glued to the screen, to Chase.

"He's shown me a love I thought only lived in my imagination," she says, eyes glistening. "I never expected to fall in love with Ethan, but it's the most incredible Christmas gift I've ever been given."

My vision blurs. *Fuck, I'm crying.* She actually loves me.

But she's still leaving. Why the hell is she bolting if she loves me?

And then, like a wrecking ball to the chest, it hits me. She's scared. Just like I am. Because what we have... It's not some bullshit PR stunt. It's raw and real, and it's fucking terrifying.

The lights come up. The video's over. My heart's hammering, my palms slick with sweat.

What the fuck do I do?

I promised to perform her words exactly as written, but right now? I want to light that promise on fire. Screw the network and this manufactured engagement crap. I'm done with this fake bullshit. I want to tell Chase I love her—actually fucking love her.

I shove the ring box into my pocket and step into the spotlight. The crowd roars, but I'm only thinking about Chase. How do I make her understand that being afraid together outweighs being safe apart?

I'm in full performer mode, but my brain's doing backflips. No way am I letting her ghost me after this is over. Not without one hell of a fight.

"Who's ready for the premiere of *Fa La La Love*?" My voice booms through the speakers, steadier than I feel.

The crowd roars. I glance at the subscriber counter: 994,703... 705... 712... So close, but we're not going to make it.

Stick to the script, Barrett. You can fix things with Chase later.

"But first..." I inhale deeply, centering myself. "It's time for my Christmas wish. Let's bring out the film's director, Chase Pemberton."

The camera pans to Chase, who is holding a clipboard and wearing a perfectly positioned headset. She pretends to be surprised at being called up, but I notice her eyes narrow slightly, a clear sign that she's on guard.

God, I want to grab her hand, admit everything. But I can't. Not yet.

"Chase and I have been secretly dating for months," I say, the lie tasting bitter. "We tried to keep it quiet at first."

"My fault," she quips, her laugh a touch too high. "I blurted it out in that interview."

The audience laughs, oblivious to the tension crackling between us.

"Yeah, you threw me for a loop with that one," I reply with a chuckle before announcing, "But now it's my turn to drop a bombshell on live TV."

I drop to one knee, my heart pounding so hard I swear the front row can hear it. The velvet feels like sandpaper against my sweaty palms.

"Chase Pemberton," I start, willing my voice not to shake. "You're everything to me. You're the girl—"

"*STOP!*"

A high-pitched shriek rips through the air. *What the actual fuck?*

A blur of red hair streaks across my vision. Gail. *Oh, shit.*

Time slows. I see Gail's wild eyes, her fingers clawed like a predator's. Chase, still processing, is totally exposed.

Protect Chase. Nothing else matters.

I lunge forward, but I'm too fucking slow. Gail slams into Chase with a force that knocks them both to the ground, hard.

"He's mine!" Gail shrieks, flailing like a demon possessed. "Ethan loves me!"

The audience gasps in unison. Cameras whip around frantically. I hear a producer shout, "Security!"

I grab Gail, trying to pry her off. "Gail, stop this!"

She twists in my grip, eyes blazing with a manic intensity. "No, Ethan! You love me. I know you do!"

Chase tries to stand, but Gail spots her and lashes out with a vicious kick that sends her crumpling back down.

"Chase!" I yell.

Gail's elbow crashes into my eye and I stumble back—pain exploding in my face.

Motherfucker!

In my moment of distraction, she breaks free, darting across the stage. *What is she doing? The ring.*

Gail snatches it up, jamming it on her finger. "See, Ethan? It fits! You're meant to marry me, not this lying skank!"

I position myself in front of Chase, shielding her. She's clutching her stomach, face pale with pain.

"You okay?" I murmur, fear and concern battling inside me.

She nods, wincing.

Gail's still going full psycho. "Stop this fake relationship nonsense! You love me, baby!"

Ice floods my veins. *Fake relationship.* She said it. On live TV. *Fuck!*

"Gail, stay back," I warn, trying to keep my voice steady despite the panic clawing at my chest. "This fantasy needs to end."

"Your relationship with her is fake!" she screeches, eyes wild. " I've got proof, assholes! It's all over my Ethan Addicts fan page!"

Security finally gets their shit together, closing in on Gail. She ducks and weaves like a cornered animal.

"They're scamming you!" she yells to the stunned audience. "This whole relationship is one big lie! You gave them exactly what they wanted—subscribers!"

The crowd's murmuring grows louder, a wave of confusion and disbelief. I can feel their eyes on us, questioning, judging.

As security drags Gail away, she lets out one final, chilling screech: "Watch your back, you lying bitch! He belongs to me!"

The stage is in chaos. The Christmas tree's toppled over, fake snow everywhere. A camera lies smashed on the ground, a casualty of the madness.

Gail's words hang in the air, ugly and accusing. The crowd's murmurs fade to static as I kneel down beside Chase. My heart's slamming against my ribs so hard I'm sure it's gonna crack a bone.

"Are you okay?" I ask, my voice raw with fear. "Chase, talk to me. Are you hurt?"

My hands hover over her, desperate to touch, to hold her close, but afraid she'll reject me. Her eyes are frantic, scanning the mess we've made like she's trying to find an escape route.

"I'm fine," she says, but the tremor in her voice betrays her. Her hands are shaking, fingers curled into tight fists, knuckles white with strain. She's holding on by a thread, and it's killing me.

"Bullshit," I growl, low and urgent. "None of this is fine."

"Gail's right," she whispers, almost inaudible over the confused buzz of the audience. "This is fake. We can't... We can't keep lying."

My heart nosedives into my stomach. This is it. The moment of truth, where our carefully constructed lie comes crashing down. She might hate me forever, might never wanna look at me again, but I have to go off script.

I'm not waiting another second.

"It's not fake for me," I admit, the words spilling out. "I love you, Chase. I love you so goddamn much, it scares the shit out of me. Love was just a word, an empty line I recited for the cameras. But then you came along and turned my life into a romance movie written uniquely for us."

Her eyes widen, a storm of emotions raging in them. Hope, fear, disbelief, longing—all there, raw and exposed.

"And I feel like I've already lost you," I continue, my voice cracking with the weight of my fear.

She looks away, tears welling in her eyes, and I hate myself for putting them there. Gently, I turn her face back to mine, my touch as light as I can manage with my trembling hands.

"I'm so sorry," I say, the apology feeling pathetically inadequate. "I let you down, with the subscribers and when we worked together on set and—"

"I don't care about that. I..." She stops, and I notice that familiar wall creeping into her eyes.

"No, don't shut me out," I plead. "Tell me what you're thinking. Please."

She takes a shaky breath. "I'm scared, Ethan. I don't know if I can do this. It's too much."

I nod, understanding flooding through me. Shit, I'm scared too. Hell, I'm terrified. But losing her? That's the kind of fear that threatens to swallow me whole.

How do I ease this tension?

How do I get her to smile?

How can I make her feel safe again?

I cradle her face in my hands. "Falling in love is like stepping under this mistletoe. It's thrilling, maybe a little nerve-wracking too. But I'm not going anywhere. I'll be right here, waiting for the moment you take my hand and say, 'Let's see where this Christmas magic leads us.'"

A small smile tugs at her lips. "Are you quoting your character from *Jingle Jokes & Mistletoe*?"

I give her a charming wink. "See, sweetheart, I CAN memorize my lines. And I'll recite every word you've ever written if you keep smiling like that."

The audience has gone quiet, hanging on each statement we make. The cameras are still rolling, broadcasting our personal drama to the whole world, like an unsanctioned soap opera.

I take a deep breath, knowing my next words could change everything. "Chase, I need you to stay. Don't quit on us. We're just getting started."

She meets my gaze, her eyes filled with doubt. I can see her hesitating, on the brink of a decision. I push forward, baring my soul.

"Say it's not just me. Tell me you feel it too." I swallow hard, steeling myself for what I'm about to say. "If you trust me with your heart, I swear I'll fight like hell every day to be worthy of it."

A laugh bubbles out of her. "Maybe you don't need me to write your lines after all." Her eyes flash with that familiar spark as she smirks. "You better believe I'm gonna hold you to that promise, Ethan Barrett."

Joy explodes in my chest. I pull Chase into my arms, crushing her against me, and kiss her like she's the air I need to breathe. The crowd goes absolutely wild.

I let the kiss consume us, my tongue exploring hers, demanding more with every movement. Her fingers press into my shoulders, anchoring herself to me, like she can't get close enough.

A loud, celebratory bell rings out, forcing us apart. We're both panting like we've run a marathon. I catch a glimpse of the subscriber counter out of the corner of my eye—it's skyrocketing past a million.

Artificial snow falls, turning the stage into a wintry scene.

"Chase, we did it! A freaking million subscribers."

"I don't care," she says, fisting her hands in my shirt. "Kiss me again."

"You're the director," I say, grinning like a fool as I draw her close for another kiss. This one is deeper, more passionate, and I swear sparks are flying between us. The lights go down, and I vaguely register our movie, *Fa La La Love*, starting on the big screen.

Without warning, I scoop Chase up in my arms.

"Ethan!" she squeals. "What are you doing?"

I tighten my grip, loving the way she fits against me. "I'm not letting you go, sweetheart. Not now, not ever." I lower my voice, just for her. "Tell me where I'm headed."

Chase's eyes darken, and she leans in close, her lips brushing my ear as she whispers, "Your trailer. Now. Let me show your limp fish dick just how much I love you."

"Really? That's how you're gonna say you love me for the first time?"

She laughs, the sound vibrating through me. "I love you more than Fernando the clit-flicking fish. That better?"

She sticks her tongue in my ear, and I nearly trip over my own feet. "Fuck, I love you," I groan, sprinting to my trailer.

I kick the door shut and set her on the couch, drinking her in. Flushed cheeks, messed-up hair, eyes blazing with love and lust. I've never seen anything more gorgeous in my life.

I'm about to rip my shirt off when her expression turns serious. *Shit. Did I fuck up already? Move too fast?*

"I love you, Ethan. Not the King of Christmas, not the fantasy, and not your handsome face. I love the real you. The guy from Florida."

My heart swells, threatening to burst. "I told you that you'd fall in love with Florida," I say, unable to keep the grin off my face.

She rolls her eyes, but she's smiling. "Shut up and get naked."

"You got it, boss."

Our lips meet, and this kiss feels like the perfect fade to black—except it's just the beginning. Chase has directed us into our own happily ever after, no scripts needed. And me? I'm not acting when I say she's stolen my heart.

This is real. This is love.

Chase Pemberton, I'm ready for my forever close-up.

EPILOGUE

CHASE

"**Everyone, if we don't** get this shot off before lunch, the boss lady is gonna have my balls for dinner!" Ethan's voice booms through the bullhorn.

I smirk, watching from my director's chair as he walks by me to his own. Both of us are laser-focused on the monitors, evaluating the scene we're filming. Well, he's laser-focused. I'm 60% focused with at least 40% of my focus on how good his butt looks in those jeans.

Cut me some slack. He's my boyfriend—it's okay if I peek.

I tilt my head over and graze the inside of his ear with my tongue, knowing how it drives him bonkers. "Or," I whisper in my sultriest voice, "we could stop early for lunch, go to my trailer, and I can have your balls right now."

Ethan's face goes serious like he is about to deliver a TED Talk. "Sweetheart, we're already over budget. We have to wrap this scene. If we don't, it's going to mess with tomorrow's schedule."

"Babe, I know. I used to do this without you," I say.

He cracks a grin. "If you hit your cues in the first take, I'll do that thing you liked in the shower last night when we get home."

"Ugh. But memorizing lines is so hard," I fake groan because I can't resist pushing his buttons *(it's basically my full-time job now)*. "Besides, it doesn't matter. We both know you're going to do your shower tongue trick either way."

He glances over, but I've switched to be all about the monitors again. I want to make sure everything is perfect for the next shot. I still can't wrap my head around it. We are making a movie.

About us.

Starring us.

Directed by us.

The set mimics the Barrett family living room at Christmas, but let's be real—no one can capture Darla's unique flair. To give it that extra, over-the-top touch, she sent me tons of Nolan-designed items from her shop. We're talking plastic flamingos in every shape and size, tacky alligators donning Santa hats, and enough floral-print throw pillows to make a botanical garden jealous.

Our Christmas movie, *Fa La La Love,* was a ratings sensation. Watching our real-life love story unfold onstage brought in a staggering 2.5 million new subscribers, probably all hoping to catch a glimpse of Ethan's abs. Not that I can blame them.

Since then, Cherish Channel viewers have been begging for a film about our relationship… starring us. The fans signed a petition with over 500,000 signatures. I'm pretty sure half of those were just Darla using different email addresses, but who am I to stand in the way of the masses and their questionable choices?

My new boyfriend and I don't always agree on how our origin story unfolded. He claims he swept me off my feet with his charm and wit. I maintain that I was simply worn down by his relentless pursuit and the Florida heat. Potato, po-tah-to.

"You know," I muse, squinting at the alligator stand-in for Bubbles, "when I was a little girl in Illinois dreaming of Hollywood, this is precisely what I pictured."

Ethan laughs. "Deny it all you want, sweetheart, but I think this was exactly your dream." He gives me a quick peck on the cheek. "Now, Miss Pemberton, if you please, return to your mark."

As I saunter back to the set, I overhear Ethan ask, "Taylor! Where are my Tums?"

I can't help but grin. Karma's a bitch. Turns out, the big director chair isn't the cozy snack fest my leading man thought it was.

With all my experience, I could make it easier on him, but where's the fun in that?

Out of nowhere, my nostrils are invaded by a familiar scent of sugar cookies and peppermint schnapps.

"There you are, hun! Oh, how I've missed you!" Darla's voice cuts like a bedazzled machete through the noise of the set. She's decked out in a flamingo-print sequin skirt and a bright-pink Chathan T-shirt. Subtle as always.

Pulling her into a hug, I nearly crush her lungs.

"Oof! Careful there, sugarplum," she wheezes. "You're squeezing tighter than the jeans I wore the night Doug knocked me up."

I giggle. I've missed her patented overshares.

"Guess who brought goodies for the crew?" She holds up a ginormous tote bag, grinning like a kid who snuck into the attic and found the motherlode of hidden Christmas gifts.

She pulls out Chathan socks, shirts, car air fresheners, and scented candles. She brings a candle to my face. "Here, take a whiff! It's like Florida came to visit!"

I edge closer, take a sniff, and gag. "Ooo-wee, smells... swampy."

Then she pulls out a ceramic sculpture that fits in her palm. "Surprise! I got some brand-new Christmas ornaments Nolan sculpted of you two. Ain't they adorable?"

I stare at the ornament, holding my best poker face. It's supposed to be Ethan and me, but our features are all wonky. You know how AI mutates faces and distorts fingers? That's this Chathan ornament. But I give mad respect to Nolan—the guy can capture the magic that is my frizzy, humidity-induced hair.

"These ornaments have been selling like hotcakes!" Darla gushes. "I featured them in the Chathan fan club newsletter so all the followers can snag 'em for Christmas in July!"

After the stage incident, the Ethan Addicts website got shut down faster than you can say "creepy stalker vibes." Nolan stepped up and created a new Chathan fan page, which Darla runs as the club president. And let's be honest, makes perfect sense—nobody's a number-one fan like Darla.

Thanks to her restraining order, we never saw Gail again. But rumor has it she's knee-deep in her new gig—posting toilet selfies for King of Thrones, a porta-potty company, where she's now their social media coordinator. She keeps trying to get #FlushGoals trending, but online pranksters just won't have it, flooding the comments with #kingofcaca and #nofloaters.

Darla reaches into her Mary Poppins tote bag and pulls out... the infamous SpongeBob sheets. "Oh, and I brought these like you asked," she says, beaming.

I hold up the bed linens, staring into Squidward's giant nose. "Why, hello old friend. We meet again."

I tuck SpongeBob and the gang back into the bag—a surprise for Ethan later. Now that's what I call getting freaky in the sheets. It's our six-month anniversary, so I wanted to make tonight extra spicy. I can already picture my man's grin when he gets into bed.

"Well, you're early for your scene," I tell Darla, trying to maintain a little control over my set. "We have you scheduled for hair and makeup after lunch. Then we'll film your cameos."

Darla pulls out a tube of lipstick so bright it could double as a road flare. "No need, hun. I brought my own," she gushes. "It's hard to get this flamingo color perfect."

I spot Doug and Nolan standing next to Ethan over by the monitors. "Hey, everyone, let's take five!" I announce.

Ethan shouts, "No, no, no. We are not taking a break! Everyone stay on set."

I roll my eyes. "Ethan, it's five minutes. Geez, why are you always riding me so hard?" I throw him a smirk that promises all sorts of fun later.

He concedes. "Okay, everyone. Five minutes."

I rush over to Doug, giving him a welcoming embrace. He's in his classic Florida dad getup—cargo shorts, a Hawaiian shirt with gators, and sandals with socks. Gotta hand it to him... He's committed to his look.

"Aren't you as lovely as ever, darlin'?" Doug says, his eyes twinkling. "I hope my boy is being good to you."

I can't resist. "No, your son is being downright awful. You wouldn't believe what a bossy director he is."

Ethan jumps in, defending himself. "Just giving my girlfriend some tough love. Chase keeps having trouble memorizing her lines."

"Eh, that's what improv is for," I say. "Besides, the words are your interpretation of what happened. I know the actual story."

Nolan laughs nervously. "I know too much of the story. All those suggestive sounds coming through the wall—the only way I could sleep was to wear noise-canceling headphones."

Taylor, assistant and keeper of the Tums, approaches our pow-wow. She hands the bottle to Ethan then says, "Lunch arrived if you want to break early."

"Sure," I say, at the same time Ethan says, "No, definitely not."

She glances between us, looking confused. "Sooooo…" she starts, but her eyes fly open. "ALLIGATOR!"

She leaps into Nolan's arms, clinging to him as if he's rescuing her from hot lava.

Doug, the alligator whisperer extraordinaire, grins and says, "Don't worry, darlin'. This here's Bubbles. He's harmless." He scoops up the reptile, who's sporting an "Emotional Support Alligator" sweater.

I pet Bubbles, scratching under his chin like he's a scaly puppy. "It's best not to show fear," I advise sagely. "And always keep a dead frog on hand for emergencies."

Clearing her throat, Taylor hops down from Nolan's arms, looking sheepish. I notice Nolan's expression change, a flirty smile creeping across his face as she smiles back.

Oh ho, ho, ho… what do we have here?

"By the way, these are Ethan's parents, Doug and Darla, and that's his twin brother, Nolan," I say, playing matchmaker. "Nolan, this is Taylor—our amazing and incredibly single assistant."

I watch her blush, and I swear I can hear the Cherish Channel executives furiously scribbling notes for their next movie.

Ethan pops a few Tums, a subtle reminder it's time to get things back on track. If his stomach takes any more abuse, he'll be of no use to me tonight. And ya girl's got plans.

"Everyone back to one!" I yell, not bothering with the bullhorn. I've perfected that *don't-mess-with-me* tone. The crew snaps back into position. "This shot happens now, or we work through lunch. Let's move."

I take my mark, shouting to Ethan, "Just remember. It's my killer writing that people love, not your artsy-fartsy camera angles."

He yells back, "Stick to the script!"

From the corner of my eye, I see Ethan scrutinizing the monitor. I take a breath and rerun the scene in my head. Acting is much harder than I gave him credit for. Memorizing lines is one thing, but remembering where to stand, keeping hand movements consistent, and showing emotional vulnerability—all while the director nitpicks the lighting, wardrobe, and—

"Chase, can you please tuck some of your hair behind your ear?" he calls out.

I grab a chunk of my unruly mane and tuck it back, but that's not good enough for Mr. Director.

Ethan groans and marches over to the set. "Just let me do it," he says, exasperated.

He fluffs my hair gently, tucking a small strand behind my ear. His hand brushes down the column of my neck, and my breath hitches. Every damn time, his touch lights up invisible sparks inside me.

"Careful now," I tease. "The crew might get the wrong idea of what's going on between us."

Ethan's eyes darken. "Who taught you how to derail a scene so well?"

I lick my lips, aware of what I'm doing. "If you wanna kiss me, we could break for lunch and do the shot after." I lean in to whisper, making sure only he can hear me, "Or better yet, take me to our trailer and I'll let you fuck my mouth."

His eyes go wide, and then he bellows, "That's lunch, everyone! Be back in forty-five minutes!"

Before I can even blink, he's thrown me over his shoulder like a caveman and is marching off set. I manage to spot Darla fanning herself with a Chathan flyer, while Doug gives a thumbs-up. Nolan and Taylor look everywhere but at us, their faces redder than Rudolph's nose.

Ethan doesn't stop until we're inside our trailer. He slams the door and claims me with a kiss that makes my toes curl. "I love you so much," he murmurs against my lips.

"No one has ever loved me the way you do. I am yours."

He starts unbuttoning my top, placing kisses on my collarbone that send shivers down my spine. "You're mine even in Florida? With 100-degree humid heat, mossy swamps, and mosquitos dying to make you their last meal?"

"I want to spend every Christmas in Florida with you—watching an alligator sleeping by the fire, putting up gaudy decorations that defy the laws of taste, and sharing it with a family who give such great hugs I'm still fucking glowing six months later."

Then, because I can't handle too much sincerity without cracking a joke, I add, "Enough sweet talk. Show me that full-blown sea monster."

"I'm the luckiest man on the fucking planet," he growls before kissing me with a force that steals my breath.

My heart is so full, it's swollen. Like a decadent meal you took a few too many bites of. I think it might burst, and there's only one reason I feel this way. LOVE. Love for Ethan, his love for me. The way his family loves each other so unconditionally. For the first time, I have a safe space—a place to treasure, to share, to breathe life into and radiate that love back.

It's the very essence of Christmas, and I'm completely hooked.

Florida, with all its quirks and contradictions, saved me in ways I never could have imagined. Ethan injected joy and wonder back into my life, melting the ice around my heart with his relentless warmth.

I'm so goddamn happy, I can't even. I'm stunned and forever grateful. Florida, you beautiful weirdo, look at what you did!

I've learned that when your heart is hardened, nothing can get in. It's like a force field against more pain. But when that shit starts to thaw, when you allow yourself to believe that maybe, just maybe, the world isn't as awful as you think it is... BOOM! Miracles happen.

Suddenly, there are people who not only don't let you down, but also lift you up.

I run my fingers through Ethan's hair, marveling at how this one man managed to rewrite my entire story. And I'm so glad I've learned to add spontaneity to the script. Because life truly begins when you're open to it.

He is mine, to squeeze and never let go. He saw something special in me when I was a complete disaster. Through the chaos, Ethan held my hand and whispered words of support when I needed them most. He is my rock.

He's my partner and my equal—and we can conquer anything.

So Merry Christmas out there, whoever you are. Believe me... No matter how you've been hurt, mistrusted, or pushed down, it gets better. Someone will come along who cares for you deeply, and they'll make you believe again.

Don't give up. Don't let cynicism and apathy win. Believe in humanity. Love is all around us... if we just let it in.

Now if you'll excuse me, I'm gonna go fuck my boyfriend.

***

You've been to Florida, now escape to italy for a hilarious vacation romance! Check out our steamy novel: Italy Can Bite Me

MORE BOOKS BY MÉLISA RYUN

STAND-ALONE TITLES

Fake It 'Til You Sleigh It

a Holiday Romantic Comedy

Live From New York... It's Love

Short Story

HOT MESS SUMMER SERIES

Italy Can Bite Me

Hawaii Can Suck It

Mexico Can Choke On It

THE DENTON SISTERS SERIES

The Love Startup

a Raunchy, Geeky RomCom

AUTHORS' NOTE

First off, can we just take a moment to appreciate that you've made it to the end of Chase and Ethan's steamy holiday shenanigans? We're raising a glass of spiked eggnog to you right now!

So, here's the deal. We (that's us, your friendly husband-and-wife writing duo) had this totally insane idea. What if we threw an uptight director and a smokin' hot actor into a fake dating scenario, added a dash of family chaos, a sprinkle of Florida heat, and oh yeah, let's not forget the pet alligator? Because nothing says "holiday romance" quite like a reptile named Bubbles, right?

But let's get real for a sec. We didn't just write this to torture Chase with Ethan's abs *(okay, maybe a little)*. We wanted to dig into something we've both felt—that feeling when the holidays start to lose their sparkle. You know what we mean? When you're a kid, Christmas is all magic and cookies. Then adulthood smacks you in the face like a runaway sleigh, and suddenly you're more worried about credit card bills than busting Santa for trespassing.

Writing this book together was like our own little Christmas miracle. Picture lots of late-night brainstorming, debating over who writes the steamy scenes *(spoiler: we take turns)*, and maybe a few arguments over whether alligators can wear Santa hats. But at the end of the day, it reminded us that the best things in life—like love, laughter, and yes, even writing—are better when shared.

So this holiday season, we dare you to channel your inner Chase. Let your hair down. Kiss that hot co-worker at the office party *(with consent, obviously)*. Build a sandman instead of a snowman. Whatever it takes to rediscover that holiday joy.

And hey, if all else fails, grab some gravy mix, whip up your own gator punch, and re-read your favorite scenes. You know the ones we mean.

Thanks for going on this crazy ride with us. We love you all more than Ethan loves walking around shirtless *(and that's saying something)*.

Happy Holidays! xo, MéLisa and Ryun

P.S. No alligators were harmed in the making of this book. But Bubbles would be thrilled if you could do us a favor and leave an awesome **AMAZON REVIEW!**

ACKNOWLEDGMENTS

Huge infinite gratitude to our new friends and mentors who continue to inspire and help us along our writing adventure.

Thank you mom and dad, for turning every childhood Christmas into something magical. We recognize what a gift that was.

- All Write Well

- Author Ever After

- TCP Authors

- Joquena and Renee Lomelino

We appreciate you, lovely reader. Thanks for checking out our book, you fun soul with a zest for life. Your support is huge, so don't be shy. Kindly leave us a review, a follow, or a message next chance you get. Now we gotta go, it's writing time!

ABOUT THE AUTHORS

MéLisa Ryun is our combined pen name, and we're a husband-wife duo who've been finishing each other's sentences (and steamy scenes) for nearly 30 years. We left the glitz of Hollywood for the glitter of Vegas. Despite calling Sin City home, we say what happens in Vegas should definitely not stay in Vegas—not with our scorching hot romcoms.

We spend our days in a death match of yoga and joke-writing. Living out our happily-ever-after while making silly social media videos together. **Snark. Swoon. Spice!**

VISIT MELISARYUN.COM
FIND US ON SOCIAL MEDIA @MELISARYUN

9 781947 775107